Praise for Jack Todd

For *Rose & Poe*

"Shades of William Faulkner! We have known for years that Jack
Todd is one of North America's great sportswriters. With *Rose &
Poe* he elevates his game to fiction — and does so magnificently."
— Roy MacGregor, author of *The Home Team* and *Canoe Country*

For *Rain Falls Like Mercy* (2011)

"The hard-hitting final volume of Todd's trilogy about the Paint
clan (after *Sun Going Down*, 2008, and *Come Again No More*, 2010)
covers the years 1941–49 as it tells a sweeping story of violence
at home and abroad. Todd masterfully captures both the larger
historical moment and the more intimate details of family life."
— Joanne Wilkinson, *Booklist*

"This Western-based tale of murder, war, love, and the pursuit of
justice cuts a wide swath from Japan to Germany before returning
home to Wyoming and leaving readers breathless. A brilliant,
compelling, at times repulsive, and highly readable novel."
— *Kirkus Reviews*

For *Come Again No More* (2010)

"Todd has based these novels on his own family history, and he shows the passion of someone telling a story he wants and needs to tell. Montreal sports fans may still find it a challenge to accept that the man who's been making their blood boil for years is now a first-rate novelist with a tender touch, but the effort will be worth it. Everyone else can simply enjoy the arrival of a late bloomer on the scene."
— Ian McGillis, *Montreal Gazette*

On *Sun Going Down* (2008)

"A writer in the vein of Mark Twain . ˙. entertaining, heartbreaking, and inspirational."
— *The Ottawa Citizen*

"An impressive, grand work."
— *Booklist*

"Very few historical novels I have come across since I first read the manuscript of Larry McMurtry's *Lonesome Dove* have impressed and pleased me more than Jack Todd's *Sun Going Down*. Jack Todd has offered further proof that the big Western novel is at once a living part of our national literature and as much a part of popular fiction as ever."
— Michael Korda, author of *Ulysses S. Grant* and *Ike*

"A beautifully written link with human ancestry that will resonate with all who treasure reading. Once begun, the pages do not stop turning."
— Michael Blake, author of *Dances with Wolves*

On *The Taste of Metal*
(published in the U.S. as *Desertion*, 2001)

"Gracefully and eloquently and honestly, without falling
into the traps of self-pity or misspent anger, Jack Todd has
written a stunning account of his desertion from the U.S.
Army in 1969. In tight, powerful prose, Mr. Todd captures
the terrors and doubts and humiliations that must necessarily
accompany such acts of spiritual and political valor."
— Tim O'Brien, author of *The Things They Carried*
and *Going After Cacciato*

"If you read only one Vietnam-era history, make it Jack
Todd's memoir. It is powerful, thoughtful, and very
human. Todd writes well, remembers clearly, and forgives
his country with a grace it has not yet earned."
— *The Austin (Texas) Chronicle*

"If you missed the 60s . . . you aren't likely to find a more
unblinking, honest, vividly drawn account of their dark side."
— *The Globe and Mail*

"Through his personal story, Todd conveys, in a voice
that haunts and sings, the impact of an unpopular
war on a generation of young Americans."
— *Publisher's Weekly*

"*The Taste of Metal* is a powerful book: fresh in the
writing, unflinching, courageous, affecting."
— *Quill and Quire*

Rose & Poe
a fable

by Jack Todd

For John Xiros Cooper

If by your art, my dearest father, you have
Put the wild waters in this roar, allay them . . .

— William Shakespeare, *The Tempest*

Prologue

If you, a traveler, should one day pass along the banks of the pristine Belle Coeur River at the northernmost extremity of this great country, you will hear a dozen versions of the legend of Poe the Giant and his mother Rose, and of the events that befell them.

The people of northern New England are famously taciturn, but given a good yarn, they can't resist improving it a little. Like the child's game, the tale as it is passed from mouth to ear becomes a bit of a stretch, then expands to outright fabrication, and so on until it takes on a mythic cast, as though handed down from the gods to the first peoples on earth. If you keep a notebook close at hand, you might fill page after page with observations on Poe the Giant, and yet you will be hard put to distinguish fact from old wives' tales, because the truest thing about Poe is that he *was* passing strange, and some of the folklore that has accrued to his name is as accurate as a compass needle — although fancy more often has its way, as a sampler from our own notebooks will show:

> *They say that Poe was tall enough to grab the weather vane atop a barn and bend it so that it would always follow the track of the full moon.*

> *It is claimed that Poe had eighteen fingers and three eyes. His teeth were the size of dominoes, and just as black. A tiny troll lived inside the hump on his back and was let out at night to make mischief hither and yon.*

> *On summer nights, Poe climbed a towering beech tree and slept in its branches, like a bear, attended by all manner of mysterious and sometimes ferocious creatures.*

After the events chronicled here, the tales told about Poe Didelot and his mother, Rose, became darker, but not a whit more true. That they persist to this day is a tribute to the human tendency to cling to a falsehood, even when the unadorned truth stands before us, solid and incontrovertible as an oak tree. The fabrications of decades cannot be swept away with a wave of the hand, but there is surely no harm in attempting to set down the truth for posterity, or preparing the visitor for an excursion to a part of this country that may seem like the setting for a dark fairy tale.

The truth is simpler. Rose and Poe were of the earth itself, formed of its clay, great souls adrift in a world that grows smaller by the day. This is their story. The rest is memory and metaphor.

Goatman

Poe, at dawn

The Giant Poe, six-fingered and six-toed, clambers up the rocky hillside to the goat pasture. He is quick and agile for a man of his size, and from a distance he resembles a great black bear as he scrabbles over the rough ground, ignoring the brambles that tug at his legs, the sharp edges of granite that could slash a finger or toe, the burrs that cling to his coveralls. He is barefoot, and the extra fingers and toes help his callused feet and hands grip the rock as he works his way over stones and boulders, gullies and sinkholes, past outcrops, fissures and ravines, and through a narrow graveled draw. In his wide foot-prints, oval pools emerge, where luminescent dragonflies will skitter through the hot afternoon.

The wide gravel county road is a far easier route to the top, but Poe gave that up years ago. On the road, teenage boys in pickup trucks called him "goatman" and "mutant" and accused him of having sexual congress with his goats. He didn't understand half of what they were saying, but when they took to throwing beer bottles at him and a bottle split his eyebrow open, he took refuge on the rocky goat path. There he has remained, exchanging the ease of the well-traveled road for the difficult ascent of the narrow and craggy path.

Poe sings as he climbs, a wild song without words. In the pale wash of light just before daybreak, his face is rapturous. This is his world, daybreak and dew and the drift of mist in the Belle Coeur Valley far below. When he reaches the goat meadow, he pauses to wipe his brow with a red bandana and pulls a fob watch on its long tarnished chain from a narrow pocket of his OshKosh B'gosh bib overalls. He scans the time. The big hand licks like a black-tongued dog between the "1" and the "2." The small hand is on the "6," a number that looks like a bucket with a curved handle. It's one of the two hours he can distinguish, six o'clock and high noon. The first six o'clock means it's time to milk the goats. When the little hand joins the big hand at the top of the watch, it's lunchtime, and when the little hand meets up with the bucket number again, it's time for the evening milking.

The fob watch brings order to Poe's world, parses his days one tick at a time. He believes there is magic in the coiled metal of its innards — that the sound he hears when he presses the watch tightly to his ear and listens wide-eyed to the *tick-TOCK, tick-TOCK, tick-TOCK* is a kind of sorcery and Rose has magicked the device so that it will tell him the time. He winds it gently, careful not to twist too hard, because Rose says he doesn't know his own strength and he busts things without meaning to. He hears the distant bell toll in the steeple of the Lamb of Jesus Gospel Church, and counts the strokes using the thumb and all five fingers of his left hand, the way Rose taught him. The bell tolls six times. The watch is right on time. His lips flap with glee, a stream of spittle trickles down his chin, and he dances a little jig. *Right time right time right time.*

Poe slips the watch back into the pocket on his overalls and turns in a full circle with his arms extended, inhaling the mountain air, drinking it all in: the goat-cropped, dew-soaked grass, the tamarack and hemlock, hackberry and beech trees, the way the air trembles red and yellow where the maples are turning early. Twisted ropes of fog lie in the ravines and the rising sun is sliced through the middle by a charcoal ribbon of cloud over low mountains dark with spruce and pine. To the west, the sky is still the deep indigo of his coveralls. A woodpecker clatters somewhere, barn swallows dart after insects, a solitary crow flies due north to Canada. His friend Wild Bill says Canada is so close that Ted Williams could have stood right here in the goat meadow and hit a baseball plumb out of the country. Poe doesn't know who Ted Williams might be, but he reckons it's true if Bill says it is.

The green meadow is slick with dew and fragrant with wet grass and goat shit, riven by the bells of the nanny goats. He calls them by name: Jenny-Girl and Ostrich, the twins Bertha and Pearl, Roxie, Little Dipper, Maude, Lula May, Olive, Susie Q, Thelma Pearl, Aunt Nell, and Princess Sally, the pure white beauty of the flock. The nanny goats crowd round, bossy as church ladies. He lifts the latch and squeezes into the summer shed, where he stoops to fill a bucket with fragrant, dusty oats. The dust tickles his nose and he sneezes, banging his head on the roof of the shed. Poe rubs his head and chuckles. *Damned fool Poe,* he says, *you manage to do that just about every doggone time.*

Back in the sunshine, the goats cluster to him, nuzzling and bleating. Impatient horns beat his rump and thighs as he fills their troughs, shaking out the contents of one bucket and then another. He steps back to watch them eat. When they finish, he upends a three-legged stool propped against the shed and sits to milk the goats, beginning with Little Dipper and ending with Princess Sally, always in the same order because if he milks them out of turn they get fractious.

He crouches to wash Little Dipper's bag with Rose's special concoction, a mixture of water and Clorox. He nestles his broad cheek into Dipper's warm flank and pulls, pulls, pulls in a slow and steady rhythm. The milk sounds like *hssssss–hssssss–hssssss–hssssss* as it sluices into the battered tin buckets, bubbling and frothing like witch's brew. Two feral kittens mew at a safe distance. Poe squirts long jets of milk into their waiting mouths. When each tug yields no more than a drop or two, he moves on to the next goat. *C'mon, Susie Q. Your turn. Come to Poe, girl.*

The goats milked, he totes the buckets, two in each hand, to the gravel road, where he waits for Wild Bill De Graaff and his pickup. Bill is their nearest neighbor up the mountain. Morning and evening, Bill drives Poe and his buckets of milk back downhill, waits for Rose to empty them, and hauls the empty buckets back up to the shed for the next milking. Rose turns the milk into the finest goat cheese in Belle Coeur County and pays Bill in cheese. He eases the truck alongside Poe and waits for him to load the buckets into the purpose-built box. Poe places the buckets carefully, covers them so they won't spill, and slides his bulk onto the seat, his knees up against the dash.

"Hey, Bill."

"Hey, Poe. How're them goats this fine mornin?"

"All good. Got to bring an extra bucket tomorrow. Too much milk."

"That'll make some fine goat cheese when Rose gets through with it."

"Uh-huh. Ma always say, 'Poe, don't eat it all, got to save some for my customers.'"

"I'll bet she does. Man your size can get on the outside of a whole lot of cheese."

Poe's breakfast is waiting on a yellow plate on the kitchen table. Six eggs scrambled with a little cheese and lots of pepper, a stack of six hot pancakes with maple syrup, a bowl of strawberries from the garden, a big hunk of toast with butter and strawberry jam, a pitcher of goat's milk to wash it all down. Warm milk because he doesn't like it cold — cold hurts his teeth. While he eats, Rose stands behind him, rubbing his huge pumpkin head.

"I swear you're gettin balder every week. Your head is like a big old billiard ball."

"Yes, Mama."

"I'm gonna have to get my cue, see if I can't bank this ole head into a corner pocket."

Poe laughs. Rose can always make him laugh. When he's done, he hands her his plate and says *thank you kindly, ma'am*, like he was taught. Then it's time to go to the outhouse to do his business. He lowers his OshKosh B'gosh coveralls and counts the spiders, the way he does every morning. Nine spiders. He grins. Nine is a lucky number. It's going to be a good day.

He wipes himself with nine pages from the Monkey Ward catalog. Men's socks and underwear. He's careful never to use the ladies' panty pictures, or the girdle and brassiere ads. Those he has tucked in a little cubbyhole to the side, against the day when he has time on his hands to gaze on the bosoms at his leisure. There's no time today. He has to get back to work on Mister Sir Mister's wall. He primes the pump and washes up at the well out back. Face and hands and the back of his neck, where it's always sunburned. Rose hands him the paper lunchbag. Apples and bananas and three sandwiches, bologna and goat cheese on thick slices of homemade bread. She pulls his big head down to where she can kiss his cheek.

"You back to work on the wall today, Poe?"

"Yes, ma'am."

"You know what I say, give the man a full day's work and you'll get your reward in heaven."

"Yes, ma'am. I always does."

"That's my boy. You might have your addlements and particularities, Poe, but there ain't nobody like you on God's green earth, be sure of that."

~

The magic of stones
Poe is building a thousand-foot stone wall for Prosper Thorne, a man he knows only as Mister Sir Mister. After four years of labor, it is six hundred feet long, with four hundred feet to go. Thorne takes little interest in the wall he commissioned, but his daughter Miranda supervises the work when she's home and sometimes helps Poe find the stones that he quarries from the fields. The stones wait in piles along the unfinished section of the wall: big stones, medium stones, small stones. With a

wall this size, they ought to run out of stones, but they never do. It's a mystery to Poe, how the earth heaves up new stones each spring, gifts from someplace underground. The miracle never fails. A pasture that is smooth as a baby's bottom in October will be dotted with stones come April snowmelt.

When he sets the stones, Poe first hefts them in his palm to find the center of gravity. Once they're in place, he checks their fit by running his fingertips over the stones with his eyes shut tight. Wild Bill taught him to build walls that way. A wall like this one is built without mortar, so the stones must fit together like puppies at their mama's belly, says Bill. He says too that a man in a hurry never gets it right, so Poe takes his time. He pauses to watch jet trails crisscross overhead, listens to the ravens raising a ruckus in the spruce trees on the far side of the house, sniffs the warmth of the sun rising from the stones. From somewhere down in the Belle Coeur Valley, he hears the cough and gargle of a chainsaw and winces as the saw rips into a tree. Wild Bill says if death had to fart, it would sound like a chainsaw.

Poe is about to start work when he sees a big black car far below, coming up the hill. The car pulls into a turnout about a quarter mile off. A man gets out and seems to be looking up Poe's way through a pair of binoculars. Poe sees the sun flash off the lens. He shrugs, tugs off his coat, tilts the two-gallon water jug with one finger, and drinks deep. When he looks again, the black-car man is gone.

Poe crouches to heft a hundred-pound granite stone. Bill showed him the proper way to lift the stones, crouching to take the weight on his thighs. After the first mighty heave sets the stone in place, Poe squares it with another tug or two. Then come niggling adjustments that can take an hour or more for a single stone. A nudge this way, a nudge that. Try it and look, try again, circle around, sight along the line of the wall, walk twenty yards down to squint at it from a different vantage point, then try again with eyes closed, searching for the fit where the stone sits true, as though it had been there since the earth was formed.

Poe can't read or write. He has never learned his ciphers or his letters and he never will, but he knows stones and he knows the wall. He knows other things, too. The hollow, tinny sound goat's milk makes when it pings into an empty pail, the way the fog curls away from the rising sun, the best way to sharpen an axe and bring down the tallest tree. And he knows Miranda.

At mid-morning, Poe perches on the sun-warmed stone of the half-finished wall, the water jug propped between his ankles, mopping his brow with a checkered bandana, waiting for Miranda. He hears her footsteps on the gravel path before he sees her. He holds his breath. Miranda has slim muscular brown legs and a cascade of wild dark curly hair. She's wearing blue running shorts and a thin white shirt, the kind Wild Bill calls a wifebeater. The shirt is damp with sweat and her hard brown nipples poke through the wet fabric.

Poe swallows hard, looking at her, and a low happy gurgle bubbles from his throat. Miranda smiles. "Hey, Poe."

"Hey, Miranda. Hello hello good morning."

"Time for a break, Poe. I baked these for you, fresh this morning."

"Yes, ma'am. Hungry. Work hard."

"I see that, Poe. You work hard. Nobody works harder than you, heaving stones all day."

Poe swings his legs back and forth, banging his heels against the wall. She leans forward to peck his cheek. He breathes deep, inhales Miranda smell. *Happy, happy.*

Miranda hands him a brown paper bag with eight fresh-baked brownies wrapped in wax paper.

"Don't eat these all at once, Poe. Have two now, and then you can have four with your lunch and two more in the afternoon, when you get tired. It will give you energy, okay?"

"Two now, four lunch, two this afternoon."

"That's it. I wrapped them separately so you won't get confused. Two in one package, then four, then two again, alright? And it's hot, Poe. Be sure to drink plenty of water. If your bottle is empty, fill it in the well, but don't forget to drink. Daddy loves the wall you're making, but he wouldn't want you to get sick, so don't forget, right?"

"Poe doesn't forget."

She busses him again on the cheek. He makes the happy sound in his throat. "I've got to go get my shower now. You remember what I said about the heat, and be sure to keep your hat on, right?"

"I don't never take it off. Ma says, *Poe, keep your hat on!* and that's what I does."

Miranda laughs. White teeth and pink tongue. Her laugh tastes like maple syrup. He watches her go until she is swallowed up by the shadows in the doorway. Brown legs pretty and gone.

He stares at the door, pondering. *Is there a Miranda now? Does Miranda stop when she steps through the door and start again when she comes back out? Or does she stay Miranda?* The thoughts trouble him until he brushes at his eyes like a man wiping away cobwebs. Then there's Miranda and only

Miranda, all-the-time Miranda. The thought of not-Miranda is gone and he has only her brown legs and firm buttocks and wild dark curls and the way the muscles in her legs move when she walks.

Poe hoists the jug and drinks, letting the icy water sluice down his neck and chest. He will remember what she is wearing. He can call to mind every outfit she has worn since she came home in the spring from the town where she goes to school, a place called Cane Bridge where there are lots of smart people and no nanny goats to milk. He recalls the striped pattern of an ocher blouse, the whorls of color on its buttons, the scarf that she wears on windy days — pale streaks of turquoise and amber and rose. Running shoes some days, yellow and blue and gray. Hiking boots other times, gray with blue, tied with blue shoelaces.

On the hottest days, Miranda wears flip-flops, one pair blue, one pair green. Sometimes her toenails are painted red, sometimes green. Sometimes no paint at all. She had red toenails the afternoon of the thunderstorm when the ravens streaked across the valley ahead of the black towering clouds. She hurried back to the house, telling Poe to run after her, with the rain pelting all around and turning to hail, and she held the door open for him as he ducked inside, her hair dripping rainwater and her face shining and wet as she watched the storm from the kitchen window. Then she baked muffins and poured a big glass of milk for Poe and he sat eating hot muffins as the thunder cracked and Miranda loved the storm and Poe loved her wet hair and the way she couldn't sit still and kept jumping up to look outside.

Nights after the light goes out, Poe takes out his remembers of Miranda and pages through them like going through the Monkey Ward catalog until he falls asleep. During the long winter when she is away at Cane Bridge, he goes back to the summer remembers until Christmas, when she comes home to ski and knocks on the door of the little yellow house in her blue jacket and red hat. *Hello, hello Poe, I didn't forget you, I brought you the saltwater taffy that you like.*

I loves you, Miranda, he whispers to himself, words he has heard at the moving picture show. *I loves you Miranda all my life heart and soul goodnight.*

Poe returns to work on the stone wall. The scent of her skin in the air. He chooses a sun-warmed stone, hefts it into place, and nudges it a hair's width at a time, this way and that, searching for true.

~

Watching Miranda

Thorne watches from the kitchen window. Miranda with her brownies, strolling out to visit Poe. The way the poor devil lights up like a Christmas tree when he sees her. If he were a dog, he'd be wagging his tail.

He breathes in the mingled scents of fresh brownies and Miranda sweat. Scent of a woman, not some pricey glop cooked up in a laboratory in Paris. God he loves it when she is home. As though life begins again.

He sees Poe smile and nod and beam, repeating Miranda's instructions, like a creature spellbound. He can't blame the poor bastard. Miranda is a distillation of pure light. She has that effect on people. Doctors, parking attendants, cops, shoe clerks, surly waiters. Her own father. They all light up when she is around.

It's always been that way, but now she's all grown up, with

a woman's charms. Miranda is all the more attractive because she is so unaware of how beguiling she is, like an enchanted creature on a desert island, with her shock of dark curly hair, her olive skin, the flash of her white teeth. Spitting image of her Greek mother. The Irish half, Thorne's contribution to the making of her, is invisible except when she shows a flash of his temper. Otherwise, she is her mother, a constant reminder of Elena in the flesh. Smiling, moving, breathing. Elena, ten years gone, lives on in Miranda, in every detail.

Thorne sees her kiss Poe on the cheek and walk back to the house. His heart floods with love for her, but when he sees her breasts sway under that sweaty top, he feels a stab of annoyance. *Good God, you'd think she would at least put on a bra.* What must it do to Poe, the sight of those candy-apple breasts in motion, the brown nipples through sheer damp cloth? He's tried to explain it to her, but there is no way to put it that doesn't sound crude. She thinks it's silly, especially where Poe is concerned. *Daddy, I've known Poe since I was a little girl. He taught me to fish. He's my friend. He doesn't think of me that way.* And Thorne has to stop himself from saying, *Everybody thinks of you that way.*

He hears the front door open. Miranda dashes up the stairs, two at a time. That's his cue to get breakfast going. Breakfasts are his domain. She makes lunch and dinner, but he insists on preparing breakfast. He tells her that it pleases him to do things for his daughter, but he is also very particular about breakfast and no one else gets it quite right, not even Miranda. He puts the cast-iron skillet on the stove to warm, adds a dollop of oil to the pan, sprinkles chopped garlic and onion and peppers and works it with a wooden spatula until the onion begins to turn translucent and stirs in two carefully beaten eggs and a freshly shredded strong cheddar. He flips the omelet at precisely the right moment, leaves it for another thirty seconds, then slides it onto a plate, and sets the plate in the oven to keep warm while he starts a second omelet made with beaten egg whites and peppers for Miranda. Once it's in the pan, he pops two slices of whole-wheat bread into the toaster.

As he waits, Thorne catches a distorted reflection of himself on a copper pan dangling over the stove. In the years of his exile, he has come to look like a biblical prophet. In the hallway, there is a framed cover from an old issue of *TIME* magazine, showing him twenty years younger and wearing a flawlessly cut dark suit next to the headline: "The Toughest Trial Lawyer in America." He barely recognizes that man. His hair and beard are now long and unkempt and as white as fresh snow, and he has more the look of an aging hippie in Haight-Ashbury than a trial lawyer. And he has grown larger in his dotage. The shoulder seams of shirts that fit perfectly ten or twenty years ago look as though they're about to split. His belly strains at the buttons. He should probably confine himself to a couple of egg whites and a grapefruit for breakfast, the way Miranda does, but that wouldn't seem like breakfast at all.

When the toast pops, he butters it, then slides the second omelet onto a plate, and cuts the toast precisely in two. He arranges her plate with care, cuts slices of banana and orange to give it color, shakes a few grains of sea salt onto his palm and dusts it over the eggs. He reaches into the cupboard for two glasses, sets them on the counter, and digs into the refrigerator for the jar of fresh-squeezed orange juice Miranda has prepared for him. Then he pours the orange juice, slowly and carefully, over the omelet and toast, replaces the cap, and returns it to the refrigerator.

He's about to retrieve the first plate from the oven when he sees the mess he has made: an egg-white omelet and a slice of whole-wheat toast, floating in a pool of orange juice on a blue plate. Miranda's plate. His hands tremble. His gorge rises. He slides the mess into the garbage under the sink and begins a fresh omelet, but he's too frightened to concentrate on the task. He knows what's happening to him. It happened to his father. His mind is beginning to fray like an old cotton shirt. Soon it will be in tatters, and he will be able to summon only fragments of himself.

He wants to call out to Miranda, but he can hear the water still running. He has a brief, disturbing image of her naked in the shower, of water streaming over her breasts and her brown belly and thighs and the thatch of dark silky pubic hair like her mother's. Another difficulty with his mind: it dwells on things best left untouched. He stands at the kitchen counter, forcing himself to take deep, steady breaths, willing his hands to stop trembling, his heart to cease its panicky fluttering against his rib cage.

Thorne hears the shower turn off. By the time Miranda starts down the staircase, he has composed himself enough to dexterously flip the omelet, pretending that all is well with his world. In the heat of the kitchen, he pauses to embrace the womanly warmth of her in her thin terry-cloth robe, inhaling the fragrance of her damp hair. With his hands on the taut muscles of her lower back, he can feel his heart thudding against his ribs and he wonders if she can feel it, too. He breaks free of the embrace, pretending that he has to attend to breakfast.

Miranda gives him a sharp look. "What's wrong with you, Daddy? You're pale as a ghost. Look at you, your hands are shaking."

"Nothing is wrong. I need my breakfast. My blood sugar's low."

She looks doubtful, but she takes both plates and leads the way out to the veranda, where they can breakfast with the splendid view from the top of Manitou Mountain north into Quebec. "Really, Daddy, you have to get out more. You don't see anyone but me, and I'm only here a couple of months a year."

"You forget Poe."

"No, I don't. But Poe almost never sets foot in the house. I don't know how you can live like this. Before Mama died, you were out almost every night."

"I'm not lonely. I have my books."

"All those dusty old books. Not much for companionship."

"They're not dusty. I dust every one once a month, without fail."

Miranda tilts back her head and laughs. So like her mother when she laughs that way. If Thorne forgets everything and only one thing is left in his mind, he wants it to be that — her rich, husky laugh. But she's not going to let him wriggle away.

"What was wrong before? When I walked into the kitchen?"

"I had what they call a senior moment. I had breakfast ready, but then I absentmindedly poured orange juice all over your plate."

Miranda laughs. "That could happen to anyone. My friends do stuff like that. They're caught up in something, and they head out the door wearing pajamas and flip-flops in winter."

"This is different. I've had episodes. They seem to be getting more frequent. Sometimes I can't remember your name. I'm sitting right here looking at you and I blank on your name."

"That happens, too. I find it happens especially to very brilliant people. Some of my professors recall things they learned in middle school, but they can't remember the name of the secretary they've worked with for the past twenty years. If you're having problems, I think it's the isolation, Daddy. Your mind is fine, but no man was meant to live like this."

"No man is an island?"

"That's not what I meant. You can't live as though you're on an island."

"But we are on an island, of a sort. Belle Coeur County is a lot like an island, have you ever thought of that? Canada on the north, Manitou Creek on the east, Hannibal Lake to the south, and the Sebasticook River on the west. We're completely surrounded by water and Canadians in all directions. Cut off from the world. We're trapped."

"Only because you choose to be cut off. I worry about you . . ."

He raises a hand. "Enough. I'm the last person on earth you should worry about. At your age, you should be entirely involved with yourself. When you're not yet twenty, you're expected to be selfish. Didn't you have some important errands to run today? Shopping at the Grand Union or something?"

"You're trying to get rid of me, aren't you?"

"Yes."

Miranda stands, kisses his forehead, ruffs his long white hair with her fingers. They are passing through a portal in time, that moment when the child becomes the parent, when he can no longer hide his dependence, when she can no longer conceal her concern. He knows it, she knows it. She has no wish to mother her own father, but the day is coming when it will be unavoidable. Perhaps it already is.

~

A gradual fading, as of the light
Thorne sits at the great oaken desk on the north side of the house, an antique volume of the works of John Dee open in front of him. He hasn't read a word. Next to it is the old Smith-Corona manual typewriter on which he is meant to be composing his autobiography, titled *The Truth & Nothing But* . . .

After seven years, he has written only the final sentence: ". . . and then I shot the sonofabitch right between the eyes." His intention was to work back from there to tell his story, but he has never been able to get any traction with the book, and now he knows he never will. Instead, he stares out the single large window that is his eye on the world and watches Poe at work.

He might have told Miranda more, if not for his desire to protect her. His most profound fatherly wish is not to be a burden. If he can prevent it, he will not allow the strain of his unraveling to fall on Miranda. No child should have to endure that, especially not Miranda. In any case, there is no need to worry her until a doctor confirms his self-diagnosis of dementia. Perhaps that's why he's already postponed that doctor's appointment a half-dozen times.

He tries to collect himself by listening to his favorite music, the Jacqueline du Pré recording of Max Bruch's *Kol Nidrei* that seems to go deeper into the heart of the human dilemma than anything he has ever heard, but his mind skims the surface of the music like a dragonfly over water, refusing to settle. He thinks of all the things he might have confessed to Miranda: That his image in a mirror appears increasingly vague and blurred around the edges. That he's often confused. That he walks into a room and turns round and round like an agitated dog, trying to recall what brought him there in the first place. How he rips up two or three checks for every one he's able to write. How he sometimes gives in to the temptation to browse old photo albums and emerges hours later, blinking in the light, to discover that time itself has become a fluid, silvery thing, like mercury in a flask, refusing to be pinned in any specific moment.

Given his occupation and his high-profile criminal clientele, Thorne had once anticipated a quick death for himself. A bullet in the back of the head or a bomb planted under the Mercedes. That was how Silverberg got it. Silverberg had just made partner. They hadn't even gotten around to changing the nameplate on the door from "Thorne & Coyle" to "Thorne, Coyle, and Silverberg" when pieces of Silverberg and his automobile were scattered for two hundred feet along a quiet, shady street in a residential neighborhood. Silverberg had set his mistress up with a nice little house there. One minute, he was getting laid. The next minute — *kaboom!* Silverberg was lawn confetti. Thorne knows there will be no such exit for him, only this gradual fading, as of the light.

~

The man with the cobalt eyes
Thorne is still lost in contemplation when the face of an oddly shrunken man appears upside down at his window. He jumps back, spilling cold tea, narrowly missing the precious volume

of the works of John Dee.

"Airmail! Dammit! How many times have I told you not to do that?" The sprite, still swinging by his legs from a branch of the massive oak tree outside Thorne's window, grins maliciously. When Thorne opens the window, Airmail executes a perfect flip in the air, lands on both feet, and performs an elaborate bow.

"I bid thee good afternoon, kind sir. Thy wish is my command and all that."

"I'm working, Airmail. This isn't a good time."

"No, you're not. You're staring out the window. Like always."

"How would you know?"

Airmail rolls his eyes. "I *know* things. If something happens in this county, Airmail is *always* the first to know."

Thorne hasn't the energy to dispute that statement. From what he knows of the man, Airmail has been around as long as the granite, yet he doesn't look a day over twenty-five. He has a mop of curly reddish-blond hair, eyes that are an unreal shade of cobalt blue, and the build of a gymnast on a frame that is barely taller than four feet.

Airmail gets his nickname from his occupation: he tears around the county on a silver-and-black Kawasaki Ninja, delivering things. He runs a courier service for which he is the one and only courier. There's a number you call. No one answers, but you leave a message and Airmail comes zooming to your door at speeds that are illegal everywhere in the world, even on the German autobahn — and yet Airmail never seems to get caught. More than once, Thorne has been on the highway, cruising along in his Volvo at a safe fifty-five miles per hour, when suddenly there's a sound like a jet plane bearing down on him and a flash in the rearview mirror, and Airmail on his Ninja goes shooting past, a gray streak on black asphalt. Yet somehow, Airmail seems equally immune to death and the constabulary.

Despite his failing memory, Thorne is certain there have been times when he did not place a call and Airmail came roaring up anyway. He hears the distant roar of the Ninja, and then it occurs to him that he does indeed have something that urgently needs to be sent to Bunker's Corner or Hartbury, or even as far away as Boston or New York. Before the thought has even crossed his mind, Airmail is there, ready and waiting.

When he isn't hurtling hither and yon, Airmail seems to make it his particular business to annoy Thorne. He drops in at all hours and makes himself at home, complaining when there's no Sam Adams in the fridge, helping himself to double handfuls of the jellybeans Thorne keeps on his desk, propping his tiny cowboy boots on the furniture.

Airmail plunges both hands into the jellybeans. "I have something for you," he says.

"A delivery? Where is it?"

"Nothing you can hold in your hot little hand. I have *intelligence.*"

"You could have fooled me."

Airmail ignores the crack. "I have information you want."

"Such as what?"

"Got a beer?"

"You know where to find it. You always do."

Airmail darts into the kitchen, returns with a Sam Adams for himself and one for Thorne. "Here's mud in your eye," he says. They touch bottles. Airmail drains his, greedily, and wipes his mouth with the back of his hand.

"That is saintly beer."

"Yes, it is. You said you have something for me?"

"What's the rush, captain? What's the rush? I need another beer. You know how it is — the first one doesn't touch the sides."

Warily, Thorne follows Airmail back to the kitchen and out the door onto the veranda. As much as possible, he tries to keep Airmail out of the house. He's like bad feng shui. Airmail sits without being asked, tilts his chair back, and puts his feet up on the table. "Here's the deal. There's a fella in town and he's got eyes for your girl. Don't think she's eyeballed him yet, but he's been following her around."

"Miranda is the loveliest young woman in Belle Coeur County. It's hardly surprising that she would attract the attention of various males."

"Ah. She is a lovely thing, Miranda. Lovely. Hence the need to keep the old shotgun oiled and loaded. But this is rather a different case. One that you might find especially appalling."

"Why is that? A man is a man. I'm sure Miranda can sort out the wheat from the chaff without my help."

Airmail grins, his teeth a tiny row of sharpened fence stakes. "See if this rings a bell. Dirty-blond hair. Spectacles. Looks about thirty, give or take. Kind of your weedy type, but with money. Family money, I'm guessing. Not his. The appearance of a man who has never done an honest day's work in his life."

"That doesn't mean a thing to me."

"Oh, it will. It will. He goes by the name Sebastian. I checked the register at the Manitou Mountain Motel. Sebastian from Boston."

Thorne's face clouds. His voice, when he speaks, is thick as cold molasses. "From Boston, you say? Sebastian from Boston? Sebastian *Coyle* from Boston?"

~

In the heat of the afternoon, Skeeter and Moe follow Poe's trail up to the goat pasture. Flies buzz over the wide saucer-shaped footprints where Poe had stepped at dawn. The sign left by his bare feet is plain as a freeway.

Skeeter and Moe are city boys staying at the Kids Kamp down by the river, the one run by Alf and Maeva Miller. Alf and Maeva solicit donations to send city kids out to the country for a little fresh air, then house them in a run-down motel. Most of the time, Alf and Maeva are too wasted to make them do actual camp things like hiking and canoeing, so the boys run wild over the countryside. Some of them get up to real mischief, but Skeeter and Moe have discovered tracking, and that's how they spend their days. They amble along until they spot the trail of some wild beast, and then they follow it as far as they can, pretending that raccoons are bears, deer are buffalo, domestic cats are mountain lions.

They're out prowling for bear tracks when Skeeter spots the footprints in the mud, prints so vast he could line up both his size-seven sneakers inside one with six inches to spare. "Check it, Moe! Lookit this! It's the Bigfoot, sure!"

"Man, you're foolish *and* dumb, Skeeter. That ain't no Sasquatch track."

Skeeter bends to get a close-up squint at the footprint. "I didn't say nothin about Squash-hatch. That's Bigfoot. Got to be! Who else you ever seen has feet like that?"

"I don't know. You need to read up on things, Skeet. Bigfoot, Sasquatch, Yeti — that's all the same thing, pretty much. The Abominable Snowman, too. But this ain't no Sasquatch. You think somethin that big could live around here and nobody notice? C'mon, fool."

Skeeter points again at the tracks. "Count. Them. Toes. You know-nothin bastard, count them toes. Plain as day. One. Two. Three. Four. Five. Six. Six toes. Right foot. Left foot. Six toes. What kinda man you know got six toes? Anyhow, what kinda man goes around barefoot in rough country like this? Bigfoot, that's what kind."

"A man can have six toes. I heard about it once."

"If you're so smart, what else got feet that big? What?"

"Poe, that's what. Poe got feet like that."

"Poe? Even Poe ain't got feet big as a manhole cover. Shut up, now. You're gonna scare him off."

"Scare who?"

"The Sasquank, that's who. The Yechi."

"It's Sasquatch and Yeti, Skeeter. *Sasquank* and *Yechi*. Don't you never read no books?"

"I read plenty books. Spiderman. Superman. The Insatiable Hulk."

"Them's comic books, and all you done is look at the pictures. You can't read, for a fact. Twelve years old and can't read. I ain't but eleven, and I been readin five years already."

Skeeter swats a wasp away and lets it go, intent on his tracking. A hundred yards farther on, he calls a halt to pee. "How big you think Poe is, anyhow?" he asks. "Maeva says he's nine feet tall and he weigh seven hundred pounds."

Moe pauses to ruminate, peeing next to Skeeter the way boys do, in golden six-foot arcs that doused the milkweed.

"That Maeva is crazy as a betsy bug. I seen Poe down by the bus station in Bunker's Corner when we came in. He ain't a inch over eight feet."

On the way back to the camp, Skeeter and Moe are passed by a man in a big black Cadillac, going real slow on the county road. He drives alongside them for a full minute, staring out the window. Moe thinks maybe the fellow is about to offer them a ride, and maybe he's the type who likes to prey on young boys, but then he stomps on the accelerator and the back tires of the Caddy spray the boys with gravel. Skeeter curses and flips the bird at taillights vanishing in the dust.

"That man is up to no good," Moe says.

"No word of a lie. Rich white man, they all up to no good."

"Not like that. He's up to some kind of special bad."

"Like what?"

"How do I know what kind of bad? *Special* bad, that's all I know. What else he doin up here?"

Skeeter shrugs. "I dunno. I never seen him before."

"Nobody seen him before. He's outta state. I couldn't read the plate, but it ain't local. How many strangers from outta state you see up here?"

"Not many, I guess."

"Not none, is how many. Unless they're out on the highway, hurryin from someplace to someplace. They don't come nosin up this road. What's up here? Nothin but goats and sasquatch tracks. That fella is up to *industrial* bad."

Skeeter nods, taking it all in. "Well, shoot."

A Rose Is a Rose

Girl on a swing

Rose is doing the washing up when she gets to thinking about the old porch swing at her father's house. It's been years since the swing crossed her mind, but something nudges her memory, and it's so real that she can feel the bottom-worn boards and the chipped paint under her bare thighs and hear the creaking of the chains as she swung back and forth.

Roses's daddy, Guy Didelot, had built the swing as a birthday present for her mother, Sharon. When Rose perched on it, her legs dangled because they were too short to reach the floor, so her father would use his long legs to rock them back and forth. Through the open window, they listened to Sharon hum the "Tennessee Waltz" as she washed the supper dishes, while Rose and her father sat outside counting the fireflies. They were up to thirty-six. Rose had only counted the first five because that was far as she knew how to count, and five was how old she would be in a week. He was trying to console her. Rose had cried a bit, and she was still pouting because her parents were going to a dance on the weekend, and she was going to have to spend the night with her grandmother, Huguette.

"I don't wanna stay with Grandma. I hate her."

"Why do you hate her, Rosie?"

"Because she's mean to me, and she only talks French."

"French is the only language she knows. How is she mean to you?"

"She don't let me play my games and she don't give me nothin to eat but bread and water. She sets right there eatin roast beef and she won't give me a single bite. Then she has apple pie all for herself, with *ice cream,* and she don't give me none, and I got to set quiet and watch her eat, the mean old thing."

"She does that? Maybe it's because she thinks you're a big girl. And she doesn't want you to get too big."

"You mean fat."

"No, honey. I don't mean fat. You're just a big girl. Big-boned, like your Grandpa, God rest his soul. My daddy. He was as big as they come. You're gonna be a big strong gal some day, and you're gonna be a real help to your daddy."

"You mean that?"

"I mean it. You can come to work with me when you're old enough."

"Is that tomorrow?"

"No, honey. Tomorrow you're staying with Grandma while your mama and I go to that dance in Rutland. You'll be fine. I'll tell her to feed you up and not to be mean to you, or else."

"Or else what?"

"Daddy will come home and spank her, that's what."

"You'd spank Grandma?"

"I would if she was mean to my little Rosie."

Rose laughed. A tinkly laugh. The way she laughed when her father teased her and poked his big blunt fingers into her ribs. He smelled of Aqua Velva, which he splashed on after supper, because he said it made her mother randy. She couldn't imagine why he'd want Mama to be randy, because Randy was a mean boy down the block who called her fat and threw dirt clods at her. Adults wanted funny things, like to go to a dance and leave their little girl behind.

The dishes were done, and her father said he had to go because Mama was going to be randy, so Rose had to get to bed because they all had a big day tomorrow, with the dance and all. From her bedroom window upstairs she tried to count the fireflies again, but she got only as far as two and then she fell asleep.

She cried when they dropped her at Huguette's the next afternoon. Cried and kicked her legs and hung on to the car door so that Sharon and Guy had to drag her off it, with Huguette standing in the doorway saying they had spoiled the child rotten and she would never allow a kid to act that way.

~

The syrup truck

They said it was somewhere between two and three o'clock in the morning and it was raining like the twentieth day of Noah's flood. Guy and Sharon left the dance around one o'clock, and Guy had been driving along the unfamiliar stretch of Highway 5 north of Ascutney, through darkness like the inside of a molasses barrel, for what seemed like forever. The left headlight was out in their old station wagon and he had only one slender beam to light the way through the downpour.

The truck appeared directly in front of him as though it had been conjured there, straddling the white line on a down-hill grade. It was carrying a heavy load of maple syrup from Quebec, the driver frantically downshifting to keep from burning his brakes. Guy saw it in time to brake hard, but it was maybe the worst thing he could have done. The wagon skidded sideways, hydroplaning in two inches of water on the blacktop. Sharon raised her head from his lap just as the undercarriage of the truck sheared off the top of the station wagon, peeling it open like a can of tuna.

When the state police arrived, the truck driver was sitting cross-legged in the middle of the road, trembling and weeping. Hundreds of bottles of maple syrup had been smashed on the wet asphalt, and the runoff from the rain sluiced away gallons of the sweet sticky stuff, mingled with blood and water and fragments of broken glass, all that was left of Guy and Sharon. They were buried side by side in the Hartbury cemetery on Rose's birthday. When she and her grandmother got back to the house after the funeral, Huguette stuck a candle in a cup-cake and said that was her birthday present and told her never to expect another present for the rest of her life because her parents were in holes in the ground and they weren't coming back and Rose was lucky to have a grandmother to look after her so she wouldn't end up in an orphanage.

A couple of years later, an older boy at school told Rose that her parents had been *decaptivated* when that big old truck hit their station wagon. Rose had no idea what the word "decaptivated" meant. By the time she figured it out, she was twelve. After that, night after night, she dreamed that her headless parents had come to fetch her and take her back to the house with the porch swing. They were amiable folk who looked exactly like their photographs, except that they carried their heads tucked under their arms.

~

The hayloft

The loft smelled of hay. It was the scent of Friday nights, always the same. Rose was fifteen years old, and she was in love for the first time in her life. First Rose watched the football game from the very back row, sitting alone with a blanket wrapped around her legs, her eyes on number seventy-two, Rafe Skilling, then they went on to the hayloft.

Rafe was a doctor's son and a star football player. He was a senior and she was a sophomore, two grades behind him. In her high school, he was a god, untouchable, far beyond the reach of the likes of the orphan girl Rose. But one rainy afternoon, she was walking home after school and a car pulled over beside her. It was Rafe Skilling, asking if she wanted a lift. A quarter mile from her house, he pulled into a wooded area where they couldn't be seen from the road. Rose looked at him, wondering.

"Why are we stopping here?"

"'Cause I want to talk to you," Rafe said. "I've seen you around school. I think you're beautiful."

Rose blushed. "I ain't beautiful. Nobody thinks I'm beautiful. I'm a big-boned gal. That don't bother me none. I am what I am."

"Well, I think you're beautiful just the way you are. You have gorgeous red hair and green eyes and skin like fresh cream and you're beautiful, and I like that there's a whole lot of you. Anyhow, I'm a big-boned fella, myself."

She giggled. "I expect you are at that."

They sat and talked for an hour. Rose couldn't say why, but they seemed to hit it off. And she could see that Rafe was mesmerized by her breasts, which were much larger than any other girl in school. He kept staring, and finally she smiled at him and undid the buttons on her sweater. "You can touch my titties if you want, Rafe. Suck 'em, too, 'cause I like you."

One thing led to another. They could never be seen anywhere together because Rafe was afraid his parents would find out, so Rafe picked her up from out back of the high school or behind the football stadium after games, which was when they started going to the hayloft. First he went by the drive-in and Rose crouched low with her head in his lap while he ordered hamburgers and cherry Cokes. Then they drove out to his grandfather's farm because the old man was deaf as a post and never heard a thing, and they climbed up into the hayloft, where Rose couldn't wait to finish eating and get her clothes off. She would rub the places where he was bruised up from football, then she would take him inside her, his big strong shoulders over her, his mouth on hers, and the sweet smell of hay and Rafe all mixed up while the moonlight streamed through the cracks between the weathered shingles of the old barn.

Halloween night was the sweetest. Rafe buried his face in her neck and she opened her thighs to him, her body fertile as the sea. He made her feel so good her foot started to tremble, then the trembling went up her leg and seemed to explode where he was inside her, and it went on and on like an earthquake, gripping her with such power that she lifted her weight and his with the strength in her hips and legs, driving up into him and shuddering from head to toe. It had never happened to her before, but she knew that it was a climax like at the movies because she had heard girls talking about it, and she was pretty sure it was the most wonderful thing that could happen to a person. When they were done, Rafe drove her home, taking the back roads so they wouldn't be seen.

"Y'know, Rose," Rafe told her as he drove, "I could get to like you a lot, but my folks and all. They expect me to be a doctor. It wouldn't do."

"I know it wouldn't do, Rafe. A boy like you with a girl like me. I know it wouldn't do, you don't got to tell me. You're smart and rich and I'm dumb and poor. It don't bother me; that's how things are."

"Thanks, Rose. I knew you'd understand. But you aren't dumb, not at all. You're smarter than people think. You might not have money or do good in school, but you're smart — smart enough to make something of yourself someday. Far as I'm concerned, you're the prettiest girl in school, too. I'd marry you if I could, I really would, but it wouldn't do. It's a damned shame in some ways, but it wouldn't do."

Rose understood. She knew how it was. Rafe had to go because it was Halloween. The boys would be out pulling one of their pranks, like tossing toilet paper all over Mrs. Bunker's mansion or turning livestock loose in the high school.

Rose tiptoed into the house, ignoring Huguette when the old woman screeched at her, wanting to know where she had been so long. She crawled into her narrow bed with the sweet smell of hay and spunk still in her nostrils and lay there with her hand between her legs, remembering.

When her belly began to swell, Rose knew Rafe was the daddy. She knew how it worked from the livestock. She had watched cattle breed, and horses, and pigs, and goats, how the females took the seed from the male, gave it a place to grow.

Because she was a big girl, Rose was six months along before anyone noticed. She hid it from Huguette, but a teacher at the high school noticed her condition and sent her to the principal, who sent her to the doctor. Doc Boudreau said she was due in a couple of months and that she was healthy as a horse, although she could stand to lose some weight. The high school principal informed Huguette, who threw a fit when Rose got home, hissing and screeching and throwing things. Huguette wanted to know the name of the father. Rose refused to say a word. She had another meeting with the principal, who informed her that because she was in the family way, she was no longer allowed near the school, where she might corrupt other girls. Once the child was born, she could give it up for adoption. Then she would be allowed to return to school, though she would be banned from all activities, like cheerleading and the chess club.

"I don't play chess and I don't want to be no cheerleader."

"Then I guess you won't miss those things."

"No, I won't. But I ain't givin my baby to nobody."

"I don't think you have a choice, Rose. You're fifteen years old."

"Don't matter. Ain't nobody takin my child."

"We'll see about that later. If you don't give it up, you can't come back to school. That's all there is to it. We're crystal clear on the rule."

"Then I won't be back, mister. Ain't nobody snatchin my child."

When she passed Rafe in the hallway, Rose nodded to him. That was the signal for him to pick her up behind the school in the afternoon. He drove to the place where they had talked the first time he gave her a lift home. He parked the car, and she turned to him and said what she had to say.

"I'm carryin your child, Rafe. Have been for a while."

Rafe turned pale and dropped his head onto the steering wheel. "Oh, my God. That's awful."

"No, it ain't. I aim to have this baby."

"You can't do that! My parents would be horrified. I can arrange something, pay to get it fixed. My dad is a doctor. He can take care of things. There's no reason you have to have it."

"Maybe there isn't. But I'm having this baby."

"You can't force me to marry you, Rose. I'll bet there have been other guys. You're pretty easy, you know."

Rose flushed with anger. "I'm easy for you, maybe. Nobody else. Never. I never done a thing with anybody before you, Rafe Skilling. Not even a kiss. You ought to know that much. Anyhow, you don't have to worry. I'll never tell nobody who the father is, but I'm havin this child."

Rafe stared out the window. "Maybe I can help you a little, pass you some cash from time to time."

"I don't want your damned money. Only reason I wanted to talk is that I thought you should know. Now I'm sorry I did. You go your way, and I'll go mine. Don't you worry, I won't never ask you for a thing."

Rose got out of the car and walked the rest of the way home. If Rafe had offered to do the right thing, to marry her, she would have said yes. She had made up her mind about that before she talked to him. But she knew he was right: it wouldn't do. A girl like Rose marrying a boy like Rafe, it would be the scandal of Belle Coeur County. Anyhow, she didn't need Rafe nor anyone else. She knew what she was going to do, and there wasn't anyone who could stop her.

~

Poe, his birth

Huguette said that if Rose wasn't going to school, it was time she earned her keep. Old lady Bunker needed someone to clean her house, and so did the banker Edgar Watson, and the Skilling family. Rose could start with those while Huguette drummed up more customers. She would make five dollars per house, and she was to bring every dime of it home to her grandma.

Rose didn't mind cleaning houses for rich folks. Anything was better than staying home under Huguette's thumb, with the old woman reminding her every hour that she was a sinner who had disgraced the family name. As her belly grew heavier, she spent her days on her hands and knees scrubbing toilets, waxing floors, scouring ovens.

Three months after she left school, Rose was cleaning Priscilla Bunker's home when she began to feel a little odd. Priscilla was the wealthiest woman in the county, the last living descendant of Prescott Bunker. The drafty old house was a brute to clean, but Rose found it fascinating. Never in her life had she seen so much *stuff*. Commodes, pitchers, wardrobes, carvings, oil paintings, knickknacks, books. More books than the town library, as far as she could tell, bookcases in every room.

Rose was cleaning the old woman's bedroom when she came across a slender and ancient volume of poetry by a man named Edgar Allan Poe. She sat down to rest on the four-poster bed and the musty old book fell open to a poem called "The Raven." Rose had puzzled her way as far as the line ". . . *In there stepped a stately Raven of the saintly days of yore*" when the first pains hit. At first it felt like dying. Then it let up and she thought she was fine and went back to reading, but it happened again and then again, until her screams sent the ravens flapping away from the house. Then a six-fingered, six-toed baby boy came squalling into the world, blood and afterbirth spilling onto a fine-stitched heirloom quilt that depicted the tale of Paul Revere's ride, with the famous patriot on a fine black horse, waving his black hat rather gaily as he galloped over the cobbled streets past a church with a tall white steeple.

The baby wasn't two minutes old when Mrs. Bunker returned home, stumbled over a bucket of filthy mop-water in the kitchen, and came marching upstairs to find Rose, her pale thighs splayed open, holding aloft a bloody six-fingered child with a bald head the size of a pumpkin.

Once the fuss over the heirloom quilt had died down and Rose promised to pay to have it cleaned, she cut the cord herself with a paring knife, rinsed the child with cold water at the well out back, wrapped him in a strip of gray cloth torn off her dress, and set off on foot to present her baby to Doc Boudreau.

The baby was born large and odd. Eighteen pounds, six ounces, on Doc Boudreau's scale, the largest birth ever recorded in the state. Six fingers on each hand, six toes on each foot. One eye brown and one eye green. There was a hump of gristle on his left shoulder, and from his right cheek, in a widening band down and across his broad neck, there was an immense ruby-red port-wine stain in the shape of the continent of Africa, with Cairo at his right cheekbone and Cape Town over his left nipple.

To Rose, he was the most beautiful, flawless child in the universe. She decided to name him Poe Revere Didelot, in honor of Edgar Allan Poe and Paul Revere. Others failed to perceive Poe's beauty. "Mark of the devil!" Huguette hissed when she saw the baby in his borrowed bassinet, with the port-wine stain like a blood sign splashed on his face and neck, the hump on his back, and the strange eyes of two different colors. "Spawn of Satan!" The old woman crossed herself three times and spat in the baby's face. Rose, watching over this miracle of her creation, turned slowly to face her tormentor.

"Don't you ever do that again," she said, and she drew back her thick right arm and shattered Huguette's nose with a single blow from the heel of her hand.

~

Rose versus the state

A week after Poe's birth, Rose was nursing him when there was a knock at the door. Huguette was out, and Rose answered the door to find a dour man and a sullen woman waiting. They both wore dark suits and looked like funeral directors. The man's shoulders were a snowstorm of dandruff and the wom-an's bloody lipstick made a savage slash across a cruel mouth.

"We're from the state."

"State of what?"

"The state. Don't you know what state you live in, girl? We've come for the child. It's for his own good."

"No, it ain't. Ain't nobody comin for my Poe."

"You have no choice, young lady," the woman said. "You are a minor. We're here to look after his welfare."

"No, you ain't. *I'm* here to look after his welfare. You're thieves come to snatch my baby in broad daylight. What's good for Poe is his mama. That's me. I can look after him better than any state."

"You have to understand, miss."

"My name's Rose, and I understand you perfect. But I told you already, ain't nobody takin this child. I'll chew your goddamn ear off and swallow it whole before I let you kidnap my sweet baby. I think I been clear on that."

"We'll see you in court," the woman said.

"And I'll see you in hell. But it's like I told you, you ain't takin my child, in court nor no place else."

Poe's fate was to be decided in the stately Belle Coeur County Courthouse, where dust motes floated in the odd shaft of light from the world outside, the only hint that there *was* a world outside. Rose walked the three miles to the courthouse for the hearing and sat nursing Poe while the proceedings rambled on. The judge frowned when she drew out a creamy breast. "Is that really necessary in my courtroom?"

"Yessir, it sure is. The child is hungry. If I don't feed him, he'll wail like a banshee. That ain't a sound you want to hear. It cuts right to the quick." She hauled Poe off her nipple and held him aloft. The baby obliged with a howl that rattled the courthouse windows. The judge endured it for thirty seconds, then gave her permission to go ahead and nurse. Rose did so, listening intently while the people from the state had their say. She had money in her shoe and she had a plan. If the judge ruled that she had to hand over her baby, she was going to say that she had to go home first to get his things. She had already packed clothes for herself and Poe in an old backpack from the army surplus. She would hitchhike to California and raise her baby among the orange groves.

But Judge Bartram saw something in her that the others missed. The child-welfare people insisted that Rose was incapable of caring for her baby because she got poor grades in school, but the judge found that the girl was a good deal sharper than folks believed. She had battled the state bureaucracy to a standstill, so she was no fool when it came to protecting her child. She was strong of body and great of soul, and she loved that huge ungainly baby.

The judge had seen plenty of hate in his courtroom, where married couples came to claw one another to shreds with the help of unscrupulous lawyers who poured kerosene on the fire, because the madder people got with each other, the more hate there was and the more money the lawyers made. Love was an emotion he saw less often. He saw how tenderly she held her baby, and he believed she could give him something no one else could. Such a child would never be adopted. Without Rose, he would become a ward of the state in perpetuity.

Judge Bartram banged his gavel: Rose Didelot, aged sixteen, was granted custody of her offspring in perpetuity. When he saw the puzzled look on her face, the judge repeated his judgment in words she could understand: Poe was hers forever more.

~

Mother and child

The abandoned Pullman car was parked on a rusty spur line of a railroad that had gone bankrupt back in 1932, in a section of forest so dense that you had to know exactly where it was or you would never find it. Apart from a hundred-foot stretch under the car itself, the railroad track had been torn up and sold for scrap long ago, but underbrush and a pine forest hid the Pullman from sight, and when Rose needed a home for herself and her baby boy, it was sitting there waiting, not doing much except providing a home for scuttling woodland creatures and nesting birds. Pullman cars had once been considered the height of luxury, and Rose was determined that this one would be luxurious again. She moved in, evicted the forest creatures as gently as she could, scrubbed every inch of the old Pullman, removed most of the seats, hung frilly pink curtains in the windows, rigged a coal furnace scrounged from the dump, and even put in a sink to give the place all the comforts of home, although she still had to tote water from a well a quarter mile away.

To keep body and soul together, Rose went back to cleaning houses as soon as she was able, with Poe on an improvised sling on her back or resting in his bassinet. After three years of backbreaking work, she had saved enough to rent a place with running water at the Split Rock Trailer Park. From the start, they were Rose and Poe, Poe and Rose, their names usually run together into a single word: Rose'n'Poe. Mother and child, inseparable. Rose scared off those who threw rocks and bottles and rotten tomatoes at him and called him *moron* and *idiot* and *freak*. She saw her unusual child as a gift from God and maintained her faith in the Good Lord above and her own strong back to provide for him.

Six years to the day after Poe's birth, Huguette dropped dead over her ironing board. The hot iron seared a brand into her withered cheek before she was found. Rose stood dry-eyed while the preacher said what he had to say at the old woman's graveside. She lingered until the gravediggers had finished their task and left, then with Poe keeping watch, she planted one size-twelve boot on either side of the freshly piled dark earth, hiked up the skirts of her best Sunday dress, and peed a thick yellow stream on the old woman's grave.

Rose's life became a little easier after Huguette's death. She was surprised to learn that the old woman had never gotten around to changing her will, so they were able to leave the Split Rock Trailer Park and the lecherous landlord who wanted her body in lieu of rent and move into the little yellow house. The will left everything to Rose's father, Guy. But Guy was dead and so was his wife, Sharon, and Rose was their only heir, so she got the house and the land it was on and even the $2,246.87 Huguette had squirreled away in a safety deposit box at the First State Bank. Rose didn't trust banks, so the first thing she did was withdraw the money and hide it in the metal box where Huguette had kept her other valuables, behind the jars of pickled beets and crabapple jelly in the cellar.

Rose towed Poe to the Henry Wadsworth Longfellow Elementary School in Hartbury on a wagon in summer and a sled in winter. He was capable of walking, but he loved to ride, and Rose indulged him. When the afternoon bell rang, Rose was waiting at the gates, her face pressed to the chain-link fence.

The kindergarten teacher was the first to call Rose in for a chat. Poe wasn't learning. It was possible he was incapable of learning. The teacher used the word "imbecile." Poe disrupted the class. He sang odd songs, wordless incantations that sounded like trucks or trains or wind moaning in the trees. The other children were afraid of him because he was so large and odd.

"Are you saying he can't go to your school?"

"Not exactly."

"Then there's no reason for this meeting."

"He belongs in a special place."

"He *is* in a special place. His home. Are you threatening to send him off someplace else?"

"I don't have the authority to do that."

Rose glared down at the teacher. "Then teach the child. That's what you're paid to do, ain't it?"

After that, the teachers simply passed Poe on from grade to grade, even though he never learned to read, write, or do basic arithmetic. Rose explained how it was to anyone who would listen. *Poe has his addlements and particularities. That ain't to say he's nobody's fool, only he don't do no editions nor suttractions, and he can't read for squat. But he's a good boy. He does right by his mother, and he does right by other folks. I believe that's worth more than ciphers.*

In high school, the football coach refused to believe that a boy Poe's size couldn't play football. He was six foot eight and over three hundred pounds by his fifteenth birthday and strong as any man. Surely he could learn to play a little game like football. But Poe never grasped that the purpose of the game was to move that ball downfield if you were on offense and to tackle the player who was carrying it if you were on defense. He made it as far as his first game, when his career ended after the first play. When the ball was snapped, he remained rooted to the ground like a marble statue, wondering why a blocker half his size kept hurling himself at his legs. He stood with great fat tears running down his cheeks, looking to Rose for guidance. *What'd I do? I didn't do nothin. Why's all them guys mad at me? I didn't do nothin. Why's they mad at me?*

Rose heaved her bulk out of the bleachers and strolled onto the field, ignoring the players in their colorful uniforms leaping and tackling and spitting blood and cursing all around her, the referees' whistles, and the catcalls from the crowd. She marched up to the coach and explained the facts of life to him. "My Poe ain't like most young fellas. He's strong as a Clydesdale, but he ain't been raised to hurt nobody. You want Poe to hurt them poor little children out there but he ain't goin to do it, for you nor nobody else."

Then she took Poe by the hand. "Come, Poe. We're goin home. Mama's goin to make you a great big bowl of pea soup with a corn dodger and then I'll read you to sleep." Poe followed her home, still in the oversized football gear the coach had ordered all the way from Boston, docile as a lamb.

When his supper was done and the dishes had been cleared and washed, when they had listened to the Grand Ole Opry on the radio and Poe had changed into the pajamas Rose had sewed for him because there were none in the Monkey Ward catalog near big enough, she tucked him into his narrow bed and sat next to him on her rocking chair and took out the only book she owned other than the Bible, a volume of poems by Edgar Allan Poe acquired for thirty-five cents from a book bin in Bunker's Corner. Then, only pretending to read, she recited the poem she had learned by heart.

> *Once upon a midnight dreary,*
> *while I pondered, weak and weary,*
> *Over many a quaint and curious volume of forgotten lore*

Once Poe was old enough to help, he and Rose found plenty of work. Word got around. If your septic tank was backed up, if your kitchen hadn't been cleaned in months, if your barn needed to be mucked out, if you had a tumbledown stone wall that needed to be put back up, someone would say, "You need Rose'n'Poe. They can handle most any job, and they work cheap, 'cause they don't know no better."

One phone call and the pair of them would show up at the appointed time on the appointed day, with Rose leading the way and Poe following in her wake like a great amiable water buffalo, Rose in her work boots and shapeless gray smock, Poe with his shoulders straining the seams of an old peacoat, a battered and sweat-stained Red Sox cap perched sideways on his enormous head, his OshKosh B'gosh coveralls stuffed with odds and ends in every pocket. As the first item of business, Rose always explained how it was with Poe's addlements and particularities.

~

Don't let the stars get in your eyes

Poe barely had time to blow out the eighteen candles on his birthday cake before the Belle Coeur County draft board sent him for a physical. He was classified 1-A despite his size, extra digits, and obvious lack of reading, writing, and arithmetic. A month after the physical, Poe received a letter from the president himself. *Greeting. You are hereby ordered to report for induction in the armed forces of the United States.*

Rose knew all the words except "induction." She paid a visit to Pastor Hendricks at the Lamb of Jesus Gospel Church to make sure she was clear on the meaning. "Poe can't do the army. You know what he's like."

"The army has lowered its standards because of the war," the preacher said. "Still, you're right about Poe not belonging.

I'll make a call to the draft board and see if there has been some mistake."

"I'd be grateful."

It took the reverend most of the afternoon to get through to someone at the Selective Service. The way he explained it to Rose after, Poe had won the lottery that decided who got that letter from the president and who didn't. Poe's lottery number, based on his birthdate, was three, which meant that as long as he was in good physical health, he was bound to be drafted.

Rose had seen the war on her tiny black-and-white TV set. Helicopters coming in *whuck-whuck-whuck-whuck*, soldiers jumping out and running into the jungle. Machine guns firing at them from somewhere in the tree line. Men falling, other men picking them up and carrying them on stretchers and loading them onto the helicopters. Alive or dead, you couldn't tell. Three boys from Belle Coeur County were sent home in body bags, and others came home in pieces even though they could still walk and talk and seemed alright on the outside. Rose didn't know much about war but she knew about hunting. Hunting Poe would be simple. He was big as a moose. He was inclined to get dazed and confused and just stand there. If he went to the war, he'd come home in one of them body bags, if they had one big enough.

"Where do you suppose they'll send him? He'll be hereabouts, won't he?"

"I can't say, Rose. There are forts all over these United States. There's Fort Dix in New Jersey, Fort Benning down in Georgia, Fort Lewis all the way out in Washington, almost to the Pacific Ocean. I was in the army myself, during the Korean thing, and they sent me to a fort down in Texas."

Rose sat pondering this calamity that had come into their lives. She rubbed her face with her hands, a habit she had when something caused her great stress. Then she seemed to make up her mind.

"I thank you kindly, Reverend. Wherever they send him, I expect I'll have to go along to look after my boy."

"Oh, they won't allow that, Rose. He'll be on an army base. You won't be permitted there."

"Well, I'll be close by, then. They won't keep him long. Poe ain't suited to no man's army. When they figure that out, I want to be right there handy to bring my boy home."

Rose took the bus to the airport with Poe, so they could practice making the call and he could tell her where he was being sent. She located the pay phones inside the airport and showed him how to pick up the receiver, dial "o," and wait for the operator's voice, then ask to make a *collect* call to Miss Rose Didelot.

The day he was sworn in, Rose couldn't clean house, she couldn't make cheese, she couldn't do a solitary thing but wait for the phone to ring. The squat black machine sat there on its little round table next to the davenport, silent as the grave. Rose had dozed off when it finally rang. She fumbled for the receiver.

"What?"

"I have a Mister Poe on the line for a Miss Rose. Will you accept the charges?"

"How's that?"

"I said I have Mister Poe on the line. He wishes to place a collect call to Miss Rose Didelot."

Poe on the line. Rose's mind was still in a fog after her nap. Whatever did the woman mean by that? She thought of a fisherman reeling in Poe, the rod bent double with his weight. Then it clicked. "Oh, you mean it's my boy Poe calling? Why didn't you say so? Sure, I'll accept the charge, ma'am. You just go right ahead and put him through. Poe? Poe, is that you?"

There was a click, a hollow sound like the phone was empty inside, then his voice, so oddly high-pitched for such a big man. Funny how she never noticed that when he was standing right beside her. "It's me, Mama, callin from the airport like you said. They let us all make a call."

"All of you? There's more than just you?"

"There's a bunch of us, Mama."

"At least you have company, then. Did they tell you where you're goin, Poe?"

"Yes, Mama. We got to take this airplane to Fort Lewis. They says that's in the state of Washington. Do you know where that is, Mama?"

"I'm not exactly sure, but it's a long ways from here. It might take me a week, but I'll get on a bus and make it out there. When I get there, I'll find some way to let you know. Meantime, you be a good boy and do what them soldier fellas tell you, right?"

"I don't like you bein so far away, Mama."

"It won't be for long. I'll be there right quick."

That evening, Rose had to milk the goats alone.

~

Poe, soaring over America
A sweet-smelling flight attendant with curly red hair told Poe he could sit up front. She said the flight to Seattle would take almost six hours and that the bulkhead seat was the only place where a man his size could be comfortable. She pulled the

armrest up to allow him to spread out over two seats and let his seat belt out as wide as it would go to help him fasten it. He had a panicky moment when the belt closed around his belly and he realized he couldn't move, but she patted his shoulder and showed him how to release it with one finger and how to snap it closed again.

The takeoff frightened him a little, the roar of the engines and the giant hand that seemed to press him back into his seat, but then he could see cars like toys on the highway below, and after that came rivers and the Adirondack Mountains and big cottony clouds so close he could reach out and grab one, and he pressed his face to the cold window and kept it there most of the flight. He didn't realize that he had begun to sing his wild song until the red-haired flight attendant came running up front to ask him what was wrong.

"Nothin, miss. I'm just fine."

"But you were making that strange noise, sir."

"Oh, that's my song, ma'am. When I feels good, I sings."

"I don't believe we can let you sing like that on this flight, hon. You'll disturb the other passengers. I'm gonna have to ask you to be real quiet the rest of the day, okay?"

Poe nodded, but every few minutes he forgot himself and started singing again while the other recruits on the plane hooted and hollered from the seats behind him. The flight attendant kept asking him to stop, but Poe kept forgetting himself, and she finally gave up.

"I guess we should let the poor devil make whatever racket he wants to make," she said to the crew chief. Her fiancé had been killed in the war. She knew what it was like over there. "He's going to make an awful big target, where he's headed. I don't suppose he's long for this world. He ain't doin no harm."

It was dark by the time they landed in Seattle. At the airport, they were all loaded onto a school bus for the trip to Tacoma. On the bus, the only place Poe had room to sit was in the middle of the back row, where there was room for his legs. The others were all laughing and joking, so Poe laughed, too, although he didn't understand what was so funny.

It was near midnight when they arrived at the fort. Peering out the window of the bus, all he could see was long low buildings and the occasional streetlight. The bus drew up next to one of the buildings and stopped and a sergeant appeared at the front, a big black man whose uniform looked as though it had been ironed onto his body. He talked to them in a low, comforting voice.

"Good afternoon, ladies. Welcome to the Fort Lewis Holiday Hotel. We're a full-service hotel with all the trimmings. We hope you enjoy your stay with us, but if you don't, that's just too damned bad. Now, you got about eight seconds to get off this bus before I unscrew your head and shit down your throat. On my command, ladies: MOVE! MOVE! MOVE! MOVE!"

The others scrambled to get off. Poe tried to hurry, banged his head on the roof, and sat down again, confused. The next thing he knew, everyone else was lining up outside and he was still sitting on the bus, alone. The sergeant was standing over him.

"Who told you to sit, you big idiot? I said MOVE! Get your fat ass off this damned bus!"

The sergeant led the way. Poe grabbed the bag Rose had packed for him and followed as best he could, banging his head twice more on the way out. Where the others had lined up, there were more sergeants, all of them screaming at once.

Poe dropped his bag, and one of them shouted at him. He picked it up, and someone else was shouting. It seemed like they were telling him to do ten different things at once: stand up, sit down, pick up your bag, drop your bag, turn around, get in line, turn that way, turn this way, do fifty push-ups, stand up again.

He stood on the asphalt, turning in slow confused circles, watching their mouths, trying to understand what it was they were telling him. Tears of frustration rolled down his cheeks.

"What'd I do?" he asked, over and over. "I didn't do nothin. Why're you all so danged mad at me? What'd I do? I didn't do nothin."

~

Harvest Moon

Rose packed a few things in a battered suitcase that had belonged to her father. When she needed a lift to the bus station, she turned to her regular beau, the tinker Joey Ballew. Joey wasn't much bigger than one of Poe's legs, but he was a good soul and he was so sweet on Rose that he would tag around after her like a puppy dog if she'd let him. She made it clear to Joey that he wasn't the only fella in her life, and as long as he understood that much, they'd get along swell.

After Joey dropped her at the station, she boarded a big Greyhound bus. She was already farther from home than she had ever been in her life. In a little notebook she bought for her trip, she noted the names of the towns that flew past: Glens Falls, Saratoga Springs, Albany (where she changed buses), Schenectady, Amsterdam, Utica, Syracuse, Rochester, Batavia, Buffalo, Cleveland, Elkhart, South Bend, Gary, Chicago and another transfer, then on to Milwaukee, and, finally, Minneapolis. She stayed two days in Minneapolis with Bertha, a cousin she hadn't seen since Bertha graduated high school and ran off to Minneapolis with a Navy man. Bertha was as tiny as Rose was large. The Navy man was long gone, but she had replaced him with a banjo-playing fella. He was off someplace touring with a bluegrass band. Bertha had a good job as a typist and a little girl who might belong to the banjo player or the Navy man or someone else. Bertha didn't say and Rose thought it would be rude to ask.

Rose arrived in Minneapolis on a Friday evening, and by six thirty Monday morning, she was back on the bus again, headed west through Burnsville, Albert Lea, Fairmont, Jackson, and Luverne to Sioux Falls, then on to Mitchell, a rest stop in Oacoma, and across the empty South Dakota prairie, where you could see so far it was like peering into the heart of God.

To pass the time, Rose hummed tunes she liked. When she met someone who wanted to harmonize, they sang away the miles as the bus bumped along the highway, watching the telephone wires swoop up and down and up again, birds perched on the wires like notes on sheet music. In Sioux Falls, she met a nice-looking older gent named Ned Barkley, who was traveling to Billings to visit his granddaughter. Ned sang baritone in a barbershop quartet back in Saint Cloud and he could harmonize on almost anything. Ned shared her affection for Bob Wills and Texas swing, so they sang "Faded Love" and "Stay a Little Longer," and "San Antonio Rose" for her, and they did the old barbershop tunes like "Somewhere out in the West" and "Shine on Harvest Moon" for Ned.

The bus was nearly empty that night. Ned and Rose stretched out on the long seat at the back, with the two other passengers snoozing up front, behind the driver. When it got cold, Ned offered her a tot or two of his bourbon and stretched his parka over the two of them. When he began to rub up against her, she tugged her skirt up and turned her hips to him. They moved gently together, happily rolling across the dark heart of America, making love to the rhythm of the bus.

When the bus stopped in the middle of nowhere to pick up an Air Force sergeant with a guitar case, it turned out he was a Sioux from Pine Ridge named Walter Has No Horse. He played and sang a little on Air Force radio, where he was known as "Walter the Singing Sioux." After Rose coaxed him just a little, he took out his guitar and sang "Don't Let the Stars Get in Your Eyes, Don't Let the Moon Break Your Heart," with Rose singing the high harmony and Ned the low harmony, and "Waltz Across Texas," which struck her as pretty funny because they were actually waltzing across South Dakota.

Whenever something struck her as interesting or funny, Rose jotted a few words in her little notebook about where she was and the things she saw out the window. She was especially fond of Burma-Shave signs, and she tried to write down every one she saw. If she got bored, she could page through the notebook, and it was like taking her trip all over again:

This cream. Is like. A parachute. There isn't. Any substitute. Burma-Shave.

Best burgers in Burnsville: 25 cents & don't ruin 'em with relish!

Ned Barkley from St. Cloud. Sings baratone real nice voice going to see his grand-dotter in Billings she is ten

years old and he ain't never seen her. We sung Faded
Love & Harvest Moon. Ned made me feel real good at
nite, right here on the bus.

Reana Pilbro, Egg Harbor, Wisconsin. Says she has a
dotter name Rose but the girl is with her father in Dee
Moin. That's a dam shame a child ott to be with her
mama.

Pedro. Walked. Back home, by golly. His bristly chin. Was
hot-to-Molly. Burma-Shave.

Ray's Rattlesnake Farm! 256 dedly rattlers! Take one
home for your mother-in-law, only $4.99!

Rapid City, they say Mount Rushmore is rite close to here.
I'd like to see Mister Linkon big like that but I dont dare
get off the bus for fear I'll get left behind and lost.

Maggie Jones hales from Valentine down in Nebraska,
has a big turkey sandwitch that she cant eat all of it asks
do I want some I say yes.

Doesn't. Kiss you. Like she useter. Perhaps she's seen. A
smoother rooster!! Burma-Shave!!

Walter Has No Horse: Looks real nice in a Air Force
unaform. Plays a sweet gittar. Don't let the stars get in
your eyes. Ned said Walter was a good-lookin fella who
would look even better if he had a horse. Walter laughed
and said he never heard that one before but I bet he did.

It was supper time when they got to Rapid City, and nearly eight o'clock when they pulled onto the road again, so she didn't get to see Wyoming at all. They transferred in Billings, Montana, where she said goodbye to Ned. When he teared up a little at their parting, she bussed him on the cheek and told him that she had always believed kindred souls would meet up again, even if it was in another life. The sun was up before they changed buses again in Missoula and passed through a glorious bit of Idaho, past Kellogg and Coeur d'Alene at mid-morning before hitting Spokane in time for an early lunch. After a stop in Moses Lake, they made it to Seattle at dusk. She found a grocery store where she bought bread and lunch meat and ate three sandwiches in the hour she had before the next bus to Tacoma.

In Tacoma, she hiked to six different motels before she found one that was hiring maids. The manager, a lean man named Hank with tattoos all over both arms, had just fired his maid for drinking a fifth of whiskey that belonged to one of the guests and passing out in the room she was supposed to be cleaning. Rose said she wasn't a drinker, although she did like a bottle of beer or three on a Saturday night. She needed a job and a room. Hank said she could stay for free in the unit closest to the highway, where she'd have to put up with the noise of passing trucks all night long. She said trucks wouldn't bother her, they couldn't make as much racket as the birds in the cedars back home. They shook hands on it and he drove her to the bus station to get her suitcase. Rose toyed with the radio in his car until she found a country station and sang along with Tammy Wynette on "Your Good Girl's Gonna Go Bad." Hank thumped the steering wheel in delight. "Damn! Looks like I'll be haulin out the mandolin tonight."

She was in her room less than an hour when Hank, freshened up and reeking of Aqua Velva and Wildroot Cream Oil, came knocking with a six-pack of Olympia Beer and a mandolin. She drank the beer with him and sang Tammy Wynette and Loretta Lynn songs and "Wabash Cannonball" the way Roy Acuff did it, and when the beer was gone, she let him have what he came for, with the roar of passing trucks drowning out the squeak of the bedsprings. After he went back to his room, Rose wrote him up in her little book:

> *Hank Spurgeon, from Spokane. Runs the motel where I stay in Tacoma. Hank is a Roy Acuff nut and he plays some mandalin. We hit it off just fine.*

> ~

"Tell him your mama is here"

Rose wanted to drive out to the base right away and search for Poe, but Hank persuaded her it would be like searching for a needle in a haystack, even for a man as large as Poe, and they would have a hard time even talking their way through the front gate. There were nearly a hundred thousand men at the sprawling base, and the trainees were often out on the firing range or on long marches. Hank had spent six years in the army and mustered out as a staff sergeant. He knew how things worked. He said the best thing to do was to sit tight and let Poe know where she was, then wait for him to get in touch.

"I could write him a letter," Rose said, "but Poe don't read."

"He'll find somebody to read it to him. The army is good that way."

"And I don't have a proper address."

"Don't need that either. If you've got a boy in the service, they'll get it to him."

Rose sat down and composed her letter, four painstaking sentences that took her half an hour to write, printed in pencil in large block letters in a Big Chief writing tablet Hank had scrounged up, the kind they used in grade schools. She wrote it once, asked Hank to correct her spelling, and then copied it out again before she mailed it.

DEAR POE —

I AM HERE AT A PLACE CALLED
THE RAINIER VIEW MOTEL. I HOPE
YOU ARE DOING FINE. IF YOU GET
THIS CALL ME. HANK WHO RUNS
THE PLACE IS A GOOD MAN, HE
WILL PUT YOU IN TOUCH WITH ME.

YOUR LOVING MAMA,
ROSE

Hank wrote the motel phone number under Rose's letter and added that he could call collect if he didn't have a quarter. She sent another letter every day until Rose's first Sunday morning at the motel, two weeks into Poe's basic training, when the phone at the front desk rang at seven o'clock. Rose was sweeping out the office when Hank answered and called her over.

"It's your boy," he said.

She took the phone with tears in her eyes. "Poe?"

"Hi, Mama. It's me, Poe."

"I know, honey. It's real good to hear your voice. How're you doin?"

"I'm doin okay, Mama. Except sometimes I get mixed up in drill and the sergeant gets mad at me. He says I got two left feet."

"I expect you do. I guess you got somebody to read my letters, then?"

"Uh-huh. My friend Bill. He's a real nice guy. He's got the top bunk and I got the bottom bunk. He helps me get everything squared away in my footlocker, so's I don't get in trouble. He made the call for me, too."

"That's good, Poe. That's real good that you made a friend like Bill. Are you gettin enough to eat?"

"They feed us pretty good, only you got to gobble it down quick. They don't give you a whole lot of time. I was eatin too slow at breakfast time and the sergeant, he kicked the whole doggone tray right in my face. I didn't get no breakfast that day."

"Well, I want you to know I'm right here. In case things don't go right. I got a job and a place to stay, and I'm gonna set right here until they turn you loose."

"They haven't said nothin about lettin me go."

"I know, baby. But sooner or later, they got to. You ain't suited for the army."

"Uh-huh. That's what the drill sergeant says. He says the draft board messed up. They ain't even got clothes to fit me and I got to wear my boots from back home."

"They'll figure it out. That's why I'm here. Soon as they let you go, Mama's going to take you back home. This sergeant fella? You tell him your mama is out here, alright? You show him that telephone number, and you tell him to give me a call.

What's his name, anyway?"

"Sergeant James. There's other sergeants, but he's the boss sergeant. He says I'm not supposed to call him *sir*. He sings when we're out marchin, and we sing back. Makes it go real easy."

"I'll bet it does. Nothing like music to make the hard miles easy, now is there? Well, I expect your time is about up. I better say goodbye now."

"Okay, Mama. We get to call every Sunday, so I'll call you next Sunday, alright?"

"Yes, you do that. I'll be waitin right here for you to call."

After she hung up, Rose burst into tears and sobbed her way through half a box of Kleenex while Hank tried to console her.

"I never been away from him before," she said. "Not for more than the space of a day, and then he was close by. I ain't used to this."

"I imagine it's hard on a woman," Hank said. "But if he's as you say he is, they'll turn him loose sooner or later."

"What if they don't, though? What if they send him to that war? Poe is big as a moose, only he ain't as fast and he don't know how to hide. They'll kill him sure."

"No, they won't. He won't go to no war, they'll turn him loose. You'll see. I know how the army works. It takes them hell's own amount of time, but they generally figure out the right thing after a while. I had a boy in my platoon in basic, kid named Kedore. Couldn't figure out a thing. Every time we buffed the floor in the barracks, he'd come in from a march on a rainy day and track mud right across the middle of the floor. We'd all yell at him and he'd stand there tracking more mud and bawling like a baby with a wet diaper, 'cause we was yellin at the poor devil. They finally sent him home."

"My Poe won't bawl like a baby."

"I ain't sayin he will. Only that if you're a square peg and the army is a round hole, they figure it out, sooner or later."

~

"This gun won't shoot!"

While Rose waited at the motel, Poe slogged through the cold rain with the rest of the draftees. On long marches when weaker soldiers couldn't take it, Poe would carry an extra pack or two slung over his wide shoulders, marching mile after mile under the hundred-foot Douglas fir trees that dripped rain down their necks, diving off to the side of the road when a tank came barreling through, listening to the sergeants bellow at every mistake, all of it a rain-smeared, exhausting blur.

Four weeks into basic, Poe still didn't have a helmet because the supply sergeant couldn't find one to fit his head. He wore the biggest field jacket the army had, but it was three inches too short in the arms and he couldn't begin to close it across his chest, so he had to leave it unzipped on the coldest days, and his high-water fatigue pants stopped short of the top of his boots. He didn't look or act like a soldier, but he didn't fare as badly as the sergeant thought he would. He was unfailingly cheerful, tireless, willing, and as strong as any two recruits. In combat, he would be the guy toting the M60 machine gun, provided he could be taught how to assemble and clean it.

It took a nearly fatal incident for the army to admit that the draft board had made a terrible mistake. They were on the rifle range, squinting at targets through the driving rain, when Poe's rifle wouldn't fire. He swiveled the muzzle into the drill sergeant's belly and pulled the trigger again and again, saying:

"This gun won't shoot. How come it won't shoot?"

The sergeant wrenched the rifle out of Poe's hands and ejected the magazine. It hadn't fired because the safety was still on. Two tours of duty in the war, and this was the closest he had come to getting killed in the line of duty. That evening, the sergeant spoke to his company commander, who booted it upstairs to the battalion commander, who paid a visit to the regimental commander, who spoke to the base commander, who had to call someone at the Pentagon. It took three days for the word to come down: Poe was to be given an immediate honorable discharge, with the paperwork to be expedited before someone got killed. When the discharge came through, the sergeant called Rose. Hank drove her out to the base to meet Poe at the gate. Poe was grinning and singing as he waited, rocking back and forth from foot to foot.

They spent three more nights at the motel before Rose decided it was time they were getting home. Hank was sorry to see her go. He offered her a job at a good wage, with better living quarters for herself and Poe, free of charge. He even mumbled something about how maybe they could get married and buy a little house. Rose said she was awful sorry, but she wasn't the marrying kind, and anyhow they had to get back home. She printed out her address on the Big Chief writing tablet and told Hank to be sure to look her up if he was ever in the neighborhood.

They left Seattle at mid-morning the next day, mother and son each taking up a pair of seats on a nearly empty bus, sometimes reaching across the aisle to hold hands as the miles flew by. Poe liked the bus stations where they ate at lunch counters. Rose laughed when a trucker who sat next to them in Spokane said to a poky waitress, "Do y'all need help to catch that chicken out back? 'Cause I got a rope in the truck. I expect I could get a half hitch on a pullet, if it would get them two drumsticks here before nightfall." Rose explained the joke to Poe and he laughed, too.

This time, Rose got to see Wyoming. They were in Billings at five fifteen in the morning, but it was full light by the time they arrived in Sheridan at seven thirty, with the Bighorn Mountains in the rearview mirror. They arrived in Plattsburgh, New York, in time for a Saturday night supper and a beer before the last leg home. Rose decided they could afford to spend the night in a motel, so they each had a hot bath and a good night's sleep and left early the next morning on a milk-run bus bound for Bunker's Corner. Rose thought of using the pay phone at the bus station to call Joey for a lift home, but she decided the walk would do them good after all those long hours on the bus. On the way to the little yellow house, they passed the cemetery where Huguette was buried. They'd been through the routine so many times that Poe knew what to do without being told. He held her bag while Rose marched straight to Huguette's grave, tugged down her panties, and peed on the old woman's grave until her eyes watered.

~ III ~

Fabula animi

Out of habit, Miranda looks into her father's study to ask if he wants to come along on her afternoon hike. As always, Thorne refuses. He knows how quickly she walks and he doesn't want to be a burden. He watches Miranda set out with that long, confident stride, wishes that his aging legs worked half as well as hers do, and when she is out of sight returns to brooding on the encroaching shadows of his life.

After half an hour spent staring blankly out the window, Thorne decides that he wants to go for a hike after all. He changes into his hiking boots, fills an old army surplus canteen with water, jams a battered straw hat on his head, and takes up his walking stick.

The staff is a marvel, a sinuous four-foot branch of red pine that had once tripped him up as he walked not far from the house. He had picked it up, tried its heft in his hands, gazed up at the pine that had so fortuitously dropped it at his feet, and knew that he had at last found the wood he sought. After a lifetime of carving, this would be his masterwork, his summing up of the story of man's soul. He would call it his *fabula animi* and work into it all that he knew.

As a young man in Ireland, Thorne had shipped out to sea on an ocean-going freighter and never looked back. Somewhere in the Indian Ocean, he had come across a seaman carving a scene of the nativity in a hunk of basswood. The seaman loaned him some tools, showed him the basics, and by the end of the voyage, Thorne was himself turning out passable carvings, but he had never attempted anything as ambitious as the *fabula animi.*

Thorne used a knot at the top of the cane to carve a swirl representing the birth of the universe from the point of singularity in the Big Bang into the opposing faces of God as Alpha and Omega. On one side of the staff, the head of the deity was represented as man, with woman on the opposite side above the inscription, *Deus absconditus,* a reference to the hidden god, unknowable to man. From there he descended to a carving of Adam and Eve giving birth to Original Sin in the Garden of Eden, then to Abraham preparing to kill his son Isaac as a token of his complete devotion to God, and then to Jesus on the cross.

After Christ, he carved Muhammed the Prophet pointing to the existence of one true God, then Buddha bringing enlightenment through meditation, and the symbol of Tao, the way, along with the symbols for Yang and Yin, the opposing poles of life, followed by the net by which all beings are caught, with no escape from life and death. Next he carved a Native American story of the beginning of life through the symbol of a howling coyote, along with Prometheus bringing fire to man and suffering the punishment of Zeus, tied to a rock to have his liver pecked out for eternity. Prometheus endured, however, in the form of man returning his fire to the heavens in the form of a rocket bound for outer space.

Thorne had used all his skill to carve an hourglass symbolizing the passage of time, and a pair of dice imposed over a dragonfly to signify man's dangerous bent for gambling with nature. Near the base of the staff was a naked man puzzling over the quantum theory, intertwined strands of DNA, and farther down the Four Horsemen of the Apocalypse, the cosmic result of man's tendency to play God. Thorne had turned a final knot at the base of the staff into a wood carving of the *Enola Gay* dropping a single bomb on Hiroshima as the plane banked away from a mushroom cloud. The staff had taken two full months to carve, and before he was a third of the way through the work, Thorne knew that he possessed something of great power.

On stormy days when there is lightning in the air, the stick begins to vibrate in his hands and he hears a recurring bass note, so low that it is almost undetectable to the human ear, a steady, low *thrum* that seemed to echo the stars. It frightens him a little, this red-pine staff, but he is proud of it. When he leaves the house, he swings the stick jauntily. He has forgotten Poe until the giant calls after him in that odd, high-pitched voice. "Hey, Mister Sir Mister. It's a beautiful day, ain't it?"

Thorne flutters his free hand in Poe's direction, not wanting to be drawn into a long conversation about the perfections of the wall. The poor devil would say it was a beautiful day if it were raining pitchforks, but it isn't Thorne's idea of a beautiful day. It's terribly hot for this far north this late in August, nearly a hundred degrees and humid, and as he strides along, the warm, dusty scent of pine trees fills his nostrils and his boots kick up dust. It's forest-fire weather. What they need is a good, soaking rain, but there is nothing in the forecast. Thorne has become obsessed with the weather in his old age, and he checks the forecast a dozen times a day. There is nothing ahead for the next two weeks but more of the same hot, dry weather they've had most of the summer.

A raven shrieks from a blue spruce, a tiny red squirrel chitters furiously. Thorne swings the walking stick as he hikes. It's beautifully weighted. It isn't just for show, this wonderful piece of carved wood. It really does help a man his age travel over rough ground. He's getting into a rhythm, enjoying the sweat and the dust and the solitude, when he tops a rise and sees them standing under a rocky outcrop a quarter mile or more away: Miranda, with a man.

Thorne halts. He waves, but they don't wave back. He leans the walking stick against a hackberry tree and takes a long pull from the canteen, trying to decide what he should do. He doesn't recall whether Miranda told him she was going hiking with someone, but it's quite possible she did and he has simply forgotten. Should he come strolling up and offer a big, cheery hello or veer off in a different direction and pretend he hasn't seen them? Hadn't Airmail said something about Miranda and a man? He can't recall. He decides he will simply blunder on up to them as if by accident, and then she'll have to introduce him. But as he starts after her, Miranda turns abruptly and hikes off in the opposite direction, leaving her friend hurrying to catch up. Even at that distance, Thorne can tell the man isn't much of a hiker. He thinks of trying to catch up to them, but Miranda is moving much too fast, with the man almost jogging to keep up with her. Soon they're around a bend onto the west slope of Manitou Mountain and out of sight.

Something about the man bothers him. Something familiar in his stance, his build, the way he walks. He feels an instinctive dislike for the stranger, but he can't say why. It is probable, he decides, that he is feeling nothing more than the jealousy every man feels toward the rival who usurps his place in his daughter's life.

Thorne turns for home along a path that will take him through the heavy woods that adjoin his property. Here the forest is a tangle of beech and fir and maple trees, leavened with the occasional hackberry or black oak. He pauses where shafts of sunlight pierce the heavy foliage overhead, stands with his arms spread wide, the walking stick upraised. There is magic in this forest. He can feel it. Odd creatures are birthed here, fully formed from the first moments of their existence, luminous and fantastical beasts, scales and skin and fur still damp from their birth, gliding down from the highest branches to caper in the shadows below. For a few moments, he can see them clearly, their lavender stripes, spiraling golden horns, and six-armed bodies. They drift down, their flanks quivering in the breeze. He peers up into the trees, watches as they sail one by one like seed pods and land gently in the thick vegetation around the roots of the trees before they prance away. Their large golden eyes gaze at him from the shadows, the stick in his hand seems to rise toward them of its own accord — then the light shifts and they vanish.

The creatures are symptoms of his dementia, surely. He cannot summon them simply by lifting his wand like a modern-day Merlin. Yet strange events are afoot. The rational man in him is giving way to something else, and in this forest all that he has learned is transformed in ways he still cannot grasp.

Thorne raises his staff into a shaft of sunlight, feels it tremor and dance, and then he hears it, that steady, low-pitched *thrum . . . thrum . . . thrum*, a sound he never hears unless a storm is on its way.

~

On the trail of the Sasquank
Skeeter and Moe have to abandon the Great Sasquank Hunt for a few days because Alf, in one of his unpredictable bursts of energy and dedication to the camp, has decided to teach the boys how to paddle a canoe on the lake. Skeeter and Moe already know what to do, because every summer, Alf has one of these phases where he actually tries to do something for the kids.

Moe loves the canoe. Alf says that he takes to it like a rat to water. It's the best place he knows, out on the lake, slipping along, as nearly soundless as a human can be, paddle left, paddle right, his own center precisely balanced between the two. He is strong for his age, and on this lake he finds something he has never known in his life: silence. Not complete silence, because there are bird cries, shouts from the other boys, bullfrogs croaking, the slosh of water on the shore. But it feels like silence to a boy who has spent all his life listening to car alarms, noisy arguments in the apartment next door, ambulance and police and fire sirens, the howls of the mad, frightening screams in the night.

Most of the boys don't care for Alf, even though they adore Maeva, but Moe is on familiar ground with the man. He's known guys like Alf all his life: sly, furtive, watchful, always working the angles, convinced that they are at least twice as smart as the law and that people who play by the rules are chumps — a trait that lands most of them in jail, sooner or later.

The canoeing makes for a handful of flawless summer days, but with Alf, it's only a matter of time until he reverts to form. There's a party, people turning up in noisy cars long after midnight and departing at dawn, Alf and Maeva still sleeping it off at nine o'clock, the boys free to go hunting the beast. Skeeter and Moe have both taken to calling their quarry the Sasquank. Moe likes the name because it's different, even though it isn't in the books. The beast they're trailing is unlike any other, not Bigfoot or the Yeti or even the Sasquatch, but the Sasquank.

Poe, his day's work on the wall done, ambles toward home. A quarter mile behind, Skeeter and Moe blunder along, heads down, following the broad footprints in the dew. They hear Poe's song and pull up, sudden chills bringing out the goose-bumps on their hairless forearms. Skeeter grabs Moe so hard he leaves a bruise on his bicep. "That ain't no human sound. That's the Sasquank!"

They crouch down, using a tall growth of cattails as cover, and creep along for another quarter mile, following the song. Skeeter sees him first, Poe in silhouette two hundred yards off, framed against the paler sky in the west, a massive creature with a wild cry like nothing he's ever heard, even in monster movies. Skeeter drops to his knees, quaking from head to toe, afraid he'll wet himself. "Holy Mother Mary. It's the freakin Sasquank, Moe."

Moe nods solemnly. "I think you're right, Skeeter. We found the Sasquank."

"Yessir! I had a dream about this right here, catchin the beast. Now we got him, what we gonna do with him?"

"*Do* with him? Well, I guess we'll put a dog collar round his big old neck and lead him home, sweet as you please. Is that what you mean?"

"No, fool. I mean, are we gonna tell somebody? Alf and Maeva, maybe?"

"No way. Maeva is alright, but Alf — he'd sell his mother for five bucks. We don't tell him nothin. This one time, you got to keep your rabid mouth shut tight. What we're gonna do is, we get a camera and take us a picture. Can't nobody argue with a picture."

"But we ain't got no camera."

"I know that, fool. That's why we go back to the camp and we borrow us a camera. We come out Sasquank hunting tomorrow, pick up the track again, then we get close and take our pictures."

"What if nobody loan us a camera?"

"Then we steal one. I don't go for stealin, most times, but this is special. We'll put it back when we're done."

As they watch from behind the cattails, the great beast turns and looks their way. Skeeter has to stifle a shriek.

"Oh, man! He can smell us! He's gonna *eat* us, sure. Ate by a Sasquank, that's what it's gonna say on our tombstones."

"Sasquanks don't eat people, Skeeter. He could grab you by the ass and throw you up in that tree, but he ain't gonna eat you."

"How you know Sasquanks don't eat people?"

"Because Sasquanks are vegetarians, that's why. I read it in a book."

"So what are we supposed to do now?"

"We're gonna *run*, that's what. Pick 'em up, lay 'em down. When I count three, we are outta here. But we got to run quiet-like."

"How we supposed to run *quiet*? Don't nobody run *quiet*. You gotta run, you run, that's all."

"Okay, so run loud, but run *hard*. You ready? *One. Two. Three . . . RUN!*"

~ IV ~
Deluge

Live music Saturday night

Rose sings with Matt Harrow and the Green Mountain Boys
at Gillespie's Tavern in Belle Coeur every Saturday night. It
started years ago when the boys were playing bluegrass and
Texas swing at the tavern; Poe was just back from the army
then, and Rose happened to hear the music as she was passing
by and went in for a listen. The Green Mountain Boys were
pretty good amateur musicians, but not one of them could
sing a lick. Rose listened to a set and when they started the
next set, she asked if she could join in. Matt Harrow was
used to folks thinking they could sing, and he motioned for
her to come on up and croon a tune. She asked if they could
play Patsy Cline's "Walkin' After Midnight" in C with the
shift to C-sharp on the last verse, and Matt gave her an intro.
When she wrapped her powerful voice around the tune, the

musicians grinned and nodded to one another, knowing they had found their singer at last. Rose ended up doing six encores that night, with the crowd begging for more. She was back the week after, and the week after that. After a few weeks, Dan Gillespie hung a new sign in the window that advertised: *Live Music Saturday Nite, Rose Didelot & the Green Mountain Boys.*

The sign was still there, faded and forgotten in the fly-blown window because no one in the county needed to be told that Rose Didelot sang at Gillespie's on Saturday nights. It was the highlight of her week, and she never missed it unless she was too sick to move, which was pretty much never. She had started out making twenty-five dollars a night, and over the years, Dan had bumped her all the way up to a hundred. A hundred dollars for a night spent doing something she would have done for free.

On the hottest night in August, Rose and Poe walk the four miles to Gillespie's, Rose leading the way along the dusty road, Poe shambling along a dozen paces behind. They arrive a few minutes after seven and take a table near the fireplace. Rose waves to Dan, who fetches a bottle of Schlitz beer for her and a cream soda for Poe. Poe doesn't dare touch alcohol because Rose says it makes him wild and he's apt to get carried away and tear up the place. Dinner and drinks are on the house. Rose has a steak-and-kidney pie, Poe has the New York steak with extra fries and onion rings and three hamburgers on the side, and they settle down to wait for Matt Harrow, Earl Conlin, and Dave Quenneville to set up their instruments. Matt is on the dobro and mandolin, Earl is a pretty fair flat-picker, and Dave, a hardware dealer from across the border in Quebec, plays the fiddle. He's the only one Rose has never taken to her bed because, as he explained to her one snowy night when she had invited him to keep her warm, he prefers to sleep with gentlemen.

The Green Mountain Boys are gray-haired now. They are better musicians than they used to be, but they still can't sing. It doesn't matter, because they have Rose. They always do an instrumental set without her to show off their picking, then around nine o'clock when the crowd is starting to peak and folks are through eating, Rose joins them for their second set. Tonight, she whispers "Sweet Dreams" to Matt, bows her head as Dave does the first few bars on the fiddle, and then her voice fills the room above the clack of pool balls, the roars of laughter, and the occasional crash of a beer glass hitting the floor. *"Sweet dreams of you . . ."* They are a hard-drinking bunch, the crowd at Gillespie's, and sometimes they're a hard-fighting bunch. They work hard all week and when Saturday night rolls around it's time to howl, but they always quiet down for Rose. She sings with her eyes closed and her head thrown back, rocking to the beat, the music they are making so honeyed that at times it makes her shiver.

Between sets, Rose dances with all comers. She never lacks for partners, although half of them barely come up to her bosom. She can waltz and jitterbug and do a mean Texas two-step, and if she runs out of guys who want a whirl, she'll grab a gal and carry right on. As the night wears on, some of the dancers cop a feel here and there, squeeze her bosom, or grope her buttocks. Rose doesn't begrudge them their pleasures. There's precious little solace for a working man or woman, never has been. Rose is generous with her favors because the way she sees things, if she has it to give, it would be a sin to withhold it. If the Good Lord didn't want a person to make love, why did He make it feel so doggone good? Now and then the wandering hand on her bosom belongs to a woman, and Rose will accommodate her, too, even invite her to stop by when Poe is out working on the wall, because we're all God's creatures, no matter how the twig was bent, and we all have our needs.

Near one o'clock in the morning, when the drinkers have drunk until their legs wobble and they are lining up to puke out back, someone takes up the cry. *Dance, Poe, dance! We want a dance! Dance, goat-man, dance! Dance, Poe, dance!*

Poe grins and shakes his big bald melon-head over and over, *No no no, not tonight*, but they will not be silenced until they've had their dance. He pushes the table back so he can stand and, to rhythmic clapping from every patron in the joint, rises majestically from his seat, his face lit with something that can only be called rapture. Poe is transformed. He tilts his head back. He thrusts out his arms and listens to the beat, nodding in rhythm, and then he begins to move, one toe tapping lightly on the floor and then the other. The patrons know enough to stay well back, out of his way. When he flings those mighty arms around, you need to keep your distance.

Poe will dance to whatever tune Matt and the boys want to play, but "Wabash Cannonball" is his favorite, and "Wabash Cannonball" it is tonight. The occasional strangers who have blundered into Gillespie's and have never seen Poe dance expect the human equivalent of a dancing bear, the fascination lying not in the dance itself but in the fact that he's able to dance at all. They gape with the rest when Poe displays not only a precise sense of rhythm and a light-footed agility, but also a genuine grace in motion, as though his size and bulk somehow vanish the instant he begins to dance. He prances.

He whirls. He leaps. He stomps until the floor shakes. His six-toed feet fly in their size-eighteen boots. Glasses hanging in racks above the bar clank and tremble and sometimes fall and shatter. The drinkers stand and clap as one, urging Poe on. *Dance, goat-man, dance!*

Poe dances on and on without pausing for breath until at last, when he's had enough, he hoists his arms above his head like a triumphant boxer, bows to the applause, and leaves the floor with his best work shirt and his OshKosh B'gosh coveralls soaked in sweat. Rose says goodnight to the Green Mountain Boys, takes up her handbag, tucks the hundred-dollar bill Dan Gillespie hands her into her bosom, and guides Poe to the door and out into the night. They're halfway home before Poe catches his breath.

The wind is almost still and the sky is a wild splash of stars from one horizon to the other. A buttermilk moon rises over Manitou Mountain as they walk. Rose points to the Big Dipper and to Orion's Belt. Poe gawks happily. Rose keeps a firm grip on his arm to prevent him from bumping into a tree or a lamppost as he gazes at the stars.

They're half a mile from home when Rose lifts a hand. She stands still for a moment, then turns in a full circle, her head up, sniffing the air. It's a balmy late-summer night and everyone in the pub talked about the fine weather they've been having, but Rose senses something else on the breeze. "Rain coming," she says, even though there is not a cloud in the sky. "Hard rain coming."

Poe nods. He has never known Rose to be wrong about the weather. If she says there is a hard rain coming, then it's going to rain.

~

On a raft in the river

Thorne's sheets and blankets are soaked with sweat and knotted around his body, as though he's just broken a fever. His fingers clutch and tear at the sheets so hard that he will discover in the morning a broken nail dangling from his index finger. He kicks out with his feet, trying to free himself, but the more he struggles, the more tightly the damp sheets bind him.

The dream has him in a powerful grip, and it won't let go. His eyelids flutter. His head thrashes back and forth on the pillow. He throws up an arm, as though blocking an unwelcome vision, but he can't free himself. He is shouting, trying to warn someone, but no sound escapes his lips. He sees himself on a mountain crag, a thunderstorm bearing down on him, black cloud towers and lightning flashing, and a wind that threatens to tear his clothes from his body, and he is directing it all. He thrusts his staff at the sky and commands the tempest, bringing it down on the heads of the tiny figures he can see below, the toy churches in the toy villages, cars the size of insects scuttling to and fro on pointless errands.

"Rain, goddamn you!" he bellows into the wind. "Rain! Bring down the deluge! Let the heavens open and rain! Swallow all the unholy works of our hands! Let the thunder roar and the lightning flash! Rain, dammit!"

He looks on as the elements obey his command and a catastrophic storm tears across the valley. He sees the flood with startling clarity, every droplet of water and blade of grass in high relief. Hail beats down. Great trees bow and crack in the wind. The crops in the fields are scythed to the ground by the hail, and after the hail comes the deluge, and the sea is upended over the earth. Everything will be washed away. Nothing will remain. Nothing.

The scene shifts and the storm bursts on a stark, arid landscape somewhere in the Southwest, in a valley that is nothing at all like the Belle Coeur Valley. The land is parched and arid, rocks and sand in high relief. In the heart of the valley there is a deep canyon and in the bed of the canyon there is a river, or what is left of it, a narrow trickle of water after years of drought. A man sits cross-legged on a makeshift raft that has lodged in the mud at a bend in the river and cannot be moved. He is shirtless and barefoot and his blue jeans are ripped and worn. He has the deep desert tan of a man who has slept outdoors for decades. His hair and beard are long and white and tangled. The man on the raft looks exactly like Thorne himself, except that he is thin and hard as a steel blade. He wears dark glasses and on his head a torn, greasy do-rag in the pattern of the American flag. He is meditating, legs crossed, forearms resting on his thighs, palms up.

The cloudburst hits eighty miles upriver, but there is no sign of the storm in the canyon. The man on the raft hears the roar when it is less than a mile away, a thirty-foot wall of water bursting through the canyon, bearing down on the raft. He remains motionless in the sun, face upturned, waiting.

Thorne understands. The deluge at his command will sweep him away with the rest.

~

Black clouds topple the moon
The massive oak tree next to the house moans and stirs in the breeze. The leaves on its lower boughs stroke the roof of the house like brushes on a snare drum. Out back, the tarp on Poe's rowboat works loose and flaps against the hull. The bedroom curtains billow, the blinds rattle. The geese in the

yard pelt one way or another in honking confusion, then hunker down for shelter beneath the overhanging roof in the lee of the pigsty. Towering black clouds topple the moon, pale sheets of lightning tremble ahead of the first slash of rain that precedes the storm like a harrow preparing the dark earth for planting.

Rose wakes to the moan of a hard wind and peers at the old clock on her bedside table. It's a quarter past five. She's been in bed less than three hours. She waits to be certain the storm is going to hit, lying with her head buried deep in the pillow until a bolt of lightning flares in the window like a stage prop, then swings her bulk out of bed. Her feet are on the rough pine of the floor before the clap of thunder shakes the window pane. She puts a pot of coffee on to perk, and stands at the sink watching the storm barrel across the valley. The sky before daybreak is just pale enough so that she can make out the first iron slant of the rain, the maple and spruce trees' dark shadows bowing before the wind, the jagged traces of lightning striking mountain to mountain across the valley, rain in long sheets washing across the river far below, a dove tossed across the sky like a scrap of paper.

The oak, whipped by a gust of wind, slams the house with a sharp crack. As if on cue, the vanguard of the rain lashes the gravel driveway, the cedar windbreak, the tumbledown stone wall that has been there for a hundred years or more. A granite outcrop that shelters the back porch is scoured by a drift of hail, and the rain comes down in a savage wall of water, backed by an unbroken rumble of thunder.

Rose thinks to rouse Poe, but he is in such a peaceful slumber she leaves him be. He can't think of climbing the path to the goat pasture in this storm. The lightning would incinerate him, big as he is. By the time she thinks to turn on the radio, the weatherman says Belle Coeur County has already received six inches of rain and the storm rages on. He is about to say how long it might last when the power goes out. The radio falls silent, and in the gloom of the kitchen Rose hunts for lanterns, candles, and matches, fumbling around until the first candle is lit because the room is plunged into midnight darkness.

It has settled in to rain as though it might go on forty days and forty nights. Poe wakes of his own accord a little before seven. Rose lights the propane stove to make breakfast, and they sit eating and waiting for the storm to end, but the deluge shows no sign of easing and the goats have to be milked. The thunder and lightning have eased some, and she helps Poe wriggle into his old Mackintosh and a pair of oversized fisherman's wading boots that she had found at the army surplus and sends him on his way.

She watches him go. Within fifty feet, he has vanished into the murk. She locates spare batteries in a drawer and slips them into the radio so she can get the weather report, then puts on another pot of coffee. The weatherman is talking about the Belle Coeur River, which is rising dangerously and threatens to overflow its banks. Rose thinks of the poor folk at the Split Rock Trailer Park. Most of the trailer park washed away in a flood twenty years ago, but they rebuilt it on the same ground, betting that nature would not strike twice in the same place. Now it looks like they lost that bet. Rose has good friends down there and she worries for them, especially those with kids. It's no place to bring up a child.

Two hours later, Poe is back with as much milk as he can tote, two big buckets in each six-fingered hand, heavily watered down by the rain. He says the goats are all huddled in their shed. He and Joey Ballew put it up on a concrete foundation. The shed is solid, the goats will be fine. They play a little slapjack, the only card game Poe knows, and listen to the radio.

The news keeps getting worse. All the bridges that lead out of the county are under water. The only way out is to cross the border into Canada. "They should call this place Belle Coeur Island," says the man on the radio, "because we're not going anywhere for awhile, folks. Might as well relax. Here's an oldie but a goodie. Patsy Cline with 'Blue Moon of Kentucky.'"

Rose leans back to listen to poor Patsy. She remembers hearing the news on her transistor radio when Patsy's plane fell out of the sky on a March day in 1963. They say time heals all wounds. It isn't true.

~

Sunday prayers

The rain falls for three days and three nights. Four bridges are out and the others are under water. Roads have been washed away, cars are under water on low-lying streets, basements flooded, electrical power fitful but mostly out. Nine trailers at the Split Rock Trailer Park have floated away and the rest are up to their doors in water. Most of the residents are able to get out with whatever possessions they can throw into cars or pickups, but a woman, her three children, and their two dogs have to be rescued from the top of their trailer house, floating two miles downstream in the Belle Coeur River.

The fourth day, a Wednesday, dawns clear, sunny, and warm, with a light breeze from the south. People emerge blinking from their houses to survey the damage. Couches and carpets from basement rooms are brought out to air. They mosey around the streets, comparing notes on who lost what, swapping yarns about how they survived the great flood. There is for a time a sense of neighborliness, concern for those less fortunate, a desire to help.

When Sunday rolls around, Rose decides that it's time to pray, to thank God for deliverance from what might have been. They are regular churchgoers anyway, Rose and Poe, but today is more important than most. There are two churches in Hartbury, the First Gospel Church of the Pentecost and the Lamb of Jesus Gospel Church directly across the street. There are more churches in Bunker's Corner and Belle Coeur: Methodist, Seventh Day Adventist, Episcopal, Unitarian, Lutheran, even Catholic, but Rose figures two churches in a village ought to be enough for anyone. She doesn't want to hurt the feelings of either preacher, so she and Poe put on their Sunday-go-to-meeting clothes and stroll down to First Gospel one week and attend the Lamb of Jesus the next.

Rose is popular in both churches for her powerful alto voice on the hymns and her habit of intoning *amen, brother* and *praise Jesus* and *sweet Lord above* at intervals during the sermon, so that she and the preacher seem to be working in unison to get the whole congregation worked up. She also contributes her cherry and apple pies to the bake sales, helps out with the church picnics, and invites the preachers to her little yellow house for supper once a month.

On this Sunday, she fixes an extra-big breakfast of waffles, eggs, and bacon for Poe, and after she has done the washing up they get dressed and walk to the Lamb of Jesus, where the sermon is one of her favorites, on the tale of the Good

Samaritan. They sing "Just a Closer Walk with Thee" and "Rock of Ages" and "An Unclouded Day," Rose's favorite, and when the service is over, they stand outside for a time, basking in the August sunshine and listening to the church ladies gossip about the storms.

When the congregation begins to break up, heading off in different directions for Sunday dinners and afternoon naps, Rose and Poe stroll home arm in arm. Poe greets everyone they pass, pausing to tickle babies and pet stray dogs. Now and then he comes to a halt on the sidewalk, lost in contemplation of the vast, spreading arms of a century-old beech tree or a towering blue spruce or a pair of cardinals on a branch of a crabapple tree. Rose lets him be. The natural world has never ceased to amaze him, and Rose believes that's just fine and dandy. It would be a better world if more people stood in awe of their surroundings. Back home, she fixes a lunch for Poe, sandwiches of sliced salami on home-baked bread, while he packs up his fishing tackle. Sunday afternoons are Poe's fishing time, and he never misses a one — fly or bait fishing in the summer, ice fishing in winter. Sunday evenings, they eat Poe's catch, usually brook trout, pumpkinseed, or smallmouth bass. Wild Bill taught him to fish, and in all the years Poe has been fishing, he's never once come home empty-handed.

~

"And if a woman have an issue . . ."
Poe stoops to lean his great head on Rose's shoulder, then hoists his fishing pole and tackle box and sets out. A fine morning has tilted on a whiff of breeze-borne minor key into a sullen afternoon and there is the threat of more rain. The sun is filtered through haze that thickens into cloud, and the

birds are oddly silent. Everywhere burst milkweed has scattered, and the spidery threads dangle from the maples like Halloween decorations.

The river and both the creeks he likes to fish are running too high, the water roiled and muddy and clogged with broken branches from the flood. Poe decides instead to hike the six miles to the gravel pit where he worked for a time after the army. The old pit is now a miniature lake set in a grove of trees overlooking the river. Only a few people know of its existence, and the lake throbs with fish. When Miranda was ten or eleven years old, she came here with him almost every summer Sunday. He taught her how to bait the hook and cast and reel in her catch. She shrieked with joy every time she caught one, no matter how small. Then she got to be an older girl, and she had studies to do, sports practice, girlfriends to hang out with, boyfriends maybe, and Poe went back to fishing alone.

When it was still a working gravel pit, the pit-man ran the gravel pump from a makeshift raft out on the water. The pump dredged sand and gravel from the pit and forced it up a long pipe into a ten-ton chute supported by a tower built with railroad ties. Next to the chute was a cabin equipped with an old tractor seat, a window that was a square foot with no glass, and a cast-iron lever. When the chute was full, a trucker would back his dump truck between the support posts of the tower. It was a tricky job, because the heavy dual tires on the back end of the truck would slew to the side in the spilled gravel, and if the truck hit the supports hard enough, the entire tower would come tumbling down, likely crushing the trucker and killing the chute-man, too. It was Poe's job to watch the truck back in and holler *Whoa!* when it was at the right spot, then pull the lever to dump the gravel into the truck bed and watch that it didn't overflow. When it was full, he'd close the lever and holler *Go!* The truck would pull out and Poe would sit happily, holding the lever in one hand, listening to the long *ssssshhhhh* of wet gravel from the pit pouring in to refill the chute. When the dour pump-man shut down the engine to eat his lunch or take a nap, Poe climbed down to fish. Most days, he caught plenty for himself and Rose, with enough left over for the pump-man and the truckers.

Poe would prefer to fish at the gravel pit every Sunday, except that the hike is long and arduous. If he goes by the road it's twice as far, so he cuts across country through the wreckage of the old concrete plant on the edge of town, past the ghosts of dead machines, tangles of rusted cable, torn and jagged metal, a crane with its boom lowered to the ground in a parody of prayer, tumbled heaps of mortar and bricks, dark scuttling rats that vanish before his tread. There is a crater where oil from some unseen source has seeped and pooled, a scum of dead leaves and the oil-soaked feathers of dead birds on its surface, and beyond that a reeking cesspool. Poe gives it a wide berth. Farther on are stone arches through which run abandoned tracks on a railroad to nowhere, a heap of old railroad ties soaked in creosote, a jungle of rusty razor wire where a hasty or careless man might slash himself to pieces.

On the far side of the wreckage, Poe emerges onto a gravel road where the walking is easier. He's half a mile along the road when he hears the ring of hooves on asphalt, the squeak of wagon wheels, and the creak of harness leather. He knows without looking that Elmer Hepp is taking his team of prized Percherons out for a drive, pulling an old wagon whose axles are badly in need of grease. Elmer pulls the team to a halt next to Poe and fixes him with a fierce one-eyed gaze.

"Are ye in need of some relief for shank's mare, boy?"

Poe lifts his Red Sox cap and stares at Hepp, not gathering his meaning.

"Do ye need a lift? Are ye tired of walking?"

Most folks in the county refuse when Hepp offers a ride because of his habit of reciting scripture as they trot along. Poe doesn't understand a word of it, so he doesn't mind. He nods amiably, hefts his pole and tackle box onto the wagon, and climbs up next to Hepp on the driver's seat, the wagon tilting to the right as he settles in. Hepp clucks to the horses and they set out, their matched tails snapping at flies. He begins his recitation from the book of Leviticus: *And he shall take of the blood of the bullock, and sprinkle it with his finger upon the mercy seat eastward; and before the mercy seat shall he sprinkle of the blood with his finger seven times . . .*

Elmer Hepp always wears his hat tied down tight around his ears with a woman's scarf. He wraps gunnysacks around his hands and feet for warmth and ties them with binding twine, even though it's upwards of ninety degrees and humid after the rain. They travel a mile or so before Hepp breaks off his recitation of the scripture and turns to Poe.

"Know ye the day?"

"Yessir. It's Sunday."

"That it is. Sunday. Know ye the year, boy?"

Poe thinks on it. "The year it rained?"

"Aye, the Year of the Flood, son. Sign of the End Time, ain't it? Even the village idiot knows that much. Judgment Day staggers near, my boy. The conflagration is about to come down upon us, contagion and flood, the curse of Eve. That's where we stand, Poe. Mark the time and suck your portion dry, because we'll none of us be here for long. Never forget how close ye are to the Apocalypse and the day when St. Peter separates the wheat from the chaff, the saved from the sinners."

Poe tries a solemn nod. Riding with Elmer is like being in church.

The sky turns dark as a skillet, heavy with cloud. The dark fools the birds. Poe hears a great horned owl off somewhere, a flutter of the wings of a night hunter, a frantic squeak, the death of some small scuttling thing back in the woods, field mouse or ground squirrel. He shivers. Hepp pays it no mind and goes back to reciting scripture. *Then shall he kill the goat of the sin offering, that is for the people, and bring his blood within the vail, and do with that blood as he did with the blood of the bullock, and sprinkle it upon the mercy seat, and before the mercy seat.*

Poe wants to ask what a mercy seat might be, but Elmer has a manner that does not encourage idle questions. Wild Bill says that too much scripture can addle a man, and that Elmer Hepp is a prime example of the damage the Good Book can do.

At the turnoff for the gravel pit, Elmer hauls on the reins. "This is where ye get off. I'll not be driving this fine team down that road. Nothin down that way but rusty barbed wire and old concrete rebar. There's enough out there to rip the guts out of a prime Percheron. Careful where ye step now, lad. I'd not want to tell your poor mama that ye came to a bad end."

Poe climbs down. The wagon rights itself with a noisy creak. "Thank you kindly, Mister Hepp," he says as he hoists the tackle box out of the wagon. Hepp ignores him, clucks to his team, and drives away, still bellowing a verse from Leviticus: *And if a woman have an issue, and her issue in her flesh be blood, she shall be put apart seven days: and whosoever toucheth her shall be unclean until the even.*

It's a good day to fish in still waters. The black clouds have blown over and the sun feels like a lash on the back of Poe's neck. Dragonflies skim the surface, tempting the fish from the depths. After a little more than an hour, he has a dozen fish on his string. When he's done fishing, he climbs the long ladder to the tower where he had once worked, dragging his gear and his catch up with him, each rung of the ladder bending dangerously under his weight. He squeezes through the narrow passage into the little cabin next to the chute and settles onto the old tractor seat bolted to the floor. The rusty lever is between his knees. He heaves it back and forth. It needs oil, but it still works.

Next to the lever is a wooden box built to hold an oilcan and various tools. The can and the tools are gone but the old comic books are still there, crudely drawn and graphically obscene imitations of real comics. They are tattered and water stained and stiff with age, but most of the pages still open to scenes of men and women from the funny pages having graphic sex. These comics make him feel the way he feels when he lies in bed at night, remembering the outfits Miranda has worn. After thumbing through a few pages, he pulls down the suspenders of his coveralls, undoes the buttons, and spits in his palm.

When he is finished, he's too drowsy to wipe the jism off his coveralls or hold his eyes open. He stretches out on the floor, gazes up at the sky through the gaps between the boards on the roof of the tower, and falls into a deep, untroubled sleep.

~

The stink of fish

Poe wakes to the stink of fish. Rose won't like that. *Bring your fish right home*, she says. *Don't stay out there all the livelong day, Poe, till the fish stink and they ain't no good.* He has stayed out all the livelong day and the fish stink. The air has thickened and his head throbs. He pulls the fob watch on its chain out of his pocket, but the hands aren't pointing to a time he knows. He peers through the tiny window to find the sun, but it's on the far side of the tower.

Poe sees something move in the grass up on the little rise where you can look down toward the Belle Coeur River, the spot where he used to picnic with Miranda when he brought her out here to fish. He blinks and waits for his eyes to adjust to the light, and then he sees her clearly. It is Miranda, lying on a blanket in the sun. It's magic. She was not-there before he went to sleep, and now she is there. Like when she goes into the house, Miranda and not-Miranda. He starts to call out to her, but a voice in his head says *no no no.* He wants to go on looking at her. Her long brown legs. White dress with lots of tiny buttons up the front. She's lying on a red blanket and the dress is pulled up so she can get the sunshine on her brown legs, and he can see her seeing-through under-pants. The sun washes away the shadows and he stares hard at the seeing-through underpants, and he can see a dark patch where the hair is, the down-there hair. He sucks in his breath through his teeth and looks at her. He can see Miranda but she can't see him. He's hidden in the shadows of the tower. Like playing hide-and-seek. He can hide and look at the seeing-through underpants.

Miranda has a picnic basket beside her and parked behind her is a big black car. She is reading a book and eating grapes.

Her legs open a little more. Poe makes a sound in his throat, feeling himself stir. Then he hears her call out to someone. *C'mon and eat before I gobble it all up.* Is she calling to him? He thinks of climbing down from the tower, saying *Hello hello Miranda* and her saying *Hello hello* back, happy to see him, like he feels happy to see her. But then a man comes into the picture, a blond man wearing a funny kind of hat. The man bends over and pours a glass of wine for Miranda, turning his back to her as he pours. Poe sees him reach into his pocket, and his hand moves over the glass like he's blessing it. He swirls the wine a little and hands it to her, then he pours a little in a glass for himself and holds the glass out to her.

"Alright," Miranda says, "but just a bit more, then I have to go. I said I'd come out here with you because I know you're hurting and I want to stay friends, but this is the end. I mean it. It's over. The bridges are open, you can get out of the county now. You're going to have to do what you promised. You have to leave."

Poe sees the man nod his head. *Uh-huh, uh-huh.* "I know, Miranda," he says. "You've made yourself clear. It's not a problem, really. I understand. I'll get out of your life. It's just awful because I love you so much, but I can handle it."

"Good. I'm glad to hear that. I really hope we can stay friends." They touch glasses. The man has a sip of wine, and Miranda drinks the wine in her glass and rolls over onto her stomach. The man is standing, his shadow over her, watching, not talking. A long shadow in the afternoon. When he moves, it is so sudden that Poe jumps up, startled, and hits his head hard on the roof of the cabin. He rubs where it hurts and looks again to be sure. It is that thing, he knows what it is. He makes that high keening sound he makes when fear or panic takes him, that sound in his throat. If he goes to help her the man will say, *Idiot moron mutant, you oughta be in the nuthouse.* If he doesn't go, if he doesn't go. If he doesn't go, he knows what will happen. He tries to go to help her, but in his panic his bulk is caught in the narrow opening that leads from the cabin onto the ladder. He hears Miranda screaming, he hears the thud of the punches striking her, then she is quiet and he is trapped, squirming like a fish in a net, unable to break free. He lifts his arms up high over his head and blows all the air out of his lungs and he is through, squeezing through the opening and down the ladder, in such a rush that the last four rings of the ladder shatter and he falls heavily to the ground. Poe is winded and dazed by the fall, but he gathers himself and gallops toward them with a roar like a wild beast.

Poe kneels over Miranda. Blood pours from her mouth and nose. How has this happened? The sequence confuses him. The man's shadow and then the terrible things, and now the man is gone and Poe is not sure Miranda is breathing. He shakes her gently. *Miranda? Miranda?* Her eyes roll back in her head. Her white dress is open, all the little buttons undone. One of her shoes is gone, the seeing-through underpants have been torn off. Poe can't help looking. He catches a glimpse of the down-there hair and makes the keening sound in his throat again. He puts a hand on her chest to see if she is still breathing. Her breasts with the hard brown nipples move up and down on her chest. Miranda is alive. He feels her ragged breath.

Rose's voice, the voice that is always in his head, tells him what to do. *Get help. Get help get help get help.* He can't help Miranda in this place. All he can think of is to get her to the road. He slips his arms under her back and hoists her off the ground. She is dead weight but he carries her easily at first, cradling her body against his chest as he sets out in a shuffling jog along the dirt track, stumbling and sliding and splashing through the puddles.

Poe stumbles along that way for two hundred yards before he can go no more. His bicep muscles burn; his back aches. He puts her down and bends over to ease his back, gasping for breath. *Get help. Get help, Poe, you got to get help.* Carrying her this way, the road is much too far, but there was a thing he learned in the army — how to carry a wounded man to safety. They call it the fireman's carry, the way a fireman would carry someone out of a burning building. He slips his right arm between her legs, hefts her weight so that it is balanced across his shoulders, then grabs her dangling right arm in his strong right hand. Her weight is perfectly balanced. He could carry her all the way up to the goat pasture like this.

The sky goes dark again, like someone has closed a curtain. It aches with rain. Poe has no shadow as he hobbles along with Miranda, desperate to reach the highway. Blood from her nose and mouth trickles down his shoulder. He slides through the puddles and trips over roots. Branches slash at his face and arms until he is scratched and bleeding. He tries to keep her head clear so she won't get hit by the branches as he lurches along the path. She dangles like a broken doll splayed across his broad back. His lungs burn. His thighs are like water.

He has to halt three times. Bent over, breathing like a bellows, heaving air in and out of his lungs. When he pauses the last time, he sees the woods are thinning to the highway. He takes a deep breath and jogs the last quarter mile as hard as he can, then turns to follow the line of the blacktop back toward town, looking in both directions for cars. *Get help. Get help. Get help.*

~

Living in the end time

Sheriff Jim Dunn likes the Sunday afternoon shift. It's peaceful and quiet and a good time to think. Nothing happens on a Sunday (truth be told, very little happens in Belle Coeur County any day of the week), and he's able to give one of the deputies with young families the day off by working the shift himself. Dunn has almost finished a wide circuit, checking how the bridges are holding up all around the county. The bridges that weren't washed out are still sound, and the levels of the creeks and rivers have fallen enough to make a man hopeful that he's seen the worst of it, but now the sky has deepened to the shade of black ink again, and there are jagged bolts of lightning to the northwest. The storm is going to hit any minute, and he wonders if the bridges can take another gully-washer.

Sheriff Dunn rounds a curve near the old gravel pit and something that looks like the abominable snowman lurches out of the woods to his right, carrying a half-naked woman over his shoulders. He brakes hard, spills what's left of his coffee on his pants, bangs his knee on the radio, and stalls the engine. He curses and rubs the throbbing knee, trying to see what manner of creature has emerged from the forest.

Holy Jesus Mother of God. It's Poe.

Dunn puts the cruiser in park, sets the handbrake, calls dispatch for backup and an ambulance. He climbs out slowly, not wanting to alarm Poe unduly. He considers drawing his service revolver, but he's known Poe pretty much his entire life. It's best to keep things calm, especially while Poe is still holding the girl. He approaches as casually as he can, keeping his hands where Poe can see them.

"Easy now, Poe. Easy. You're going to want to put her down real gentle now, right over there."

Poe swings Miranda off his shoulders and lies her down gently in the grass. His exhausted legs give way then and he collapses beside her, his legs burning, his lungs fighting to draw in enough oxygen to speak. He rolls onto his back and lies next to Miranda, his chest heaving, staring up at the sky where the rain is about to fall, his face blank. He whispers, *Get help get help get help*, but the sheriff doesn't seem to hear him. The first drops of cool rain wash over his face. He licks the water from his dry lips as the sheriff bends over the girl.

As the wail of a siren approaches in the distance, a pair of slender, shadowy figures watch from the heavy woods on the side of the road, one of them dangling a camera by its strap.

"Oh, man, Skeeter," Moe says. "That's Poe, ain't it? That's who we been followin all this time. Ain't the Sasquank at all, it's Poe. And that poor man is in a world of misery now. He's about to learn how black folks live. Once the man gets his hands on you, he don't let go."

They start walking back to the Kids Kamp, instinctively hurrying away from trouble. They've gone barely a hundred yards when a five-pronged bolt of lightning strikes a quarter mile away. Moe jumps two feet in the air and comes down running. "I swear, we're livin in the end time, Skeeter. We better skedaddle or we're goin to get washed right off this earth."

~

A ride on a Ninja

The machine is a gray-and-silver streak on wet blacktop. It screams like a hungry thing, bearing down on Skeeter and Moe so quickly that they barely have time to crane their necks before it is almost upon them, traveling at the kind of speed that makes your bones freeze up and your muscles turn to jelly. Skeeter comes to a dead stop, mouth agape, and Moe stumbles into him, knocking Skeeter to his knees. The streak keeps coming, its engine wound up to a sound like an eagle's shriek. It's a hundred feet behind when the rider brakes, sending it into a sideways skid that threatens to take out both boys before throttling down inches from Skeeter's toes.

The rider twists the throttle on the Ninja once for effect and lifts his visor. He is a strange little boy-man with eyes a shade of inky blue. "You boys are from the Kids Kamp, are you not? What are you doing out here, may I ask? You do realize there's a storm coming. I'm bound for Maeva's abode myself. Hop on, I'll give you a lift."

Skeeter and Moe look doubtfully at one another. They've seen Airmail making deliveries or picking up mysterious packages from Alf and Maeva from time to time. It's not like he's a stranger. Moe shrugs, Skeeter nods. Airmail pats the seat behind him. "Do climb aboard the Ninja, boys. I fear the storm will not hold off for long. There's room for three when you're no bigger than we are."

Moe climbs on behind Airmail and wraps his arms around the little man's waist. Skeeter does the same with him. Moe slips the camera to him and Skeeter tucks it under his T-shirt. Airmail giggles, twists the throttle again, and they're off as though flung from a giant slingshot. Moe, clinging to Airmail for dear life, has time to think that his grandchildren will never believe this, if he lives to have grandchildren. He has some idea what a hundred miles an hour feels like from riding with one of his fool half brothers, but this is way past anything he has ever felt in an automobile — trees a greenish blur, the wind tearing at his eyeballs, the scream of the Ninja trailing some- where behind as though they've broken through the sound barrier. The boys squeal with delight: this is better than all the carnival rides they've ever taken put together — but they moan with disappointment when the ride ends far too soon and they roar up the gravel driveway at the Kids Kamp. Airmail eases the Kawasaki past the rusty hulks of ancient and abandoned Dodge Rams, International Harvesters, Chevy Bel Airs, and Ford Fairlanes and skids to a stop in front of the main house. Maeva is at her usual spot on the sagging front porch, with a spliff in one hand and a Rolling Rock in the other.

"Come to make a pickup for Alf," Airmail says. He jerks a thumb at the riders behind him. "I also have a couple of packages for you. I found these lads pelting along the highway out by the old gravel pit."

Skeeter and Moe hop off, mumble their thanks to Airmail, and take off. They're almost past Maeva, about to turn the corner and bolt for the cabins out back, when it occurs to her to wonder why they look like they're being chased by a bear.

"You boys!" she says, and they skid to a halt. "Get over here this minute."

Moe whispers, *Don't tell her nothing*, out of the side of his mouth. They come shuffling up to the bottom of the weathered wooden staircase that leads to the porch. Maeva leans forward, her eyes shifting from Skeeter to Moses and back again.

"Where you been?"

Skeeter looks wildly to Moe for help, but Maeva's eyes are

on him. "Wherever Moe says," he replies.

Maeva takes a long toke and blows the smoke out her nose. "Wherever Moe says? Is that right? So he's the one supposed to lie for both of you?"

"No, ma'am. We ain't been no place."

"No place. This is getting curiouser and curiouser. If you stop and think about it a minute, nobody is ever no place, do you take my meaning? Unless you're dead, and then you're still someplace, 'cause you're under the ground. Well, unless maybe you gets yourself crematized and they scatter your sorry butt all over hell's half acre, isn't that right?"

Moe nods. "I expect so, ma'am."

"So let's try it again. You answer this time. What's your name — you, Noah."

"Moses. Only they call me Moe."

"Alright, Moses call-me-Moe. Where you been?"

"Hiking."

"Hiking, you say? That's it, hiking? You look like you seen a ghost."

"No, ma'am. We didn't see no ghosts."

"So where were you when you didn't see no ghosts?"

"Like Airmail said. We was out by the old gravel pit. Pretending we was tracking things. Alf taught us the Indian way. Alf says an Indian could track a butterfly through a hailstorm. We're practicing to be like them."

"So what scared you so bad that you came running back here like that?"

"Lightning. We didn't want to get fried."

"That's the first sensible thing you said."

The police radio scanner attached to the Ninja squawks to life. They hear Sheriff Jim Dunn on the radio to the sheriff's department dispatcher, saying quite clearly that the victim is on her way to the hospital and they're bringing a suspect in for questioning.

Airmail perks up. "What's that? A victim in an ambulance and a suspect in custody? I have to roll, Maeva. Must collect some photographs before they hustle this poor unfortunate inside. D'you have that package for me?"

"You know I do." Maeva turns to the boys. "You two get out of here. Me and Airmail, we got business to transact. But next time I ask you a question, you better come up with the truth right off, or you're gonna have Alf in your britches. And Alf when he's got his dander up is a sack full of mean."

Skeeter and Moe pelt out of sight. Maeva darts into the house and comes out carrying a shoulder satchel with three stuffed freezer bags inside.

"Sorry," Airmail says. "You know I always love to tarry and chat with a beautiful woman, Maeva, but this could be big."

Maeva nods. Alf is always saying something like that, *This could be big*, when most of the time it's no bigger than a half-price sale on toilet paper. She nods and watches the Ninja roar away, thinking that the little man should be dead about fifty-seven times over by now.

The first heavy scythe of rain comes before Airmail reaches the highway. Maeva hurries inside. It occurs to her that she ought to get hold of those two boys and get to the bottom of what they were up to out by the gravel pit, but the rain is building up to a full-scale storm, and besides, it's time to roll another spliff.

Airmail is already there and waiting when the cruiser pulls up in front of the county jail. He has an ambition to work as a *paparazzo*, and he never goes anywhere without a camera in his saddlebag, but there is rarely anything around Belle Coeur County worth photographing. This week has been an exception. He's already sold more than twenty photos of the storm and its aftermath, and if there's been a horrible crime, there will be more sales. He parks his Kawasaki around back, because Sheriff Dunn hates the sight of him, and peers around the corner to see what's going on.

As Poe is helped out of the backseat of the cruiser, Airmail stays back in the shadows where the roof overhangs the sidewalk to protect his bulky Speed Graphic camera from the driving rain, but he's still able to grab seven frames of the deputies helping Poe out of the car before Deputy Travis Proulx sees him and aims a kick at his backside. "Get outa here, you little parasite!"

Airmail gets, but not before he has taken his photographs of a massive and forlorn-looking Poe standing handcuffed in the rain.

~

The room with the puke-green walls
Rose is patching an old pair of pants for Poe when the phone rings. She answers on the third ring. Joey Ballew, trying without much success to thread a needle for her, sees the shadow pass over her face. She murmurs something and hangs up, looking dazed.

"What was that?"

"That was Jim Dunn. We got to go to the jailhouse to get Poe. They got my boy locked up for something he didn't do. C'mon, now. Don't dawdle."

"There's a helluva storm out there, Rose. It ain't entirely safe."

Rose is already pulling on her rain slicker. "You think I don't know that?"

Joey has trouble starting his pickup, which is so old the original red paint has faded to a blotched pink. Rose waits while he pokes around under the hood. A bolt of lightning cracks so near them that Joey can smell sulfur in the air. The engine starts on the third try, but he has to crawl along in first gear, reaching out with one hand to keep the single feeble wiper blade going on his windshield. The wind is blowing so hard that the rain sounds like hail rattling on the roof of the cab. Twice he has to stop to drag heavy fallen branches off the road. Rose pays no attention. She sits bolt upright in the passenger seat, staring straight ahead. When Joey brakes the pickup in six inches of water in the parking lot outside the jail, she hurries in through the torrent, leaving him to follow along behind. By the time he manages to tug open the door against the blast of the wind, she has already barged into the sheriff's office.

Rose has known Jim Dunn since he was a bump in his mother's belly. She comes right to the point. "Hello, Jim. I'm here to take Poe home."

"Hello, Rose. Have a seat. Helluva night, raining cats and dogs out there."

"I didn't come to get the weather report, Jim. I know rain when it's falling. Turn my boy loose."

Dunn picks up a paperweight, sets it down on a different pile of papers. This is the hard part of being a small-town sheriff. He remembers seeing Rose bring Poe to school. He was the star quarterback on the high school team when the coach tried to make Poe a football player. He buys goat cheese from Rose, and sometimes he follows with the lights flashing on his cruiser to warn drivers as Poe goes around town gathering up old Christmas trees for the goats, piling them on an old sled and letting a slew of kids come along for the ride. Now he has to break the news to Rose, and the only thing worse is telling a parent that a child is dead.

"I couldn't be sorrier, Rose, but I can't turn your boy loose. We've got the Thorne girl hurt bad, and we don't know whether she's going to make it or not. I found them myself. I was out patrolling on that stretch of Highway 116 by the old gravel pit when I saw Poe come out of the woods, carrying the girl. She'd been beaten half to death. It wasn't a pretty sight."

"You mean Miranda?"

"Yes. Miranda Thorne. We're trying to reach her father, but he hasn't been answering his phone."

"Poe's known that little girl since she came up to his knee. I cleaned house for her folks when her mama was still alive, and after she was gone I kept at it until Miranda got big enough to do it herself. Poe is like an uncle to her. He wouldn't harm a hair on that girl's head."

"Well, I hope you're right, Rose. But somebody hurt her bad."

"What does Poe have to say about it?"

"He hasn't said anything that makes much sense, and I can't question him without a lawyer present. He's out of his head a bit, keeps saying *get help, get help.*"

"Then I expect he was trying to get help for her. Let me take him home now, and I'll get to the bottom of this."

"I can't do that, Rose. The only person who can turn him loose is the district judge."

"Then get the judge in here. Poe ain't guilty. There's got to be some explanation for this."

"The judge is only in Belle Coeur County one day a week. He'll be here Wednesday morning for the arraignment. I called the public defender's office. They'll send somebody over to meet with you tonight. You'll want a lawyer there when we question Poe, and you'll need help to enter a plea."

"The plea is not guilty."

"That's fine, Rose, but you're going to have to tell it to the judge. And Poe has to do the telling himself, you can't do it for him. When that girl comes to, if she does, maybe she'll sort things out. If she says Poe isn't the one who attacked her, your boy is free to go. Right now, he's the only suspect we've got. He's in a clean, dry place, and I'll see to it he gets plenty to eat."

Dunn sees something go out of Rose then, sees her taking in how bad this could be. She takes a deep breath and lets it out before she speaks, so softly he can barely hear. "That's kind of you, Sheriff. Can I see my boy now?"

"Sure thing. I'll take you down the hall there, and they'll bring Poe out in a minute."

Sheriff Dunn leads her down a long corridor and into a drab, windowless room with puke-green walls. Poe shuffles in, escorted by two deputies. At the sight of him in handcuffs and leg irons, Rose bites her lower lip so hard she draws a pearl of bright red blood. The deputies guide him to a chair at a square table, facing her. He sits down heavily, unable to use his hands to brace himself. Rose remains standing, resting her knuckles on the table. She points to the leg irons.

"Do you have to do that to him?" she asks a deputy whose name tag says *Travis Proulx*. "Wrap him up like some kind of beast?"

"Regulations, ma'am. Poe is likely to be charged with

a felony offense. We can't bring him out unless he's fully shackled."

She waits until the deputies close the door, then she wraps her arms around Poe and hugs him. When she has just about squeezed the life out of him, she sits and holds his big hands. "Such beautiful hands you got, Poe. Even when you was a baby, you had such beautiful hands. I was always so happy you had six fingers and six toes and you was so big, 'cause there was more of you to look at."

Poe's head swivels on his neck and his eyes roll back in his head. He gnashes his teeth and he's drooling more than usual. "Get help, Ma," he says. "Got to get help."

"Do you mean get help for Miranda, son? They got help for the girl. She's at the hospital now. I'll say a prayer that she's gonna be alright."

Poe strains against the handcuffs. His wrists are already chafed.

Rose looks him in the eye. "Be honest with your mama now, Poe. Did you do this thing? Did you hurt this girl? Did you hurt Miranda? Even if it was an accident, you got to tell the truth."

Poe shakes his head frantically. "No, Mama. No. I doesn't hurt Miranda. Sonofabitch fella hurts her. I tries to get help."

"Who? Do you know who hurt her?"

"Sonofabitch fella."

"Had you seen him before?"

Poe shakes his head. "Sonofabitch fella."

There's a knock at the door and a weedy little man in a sports jacket and blue jeans enters the room. He's carrying a Styrofoam cup of hot coffee and a dripping half-broken umbrella. He puts out a hand and introduces himself to Rose.

"I'm Gerald B. Nye, ma'am. Public defender. The sheriff called me. I assume you don't have a lawyer?"

Rose ignores the hand. "Don't have no lawyer, Mr. Gerald B. Nye, and we don't need one. Poe didn't do nothing except help a poor girl who was bad hurt."

"I'm a public defender, ma'am. My services are free."

"Don't matter. We don't need no lawyer."

"That's your right. But Sheriff Dunn plans to question Poe, and he has the right to have a lawyer present. My job is to represent Mr. Didelot."

"Mr. Didelot was my daddy. Guy Didelot. Killed in a car wreck, alongside my mother. I guess you're referring to Poe?"

"I am."

"Then say so. Poe carried that girl out of the woods. He's been her friend most of her life. They got to turn him loose."

"They may release him, ma'am, but we have to go one step at a time. We need to figure out what's best for Poe. I'm thinking that the best thing might be to clear the way so that Poe can live in an institution. That way he can't hurt anyone and he won't have to go to prison."

"You mean send Poe to the nuthouse?"

"Well, that's what people call it, but those places aren't like they used to be. In this state, they're quite civilized."

"Son, you don't know me. They tried to take my boy away from me before he was a week old. If I hadn't fought the bastards, he would've spent his entire life in one of them institutions. If my Poe is in as much trouble as you seem to think, he'll need a real lawyer. No offense, son, but any lawyer with a lick of sense would know better than to take an umbrella outdoors when it's blowing a gale."

~

The storm rages on, a torrential, obliterating rain. The wind tears great oak and hackberry trees out by their roots, the rain washes out roads, the creeks flood over the bridges, and the remnants of the Split Rock Trailer Park swirl away down the river. The boys at the Kids Kamp are left to sit in their dismal cabins with nothing to do but watch the leaks drip into buckets on the floor. The phone lines are out, the power lines are down, and Belle Coeur County is an island, cut off from the world.

The hospital has switched to its emergency generator. The lights are dim and the corridors hushed. Nurses hurry back and forth on their soft-soled shoes. In room 413, Thorne sits at the bedside of his battered daughter, listening to the beep and ping of the instruments that surround her. The roar of the storm is muffled inside the hospital, but now and then a gust of wind causes the windows to ripple like the surface of a pond. When it does, he fears the glass will shatter and the wind and water will come howling in. Through the long, empty hours, Thorne watches Miranda's face. Her nose is broken, her eyes are black, there are cuts on her forehead, her lips are swollen. With that corona of wild dark curly hair fanned out on the crisp white of the hospital pillow, she looks like a battered Madonna.

Watching her, a snippet of an old song drifts through his mind: *she's come undone* . . . He can't recall the band, the singer, or the name of the song, nothing at all but that single phrase, on endless replay, like a thirty-three-rpm record with the needle stuck. *She's come undone* . . .

Miranda has come undone. His lovely, vital, athletic, brilliant Miranda is now simply a body that breathes. The list of her injuries is frightening. She has a damaged trachea, two broken ribs, three broken teeth, a broken nose, multiple contusions, vaginal bruising, some bleeding in the brain. She is unconscious and heavily sedated. For now, the doctors say, the only thing is to let her rest. They won't say that she may never wake. They don't have to.

When Thorne needs sleep, the hospital wheels in an extra cot and he curls up under a thin blanket, his jacket and shoes still on. He is startled awake a dozen times a night by the absence of her breathing. He sits up, panicked. Then he hears it again, a ragged, creaky sound like an old bellows. He waits for his heart rate to slow and drifts back to sleep, soothed by that rough sound. Breathe, Miranda, breathe. In and out, that's a good girl. Breathe.

~ V ~
The New World Hotel

The man in the dark blue suit

Lambert Cain leans back in the vast leather chair that had been his father's, watching the storm beat down on Main Street in Belle Coeur, a block from the courthouse. He has come to work as usual despite the storm, driving the six blocks to the office instead of walking the way he usually does, dodging fallen tree limbs all the way, to arrive at precisely five minutes before eight, even though he has no appointments with clients and no work that can't be postponed. He's been going to work every weekday morning for more than forty years, and in all that time he hasn't missed more than a dozen days in the office. Lambert Cain III is the third and last in his line to practice law from this office. There is no Lambert Cain IV waiting to take over, nor a Lucille Cain nor a Linda Cain, because he and his beloved wife have no children. His partners have all retired or moved on to more lucrative practices, the young lawyers he trained have left for big cities, corporate clients, and thousand-dollar-an-hour fees. Most of what remains of his practice represents the old wealth of the county. They trust him and no one else. He takes care of their wills, their petty quarrels, and their infrequent arrests for impaired driving, but it's hardly demanding work.

Lambert Cain is a long-limbed, courtly man, with long graying hair combed straight back. The suits he wears on his tall, angular frame are a uniform dark blue. He is considered a pillar of respectability in the community, although there are rumors of a dissolute past that he has never bothered to deny. For the present, Lambert is going nowhere, and he will never appear in a television ad. He plans to stay where he is until the last client has vanished or he's too sick or feeble to carry on. Then he will pack up his desk and the objects on his walls, turn off the lights, say goodbye to Gladys, and go home to listen to opera and read Russian novels, the two great passions of his life apart from his wife, Martha. He walks home to have lunch with Martha every day at noon sharp, and he feels like the luckiest man alive.

Cain is still gazing out at the empty, rain-swept street, mulling the past and the present when, at two minutes past nine, he hears the bell that announces someone has arrived in the outer office. Gladys has called in to say she can't make it, so he hoists himself out of his chair, noting the stiffness in every joint brought on by the rain, opens his door, and finds Rose Didelot standing uncertainly in the waiting room, clutching her handbag. Lambert hurries to the door and helps her to a chair in the waiting room, pours a glass of spring water from the five-gallon bottle next to Gladys's desk, and sits facing her. He waits politely until she has drunk half the water and composed herself.

"They got Poe down at the jail, Lambert. They say he attacked the Thorne girl, Miranda. Poe has known that girl since she was an itty-bitty thing, used to take her fishing out at the gravel pit. Jim Dunn himself found 'em alongside the highway, close to the turnoff to the gravel pit. Poe was carrying the girl. Jim says she was half naked and beat up pretty bad."

Cain reaches for a legal pad and a pencil and starts taking notes. "When did this happen, Rose?"

Rose dabs at her eyes with a handkerchief. "Late yesterday afternoon, I believe. Poe went out there to fish, but he didn't say nothin about Miranda coming along. I don't know how they met up. You know my Poe. He wouldn't hurt a living soul, big and strong as he is. I know he didn't hurt that girl, only I can't prove it. That's where you come in."

"I'd be happy to recommend someone, if you like. I don't do much criminal law anymore, Rose. Never did, really. It's been years since I argued a criminal case in court."

"I know that, Lambert, but my boy's in big trouble. Poe said something last night about a sonofabitch fellow that hurt Miranda, but I've got no idea who he's talkin about. He's not making a whole lot of sense right now, like he's in shock. I want you to be his lawyer because everybody knows you're the best in the county, maybe the best in the state. They sent some tomfool from the public defender's office last night, said he was gonna defend Poe. The man came in with a busted-up umbrella. He had it open outdoors when it was blowing like a cyclone. Right off, I could see that he ain't got common sense. I can't do business with a man like that."

"Who was the lawyer? Did you get his name?"

"Mr. Gerald B. Nye."

Cain chuckles. "Well, poor Gerald is a good soul, Rose, but he isn't the sharpest knife in the drawer. I can see where you might have your reservations about him."

"It's worse than that. All he wants is for Poe to claim he's insane, so they can stick him in one of them institutions for the rest of his natural life. But he ain't crazy, he's innocent. I'm not asking for your charity, Lambert. I don't have a lot of money, but you can have what I've got. If the money runs out, I'll sell the place. I'm getting too damned old to run the cheese business by myself, anyhow. All I want is to see my boy go free."

Lambert Cain hesitates, watching the tempest rage outside, thinking it over. If he's honest with himself, he has to admit that he's bored with his practice. It's been years since he took on a real challenge.

"Alright, Rose," he says. "I'll take the case. But you're going to have to listen to me and take my advice. Don't worry about the money, I'll drop by for some of your fine cheese now and again, but you can pay me one U.S. dollar. That's what we call a retainer. Then you have officially retained my services to represent your son, Poe."

Rose digs around in her purse and comes up with a greasy dollar bill. Cain takes an empty file folder from a file cabinet, prints Poe's name at the top, and clips the dollar bill to the inside of the folder. "Now, let's pay a call on your son. I imagine he'd appreciate it."

~

"I throws him away..."

Jim Dunn has just come in from checking on the storm. With bridges out, roads blocked, and power lines down, it's as complete a mess as he's ever seen. Then there's a girl in a hospital bed, the daughter of a wealthy man who was once a prominent lawyer in Boston, and Poe in a jail cell. The storm has interfered with the flow of gossip, so the good citizens of Belle Coeur County haven't heard of the attack on Miranda Thorne, but they will. They'll expect him to have a suspect tried, found guilty, and, if possible, hung by the neck until dead, all by the end of next week, because that's the way folks are.

The water is still pouring off his rain slicker when there's a light knock on the door and Lambert Cain pokes his head in. "Time for a word, Jim?"

"Nothing much else I can do right now, Lambert. What brings you out on a day like this?"

"Rose Didelot came by this morning, asked if I could represent her boy."

"And you agreed? Hell, Lambert, you haven't done a criminal case in ten years."

"More like twenty, maybe twenty-five. But I said I'd do it. Rose is the salt of the earth, and you know she won't get much help from Gerald B. Nye."

The sheriff nods. "I thought the same thing myself. Poe could be in trouble right up to his neck, and that's a good deal higher than my head."

Cain takes a seat in one of the comfortable old chairs in the office, chairs that have been there at least as long as he's been a lawyer in Belle Coeur County, and probably a lot longer. "What can you tell me, Jim?"

"Right now, the Thorne girl is in critical condition. If she pulls through, we have aggravated assault and aggravated sexual assault. If she doesn't, it's murder in the second degree. Maybe first, if the prosecutor wants to try and prove that Poe tempted her out there some way or another."

"You were the arresting officer?"

"I was. I was out checking the bridges yesterday afternoon when I found him staggering along the highway out by the old gravel pit, carrying this young woman who was half naked and half alive. Well, you know who she is, Lambert. Miranda Thorne, Prosper Thorne's daughter. She took an awful beating, I suppose you know that. Poe is claiming there was some other fellow there. I had two deputies go back out and drive up that road to the gravel pit after we brought him in, but they didn't see a thing, and in that storm we couldn't do any kind of search. Given what I saw, it didn't seem there was any reason for a search."

Cain nods. "And if there was anyone else, he's long gone by now. Probably was before your deputies went back out."

"I suppose so, although it would have been hard to get out of the county. Depends if he got over one of the bridges before it flooded again. Assuming there is such a fellow, assuming Poe is telling the truth, or even that he knows what the truth might be. I was the quarterback on the football team when Poe tried to play all those years ago, you might remember. You could never make out how much he understood and how much he couldn't soak up at all. Meanwhile, I don't want to tell you your business, Lambert, but if I were you I wouldn't try to get bail for Poe until this thing is settled. You know how folks are liable to react. He's safer in here. I don't want a lynching on my watch."

Cain finds Rose waiting outside and asks her to accompany him to his first meeting with Poe. The giant looks smaller, somehow. Diminished. Maybe it's the orange county jail suit he's wearing, along with the handcuffs and leg irons. Or maybe it's simply that he has shrunk into himself. The attorney has Rose with him to keep Poe calm, but the giant is still gnashing his teeth and rolling his eyes.

"Poe, you remember me. Lambert Cain. You've done some work around my house a few times, cleaned up some tree limbs after a storm, things like that."

"Mister Cain, yessir. I knows you. Ma says you were always a fine fella."

"Well, that's good to hear, Poe. Rose is an old friend of mine. She's asked me to be your lawyer, do you understand?"

"How come I needs a lawyer?"

"Because of Miranda, Poe. They think maybe you hurt Miranda. Is that true?"

Poe shakes his head frantically. "No, no, no, no. I doesn't hurt Miranda. I never hurts Miranda. Sonofabitch fellow."

"You mean there was someone else out there, is that right?"

"Sonofabitch fellow."

"But if someone else attacked her, Poe, what happened to him? Why didn't the sheriff see him? The sheriff didn't see anyone else out there."

"I throws him away."

"I'm sorry? What did you say?"

"I throws him away. I think his head crashed up on a car."

"So he had a car out there?"

"Yep. Big black car. I throws him away and he hits the car, bang! Then he don't move. Sonofabitch fellow."

Cain spends another ten minutes with Poe, tracking the

same circle around and back to the man in the black car, without learning anything more. He leaves Rose to keep Poe calm while he strolls down the hall to locate Jim Dunn, and pokes his head into the sheriff's office long enough to say that they're as ready as they will ever be.

"I don't know that you'll get any more than I can get, Jim," Lambert says, "but you're welcome to try."

According to Jim Dunn's log, his initial interview with Poe Didelot lasts fifty-two minutes, with the suspect's attorney, Mr. Lambert Cain, and his mother, Rose Didelot, in attendance, although what Poe has to say could have been said in a minute or less. After that, it's all repetition. "That sonofabitch fellow. I throws him away. I *throws* him *away*. Sonofabitch fellow."

"What did he look like, Poe? What did this man look like?"

"Sonofabitch. Like a sonofabitch fellow."

~

How dead feels

Poe wonders if this is how it feels to be dead, and he wonders if he's not already, like one of the dead things he's seen: a cat crushed by a cement truck, the old nanny goat Molly B., or Wild Bill's wife Darlene, who died of the cancer. He remembers Darlene at the funeral home, lying there in her open coffin like a thing made of yellow wax, while Bill stood nearby with his head down, shaking all over and sobbing because the sorrow had him in its grip and would not let go. Did Darlene in her coffin feel the way Poe feels now? Looking out at the world, able to see but unable to touch or feel or taste? He watches it all going by, but it does not feel like his world anymore.

Things lose their odor in jail. He can barely smell himself. He can't hear much over the hum of the ventilator and the heating system. The food all tastes the same, and he has no appetite even when Rose brings food from home. Inside his cell, there is a constant trickle of water from somewhere, tracking along the outer walls, dripping onto the floor. Poe figures that the people who built the jail probably didn't take much care. When he builds a thing, he builds it to last. If something is put up the right way, water won't seep through. Whoever built this jail took care to see that no human can escape, but less attention was paid to what might get in.

Spiders share his cell, as many as there are in the outhouse at home. He tries to figure out where they come from and what they eat. He's seen no flies or mosquitoes inside the jail. He can pass an entire morning watching a spider going back and forth on the ceiling or weaving a web in a corner. He doesn't fret. His only worry is that the door won't open. It's a foreign thing to him, a locked door. He and Rose never lock anything, not the door to their house, the door to the cheese shed, or the door to the barn where the goats and geese shelter in winter. When the door to his cell slides shut, there isn't even a crack where Poe can get purchase with his fingers to open it. He tries putting a shoulder against it and giving it a mighty heave, but there isn't a hint of give. He lies awake, worrying that the door will never open again, that when they press the button nothing will happen and he will be trapped in his cell until he starves to death.

He misses Miranda. He misses Wild Bill and Joey Ballew. He misses the goats. The jailers let him keep his fob watch, so when it's milking time, he closes his eyes and lets his six-fingered hands move and flutter as he milks them all in turn:

Jenny-Girl and Ostrich, the twins Bertha and Betty, Roxie, Little Dipper, Maude, Lula May, Olive, Susie Q, Thelma Pearl, Aunt Nell, and Princess Sally last.

~

Vanished

Because of the storm and its aftermath, four days go by before Sheriff Jim Dunn is able to get out to the crime scene. He takes his own battered old Jeep with the four-wheel drive rather than the department's cruiser because the track to the gravel pit is sure to be pitted with muddy ruts after the storm and because he enjoys driving the old Jeep in rough country.

Belle Coeur County has survived the storms without a single fatality, although a great deal of property has been lost or damaged, enough to keep the insurance companies busy for months. The forecast for the next week is for sunny skies and mild temperatures, so the county will have time to dry out. Crews are out already, and he can hear chainsaws everywhere, cutting up all the downed trees for firewood. There are roofs to be mended, fences to be rebuilt, and a few rickety bridges that are gone forever, but the thing about a place like this is that people will pull together and help out.

Late-summer sunshine drifts through the trees, and it feels good to be out by his lonesome rather than shuffling paper in an airless office. He's listening to Hank Snow on the radio, enjoying himself a little too much, driving too fast on a road that hasn't been maintained since the old gravel pit shut down. He rounds a corner near a thick stand of beech and maple trees and has to jam the brakes through the floorboards to avoid sailing off into the water. The Jeep skids sideways right up to the edge of a lake that is a couple of hundred feet beyond where it ought to be. He eases it into reverse and backs away as gingerly as he can to where the ground feels reasonably solid.

Sheriff Dunn parks the Jeep between a couple of tall poplars on higher ground and climbs out, his knees feeling a little watery. He walks back toward the lake in mud up to his ankles, feeling his way along from tree to tree, wanting something to hold on to in case the ground gives away. When he reaches the point where the gravel pit should have been, he sees that the old gravel tower is gone. So is the pump shack and the turnaround where the heavy dump trucks used to back in for their loads. At least a dozen tall poplar trees have vanished into the water, along with a stand of weeping willows that fringed the bank. Everything is gone, including that pretty picnic spot up on a little rise overlooking the river trail. Washed away, as though it had never existed.

This puts a whole new slant on things. He had planned to spend the better part of the day out here, measuring, marking, observing, bagging evidence. He even thought he might get lucky and be able to identify the tire prints of the car that Poe claims was parked here, but everything is gone. He walks the last hundred feet with care, probing with one boot and then the other, holding on to branches when he can, half expecting the ground to slide out from underneath him at every step. Only the roof of the old tower is visible, far out in the lake. It isn't hard to figure out what happened: all those years of pumping gravel hollowed out the ground underneath and the deluge did the rest. The artificial lake is now a few hundred feet wider than it had been, and everything that was here before the storm is gone. The crime scene is nothing but water.

Dunn moves cautiously around the fringes of the lake

until he finds an abandoned skiff with an oar hidden in the weeds. He tests it to make sure it won't sink, then paddles out to the tower and circles it carefully. There's little to see, but a dozen feet from the tower, he finds a waterlogged old comic book, with crudely drawn obscene cartoons. He lifts it from the water with a stick and bags it as evidence.

On the way back to the highway, he notes how rough the track is and clocks the mileage on the odometer. It's better than a mile and a half from the highway to the gravel pit. That's a long way to carry an injured woman, even if you're as big and strong as Poe. That doesn't tell him a whole lot, except that Poe was determined to get to the highway. If he attacked the girl, you'd think he would have left her there and tried to save himself, but that's what another man would do. A man like Poe? He's heard Rose say it a dozen times: Poe has his addlements and particularities. There's no telling how he might behave if he was alone with Miranda in an isolated spot like the gravel pit.

~

"I took the brownies out to Poe and then . . ."
On the morning of her seventh day in the hospital, Miranda flickers in and out of consciousness, like a lightbulb in a faulty socket. Her father sits in his chair by the window, watching the traffic go by. It's a glorious, sunny day, late summer slipping into early autumn. He can see leaves turning in the distance, and the sky is the deep blue you get after the summer heat has faded. The warmth streaming through the glass makes him sleepy, and he must have nodded off, because he thinks that he is dreaming when he hears her speak. *Daddy? Daddy, my throat hurts.*

Thorne struggles to focus on the sound. *Daddy? Daddy? Where am I? How did I get here?* He leaps to his feet, frantic and a little dazed. By the time he gets to Miranda's side, she is unconscious again and he is left to wonder if it was all a dream. He rings for a nurse, and the nurse checks her vital signs. Her pulse is strong, her blood pressure is normal. An impossibly young doctor looks in long enough to say they can start weaning her off the sedatives. He warns Thorne not to upset her. Thorne guesses that someone must have heard him ranting about the brutal things Poe has done to his daughter. He returns to his chair by the window like a child who has been chastised and resumes his vigil. If Miranda woke once, she will wake again. He is certain of that now.

An hour later she is briefly awake, says a few words, and drifts off. Thorne keeps talking to her, about the weather, about her mother, about her girlhood, anything that comes to mind except Poe. It's late in the evening before she is fully conscious.

"My throat hurts," she says.

"Yes. The doctors say it will heal. You just have to be very careful."

"How did I get here?" Miranda asks.

Thorne is startled by the question. "You don't remember? You must remember. You don't remember what happened to you?"

"I don't remember. What should I remember? Was I in an accident?"

"It appears that Poe attacked you, honey. Out by the gravel pit. I guess he tried to do things to you, but they say he didn't quite succeed. He beat you half to death, though."

"Poe? No. No no no no. It can't be. Poe wouldn't hurt me."

"The sheriff caught him red-handed, honey. Poe was

carrying you out of the woods. Out by the old gravel pit, where he used to take you fishing. I'm sure you'll remember if you think about it."

"Think about what?"

"The day you were attacked. It will come back to you."

"When was it?"

"A week ago today."

"I've been here a *week*? That's not possible."

"I'm afraid it is, Miranda. They didn't know if you were going to make it or not. I didn't know if you would ever be conscious again."

Thorne is weeping. Miranda reaches up and traces his tears with her fingertips. "Don't cry, Daddy. I'm okay now, I think. I can't believe it's been a week." She tries to shift her position on the bed and grimaces. "I hurt all over."

"Yes. It was worse. You're looking a bit better."

"I need water."

He holds the water glass in his right hand, his left behind her head, lifting her up. "The nurse said you can only have a bit at a time, otherwise you'll bring it back up."

Miranda nods. "I don't remember any attack. I don't remember anything. The last thing I can remember is taking brownies out to Poe."

"That was three or four weeks ago, before the first flood."

"What flood?"

He strokes her forehead. "The doctor said you might have some short-term memory loss. We don't have to talk about it now. It will come back to you."

She closes her eyes and drifts away again. Thorne stands holding her wrist, feeling her pulse, tears rolling down his cheeks.

When Miranda wakes again, it's night. Her father isn't in the room. She assumes he went home to sleep. She helps herself to a sip of water and lies staring at the ceiling, trying to remember. Her mind keeps traveling the same circuit, up to the same point. She remembers clearly the time school ended for the summer, driving her VW Beetle home, listening to the radio. She remembers things that have happened since, like looking for stones for the wall, driving out in the pickup to load them. The day Poe hoisted Bill's pickup out of the mud. She can reconstruct it all, up to the point where she made brownies before she went out for her morning run. She remembers taking the brownies out to Poe.

I took the brownies out to Poe and then . . .
I took the brownies out to Poe and then . . .
I took the brownies out to Poe and then . . .

The next thing she can recall is the pale halo of light over her hospital bed, then her father at her bedside. *I took the brownies out to Poe and then . . .*

And then nothing. A gaping void. How is it possible not to remember three weeks of your own life? She is a blank, nothing left of those weeks but the hole in her soul.

Sheriff Jim Dunn finds Miranda asleep in the afternoon. Wild dark hair spread over the startling white of the pillow, her face and neck covered with fading greenish bruises. Thorne sits at her bedside, ready to snarl at any who would disturb her.

"What do you want?"

Dunn lifts his hat. "Good afternoon, Mr. Thorne. I heard that your daughter is conscious and thought that she might be up to a question or two."

"Well, she isn't. Get the hell out of here."

Dunn stands his ground. "Well now, I could do that. I could go. But I'd think you'd want to get to the bottom of this so's we can find out who attacked your girl."

"We know the guilty party, Sheriff. Poe the giant. I want him hanged by the neck until dead. Now go do your job."

"That's precisely what I'm doing. You're a lawyer, Mr. Thorne, and a top-notch legal eagle defense lawyer at that. You of all people know how it works. It's one step at a time, and the lawman who tries to skip a few steps ends up with a case that won't stand up in court. I'll swing by in an hour or two and see if it's possible to have a word with your daughter."

"It's alright, Daddy." Miranda is awake, her dark eyes wide. "I don't mind a few questions, but I'm not sure I can help much, Sheriff. I don't remember a thing."

Dunn nods and drags over a chair. Thorne folds his arms over his chest and glares at him. With his tangled hair and beard, he looks thoroughly unkempt and half mad. Dunn can't blame the man. His own daughter is only two or three years younger than Miranda. If such a thing had happened to her, he would be in such a state or worse, but he has a job to do.

"Mr. Thorne, I have some notion how difficult this might be for you. Perhaps you might want to stroll down to the cafeteria and get yourself a cup of coffee while I chat with your daughter. It won't take long."

"How dare you? You can't force me to leave, Sheriff."

"No, I can't. You're absolutely right, Mr. Thorne. I can't force you to go. I'm not forcing you, I'm asking. It's been my experience that the victim in a case like this feels a little freer to talk without the presence of a parent in the room. Just step out for a bit and let us talk."

"I will not."

Miranda touches her father's arm. "Daddy, it's okay. Really. Get yourself a coffee and get me one of those raisin oatmeal cookies. It's still two hours until supper and I'm hungry. Please."

The effect she has on her father is magical. Thorne leans back, obedient to her touch. "Alright, I'll go. But don't let him bully you, now. If he starts leaning on you, you clam right up and wait until I get back."

"He's not going to lean on me, Daddy. I'm not a criminal."

Thorne nods reluctantly and struggles to his feet, keeping a wary eye on the sheriff. "Alright. One cookie, coming up. Anything else?"

"An apple juice. Please."

"Sheriff? I suppose you'll be wanting a coffee?"

"No thank you, sir. I'll be fine."

Miranda waits until she can hear her father's footsteps echoing down the hall, then turns to the sheriff. "Is it true? Poe is in jail for this?"

"I'm afraid so. I found him carrying you alongside the highway out by the old gravel pit. He had you slung over his shoulders and you were in a bad way. Just dumb luck I happened by when I did. Now, we don't know what happened, I've got to stress that. Poe kept saying 'get help,' over and over, so it's possible he was just trying to help you. But in the meantime, we've got to keep him in jail, for his own protection if nothing else. Folks are pretty wrought up about this and since Poe is large and odd, they're inclined to blame him."

Miranda sinks back into her pillow and bites her lip. "This is so wrong. It's got to be wrong. Poe would never hurt me. Never."

"You've known Poe a long time?"

"Since forever. When I was a little girl, he used to take me fishing out at that old gravel pit. The last few years, I've been helping him build a stone wall along my father's property. I hired him, to tell you the truth. Daddy didn't want to. But it's a good job for Poe and we're going to have a beautiful wall."

Miranda reaches for a glass of water, but the water is stale and warm and she makes a face. "I really wish I could help more, Sheriff. I don't remember a thing. Daddy told me where you found me, but I have no idea how I got there. I can't remember a thing since the day I took some brownies out to Poe. Daddy says there was a big storm after that, and then another one, but I don't remember any of it. Just Poe and the brownies. It's so awful not to remember. Like I've lost a part of myself, like I didn't exist and that time is gone forever."

"Memory is a funny thing," Dunn says. "I've run across this maybe a dozen times. Short-term memory loss. Sometimes it comes back in a few hours or a day, sometimes it takes a few weeks."

"And sometimes it never comes back at all, right? That's what the doctors tell me."

"Correct. Sometimes it never comes back at all. But I believe that's rare, certainly in my experience. It might come back to you in a rush, or sort of trickle back over time. You might remember some of what you're missing, or you might recover it all."

"God, I wish I could just concentrate and get it back. It's like I've got a math test, and I can't even remember taking the class."

Dunn toys with the hat on his knee. "You can't force it, I know that much. It will come when it comes. I surely hope it does, it would be very useful to us. You're the only witness we've got, other than myself — and I didn't see what happened. I just stumbled on the aftermath."

"You'd think Daddy would be more grateful. You probably saved my life."

"I expect it's hard for him to admit that. Listen, has Poe ever tried anything with you? Touched you the wrong way, anything like that?"

"Heavens, no. Poe doesn't even put a hand on my shoulder. Now and then I give him a peck on his cheek, that's about it. I catch him looking at me sometimes, so I suppose I have an effect on him, but he's so gentle, the gentlest man alive. I've seen Poe cry because he hurt a butterfly. It's not possible that he did this to me. I wish I could prove it."

The sheriff is silent for a time, gazing out the window. "Is there anyone else, Miranda? Boyfriend? Ex-boyfriend? Anyone like that?"

"Why do you ask, Sheriff?"

"Well, there's a pattern with these things. More often than not, when there's been a sexual assault, the culprit is known to the victim. Now you knew Poe, obviously. Is there anyone else?"

"Well, I have a boyfriend at school. Sort of."

"How do you mean that?"

"When I left school in the spring, I told him I needed the summer to think. I'm only nineteen, too young to be in a permanent relationship. He's eight years older than me, so he's looking for a wife, and he's a bit clingy. More than a bit, actually. And there's more."

"More?"

"It's complicated. I'd better warn you, Sheriff, I'll have to stop talking about this when Daddy comes back. He would have a stroke. My boyfriend's name is Sebastian Coyle. His father's name is Anthony Coyle, maybe you've heard of him?"

Dunn shakes his head.

"He's a big criminal lawyer in Boston. He took over the firm that was founded by my father when my father left. But the way Daddy sees it, he was forced out. My mother was dying of cancer and Daddy was really torn up by it and terribly distracted while he was nursing her for a whole year before she died, and Anthony Coyle took advantage of the situation to force him out of the firm. That's how Daddy sees it. The way Sebastian tells it, his father had to take over, because Daddy wasn't doing his job and the firm would have fallen apart if he hadn't stepped in."

"And how do you see it?"

"I have to support Daddy. I'm pretty sure he's right about the way he was pushed out. I'd like to be able to talk to him about it, but it's a subject I don't dare bring up. If you say the name Anthony Coyle, he just becomes completely irrational. It's a shame. When I was young, before Mama died, our families were the best of friends. We lived two doors apart in Boston, we saw each other all the time, and I had a big crush on Sebastian. Then everything happened and I didn't see him for years. When I ran into him in the quad, I knew almost no one. He's a graduate student, and he took me under his wing and showed me around. I started getting this notion that we could be like Romeo and Juliet, only instead of a tragic ending, we would bring our families together. Now I think that was pretty silly. There's nothing I could do that would persuade my father to forgive Anthony Coyle — or his son, for that matter."

"When was the last time you saw Sebastian Coyle?"

"Oh, I haven't seen him since spring. We had an agreement.

I told him I needed the summer to think, and anyway, he wouldn't dare come up here. Daddy has an old shotgun. I don't think he would actually shoot Sebastian, but I don't want to find out."

"Is there any chance at all that Sebastian could have attacked you?"

"No. None. Really. Anyway, I'm stronger than he is. He's a bit of a wimp, which is another thing I don't like about him. He's very soft, not in the least athletic."

"You're a real tiger. I've seen you play softball and hockey."

Miranda smiles. "I'm not much of a tiger now, I'm afraid. It's the first time in my life I've felt weak."

Dunn hears the heavy tread of Thorne's footsteps in the corridor. "I think we're going to have to stop now," he says. "Is there anyone else you can think of? Anyone at all? Any threats, anyone following you, anything like that?"

"No. I sort of wish there had been. It's makes me sick to think of Poe in jail."

Dunn rises from his chair just as Thorne enters the room. He has slopped coffee all over the tray he's carrying, and bought orange juice instead of apple juice for Miranda, but he is still truculent.

"Good," he barks. "You were just leaving, Sheriff. I trust you got all you want."

Back in his office, Dunn phones Brendan Savage, the state's attorney, to tell him that unless Miranda Thorne recovers her memory, she is going to be no help at all as a witness — but she is apparently out of danger, so a charge of manslaughter or second-degree murder is off the table.

The attorney isn't concerned about the gap in Miranda's memory. "We have enough without the girl testifying. The state lab called. There are semen stains on her dress and Poe's coveralls, and bloodstains on both as well. It's circumstantial, but with you catching him red-handed, circumstantial evidence can be pretty powerful in a courtroom, sometimes better than an eyewitness. I think we'll go ahead and try him. I'm under a lot of pressure here, Jim. Folks are calling me around the clock, wanting Poe to hang. Did you know the Carney brothers cut down a big oak tree to build a gallows?"

"I did."

"They say they're all ready for the hanging. I wanted it taken down, but it's on their property and they went and got a permit for it saying it's some kind of deck, but it's a deck with a beam overhead to hold a noose and a trapdoor underneath."

Dunn shakes his head. "Jesus. The things people get up to."

"Yes, they do. Anyhow, that's the kind of pressure I'm under. So if you don't object, I'm going to go ahead and bring Poe to trial. Maybe his lawyer will agree to plead it out."

"His lawyer is Lambert Cain."

"Lambert? Jesus, he hasn't tried a criminal case in decades. Why would he take this on?"

"Damned if I know. Maybe he thinks Poe is innocent."

"Innocent, hell. Well, I'm not going to lose sleep over Lambert Cain. He's an old man who likely doesn't remember all that much about criminal law. Main thing is to get Poe off the street, so he can't hurt anyone else. That's if you don't object."

"It isn't my decision to make, Brendan. You want to put the man on trial, that's your call. My instinct tells me we have the wrong guy, but I don't have a shred of evidence to prove it, other than what Poe himself is telling me."

"He's got every reason to lie to save his neck."

"That's assuming he's clever enough to lie."

"Well, Rose could've told him what to say."

Dunn mutters something, hoping it sounds vaguely like assent.

~

"Freeks not welcum"

Joey Ballew is on his way up to milk the goats when he glances at the little yellow house and slams on the brakes. The word *RAPEST!* is painted in letters three feet high on the wall of Rose's home. Next to it, right under the bedroom window, is another scrawl: "Freeks not welcum here!"

When the milking is done, Joey drives to the hardware store and buys two gallons of yellow paint to cover the writing. Rose blames herself for keeping the geese penned up at night. If she had left them to range free, they would have made more noise than a pack of dogs. Before bed that night, she opens the gate to their pen. The geese will let her know if anyone is creeping around in the dark, but it won't change how people feel. She asks Joey to stay the night. Somewhere around three o'clock in the morning, he hears her sobbing and tries to comfort her, but she shrugs him off.

"It's just kids," he says. "They don't know what they're doin. They get it from their parents."

"That's exactly what bothers me. If it was kids that did this, they got the idea from their folks. That means people are telling their kids awful things about Poe. Spreading poison, right here in this town where we've lived all our lives. We've never done no harm to nobody. There's no reason for any of this, except that Poe is different, with his addlements and particularities and all. Gentlest man alive, but he ain't like the rest, so they want to believe the worst."

Joey is stumped. He doesn't know what to say to that, so he says nothing. When Rose is upset, that's usually the best way.

Rose is on her way to her usual pew at church on Sunday when Melody Crowder, a squarely built woman in a brown dress who is married to one of the deacons, blocks her way. "I can't believe you'd show your face here," the woman says. "You who spawned that six-fingered devil!" Before Rose can react, Melody spits in her face. The new preacher, Reverend Hank Tattersall, gets between them before Rose can retaliate and leads her by the hand to his office.

"I've been thinking, Rose," he says. "It might be better if you stayed away from the service until this blows over. I know a man is innocent until proven guilty and all that, but people are awfully wrought up, to think that a girl could be attacked that way."

"Poe didn't hurt that girl."

"That's what you say, and I hope you're right. But a lot of folks believe it's an open-and-shut case, so I'll let the law decide. I just don't want any trouble in my church. You understand that, right?"

Rose looks him up and down, taking the measure of the man and finding him wanting. "I pity you, Reverend. I do. You have come a long way from the teachings of Jesus Christ, but I'll not sully your church again."

She takes Joey's arm and leads him out of the church. At the door, Eleanor Biggs catches up with her. Eleanor is old and sickly, but she was Rose's third-grade teacher and Rose has never forgotten her. "Rose, honey, I just want you to know I think that was awful. That should never happen to a person in the House of God, least of all you. I'm going to speak to the reverend."

Rose shakes her head. "Thank you, Eleanor, but that won't do. I don't want you sticking your neck out for me. Poe is innocent and once we've proved that in a court of law, I don't expect there will be any more trouble."

Eleanor smiles doubtfully. "I surely hope not. I do. This is just so wrong."

Rose wraps her brawny arms around Eleanor's frail body and hugs her tight. "Thank you, Eleanor. It's good to know there is still a kind person in this world."

Eleanor Biggs is the exception. Rose feels the loathing everywhere she goes. At the Grand Union, at the drugstore where she gets her blood-pressure prescription filled, at the filling station when Joey stops to pump gas in the pickup. People she has known for decades back away or breeze right on by as though they had never met. She understands it, up to a point. If she thought someone had done that to a girl, she'd be pretty riled up, too. But someone *did* attack Miranda, and folks are so convinced it was Poe, they aren't giving much thought to the possibility that a violent man is on the loose.

Rose's friends don't abandon her. Joey is always loyal. Matt Harrow isn't around as often as he used to be, but he had pretty much stopped coming after he had the prostate thing and couldn't get it up anymore. He makes it a point to look in a time or two every week, though, just to see how she's doing. Dan Gillespie never wavers, and even though Rose doesn't have the heart to sing on Saturday nights anymore, he buys more cheese for his pub than ever after word gets around that Rose has lost most of her customers. There are dozens of others, good people who put old friendships first, but the folks who want to see Poe hang are the ones making all the noise. Rose has no idea how far they might go if they were able to get at Poe, and she doesn't want to find out.

~

The fall

The days slip away. The leaves begin their red-and-gold dance, gliding down in search of a likely place to rot. Drunken hunters come in their pickup trucks. Deer scream and die. The world goes brown and bare. Poe is still in jail, awaiting trial the next time the circuit judge is in Belle Coeur County, which will be in December or January.

One afternoon in early November, Rose is surprised to see Maeva Miller walking up the path to her house. Rose has known Maeva since she was a little bitty slip of a thing. She was a fine girl until she turned sixteen and hooked up with Alf Miller. Alf was twenty-six at the time and rotten clear through, but Maeva had a father in jail and a drunk for a mother. She was adrift on a rough sea, looking for a spar to cling to, and she picked the wrong spar.

Rose boils water for tea, and the two women sit and chat awhile before Maeva explains what's on her mind. Alf has been arrested for dealing crystal meth. He's two cells down from Poe at the jail. State inspectors have closed down the Kids Kamp because Alf is no longer around to bribe them. Everything is falling apart in her world, and Maeva wants to know if it's possible that Rose could use a little help with her cheese business.

Rose doesn't need help, but she tells Maeva she could use her two days a week to help put her paperwork in order, if Maeva is good at that sort of thing. Rose hates bookkeeping and she is always falling behind. Maeva says she always kept track of the money for Alf, and she'd love to do the same for Rose. She's about to leave when she remembers another reason she came to see Rose. There are two boys from New York City, Skeeter and Moe, who might be useful to Poe. They stayed at the Kids Kamp three summers in a row, and the day Poe was arrested, they were out by the gravel pit. When the boys came back that day, they looked as though they'd seen a ghost. They claimed they were out on a Sasquatch hunt and they didn't mention seeing Poe, and it wasn't until after they went back to the city that Maeva put two and two together. She doesn't know if the addresses she has for them are still good, but she has a hunch they might have seen something that could help put things right for Poe.

~

The missing Ninja

On the bad days, Thorne sits in his study, staring out at the wall he thinks of as "Poe's wall," grasping the walking stick with both hands, refusing to let go. He relives the storm over and over, flinching at each bolt of lightning and each rumble of thunder, willing his *fabula animi* to tell him what happened, receiving no answer but that low *thrum, thrum, thrum* and the vibration in his palms. If he does happen to put the stick down now, he has only to reach toward it and it leaps into his hand as though magnetized. He wants to tell Miranda about this phenomenon, but he fears she will not believe him.

He is obsessed with the walking stick, and he is obsessed with Poe, and with the sprite, Airmail, who has somehow vanished.

"Airmail told me something very important last summer," he says to Miranda.

"Oh, yes? And what was that?"

"I can't remember."

"Then how do you know it was important?"

"Because I have it in my mind that it was important. I know it was. But I can't think what it was."

"So why don't you call him? You always say that you only have to leave a message and he comes buzzing around, and sometimes he comes even when you *don't* call him."

"I know. I've called him. Four or five times. That answering gadget he has never picks up. I've *willed* him to come, if you believe in telepathy, but that hasn't worked, either."

"Maybe he's on vacation. Even couriers take vacations, right?"

"Not Airmail. He's not like any human alive. Sometimes I wonder if he is human."

"Well, if you can't summon him, you're just going to have to remember. I'm sure it will come to you."

Thorne bites his lip. No matter how hard he tries, he can't remember whatever it was that Airmail told him. He stares at Miranda, his watery gaze unfocused and drifting.

"Perhaps I wrote something down? Wrote a note to myself? Put it somewhere as a reminder?"

Miranda searches Thorne's desk and all his file cabinets for a note, but she finds nothing. He drops the subject for a few days, but he keeps circling back to it.

Miranda herself has been living in a kind of limbo. She has called the university and been granted a year's leave of absence to recover, but she knows somehow that she will never return. She doesn't want to be among all those cut-throat sophisticates. She doesn't want to study law. She doesn't want to be that far away from Thorne when he needs her. She wants to find a place where she can study geology closer to home. Close enough to look after her father, near enough to support Poe in any way she can, even though she is the agent of his misfortune.

The gap in her memory is still there and it is maddening. If only she could remember what happened to her, she could clear this up in minutes, she could exonerate Poe, free him from that jail. But no matter how many times she goes over it, she can't get past the point where she took the brownies out to Poe.

Miranda is mildly curious about Sebastian, who hasn't written or called or gotten in touch with her in any way. It is not like him — he has always been so clingy. She finally writes to tell him that it is definitely over. She won't be returning to Cambridge, so it would be pointless to try to go on. When Sebastian doesn't reply to the letter either, Miranda shrugs. She had braced herself for a long campaign to win her back, weepy letters about his infernal *need*. Under the circumstances, silence is golden.

Miranda is more frustrated by Airmail's absence. She won-ders if what he told her father might have some bearing on what happened to her, if he might be able to jog her memory, but the man with the cobalt eyes has vanished. When she tries the number herself, she learns that the phone has been disconnected. She jumps into her VW and drives into Belle

Coeur. The door of the store-front office on Main Street where Airmail had worked has been left ajar. She pushes it open and finds nothing but an old desk, a worn desk chair, and a lot of dust, as though the place hasn't been occupied for years. There is a square imprint on the desk where there was a phone, but the phone is gone and there isn't so much as a scrap of paper to indicate where Airmail might have gone. She walks up and down the street, talking to the proprietors of neighboring stores. It doesn't seem possible that a man who is four feet tall and rides a Kawasaki Ninja at the speed of sound could disappear without anyone noticing, but she can't find a solitary person who can recall the last time Airmail was seen around town.

After two hours spent combing both sides of Main Street, Miranda sits on a park bench and weeps. It feels as though her last chance to understand what happened to her has disappeared, along with the strange little sprite who so annoyed her father.

~

The New World Hotel

With the trial set to start nine days before Christmas, the presiding judge knows it's likely to spill over into the holidays, so he postpones it until the fourth of January. The postponement makes sense, but it leaves Rose feeling as blue as she has ever been. She had counted on having Poe home for Christmas.

Rose mopes for a couple of days, snapping at Joey Ballew for his habit of following her around and asking if she's okay, but it's not like her to lollygag. She is tossing and turning at three o'clock in the morning, annoyed at Joey for taking up a third of the bed where she is accustomed to sleeping alone, when she hits on the one useful thing she might do. She leaves Joey the entire bed, brews a pot of coffee, and waits impatiently until the first pale wash of winter sunlight strikes the kitchen window. Then she picks up the telephone and dials Maeva Miller.

A recorded message tells her that Maeva's line has been disconnected, but Rose is undeterred. She drags Joey out of bed to help her milk the goats and do the chores, then waits while he dawdles with his oatmeal. She is sitting in the pickup when he finally ambles out, still tucking in his shirt.

What had been the Kids Kamp looks more run-down and dismal than ever, without Alf around to do even minimal maintenance. There's no answer when Rose rings the doorbell, but the door is unlocked. Rose opens it to find Maeva drinking coffee and smoking while she watches a daytime talk show on TV with the volume up as high as it will go. Two sisters are screaming obscenities at one another because they had both slept with the same man. Maeva watches as though hypnotized. Her long blond hair looks like it hasn't been washed in a month, she's wearing nothing but one of Alf's old plaid shirts, and there are huge dark circles under her eyes. Rose tries to explain what she has in mind, but she can't talk over the TV, so she reaches over and switches the power off. In the odd silence that follows, they can hear the old house creaking in the wind.

Maeva blinks up at her as though she has never seen Rose before in her life. Rose figures that she has been into Alf's drug stash and that she's having a little trouble coping with the cold gray reality of a December morning. Rose edges her chair up close and forces the young woman to look at her.

"Maeva, I have a little outing in mind. How'd you like to come to New York with me?"

"New York? You mean, like, Plattsburgh?"

"No. I mean New York City. I want to find those boys."

"What boys?"

"Skeeter and Moe. The two you told me about? The ones who might've seen Poe out at the gravel pit the day the Thorne girl was attacked?"

"Oh, them boys. I dunno, Rose. New York City is a big place. I've been there with Alf. It can scare the hell out of you."

"You'll be safe with me. Folks never give me trouble. I called the station in Bunker's Corner and there's a Greyhound bus that leaves at ten. I'll pay all our expenses; it won't cost you a thin dime."

Maeva manages a half smile. It's the first sign of life Rose has seen in the woman. "Where we gonna stay? A hotel?"

"I haven't thought that far ahead. We'll find a place, and I'll feed you good. You could use a little meat on your bones. I swear you've lost ten pounds since the last time I seen you, and you was skinny then. You look like one of them bony little girl country singers. They don't eat because they think they got to look like a fashion model, and they end up with voices as thin as a poor man's soup."

Rose brews a pot of coffee. The milk in Maeva's fridge has curdled and the sugar is full of ants, but she gets Maeva to drink two cups, then accompanies her into the bathroom. There's no soap but there is an almost full bottle of baby shampoo and Rose uses the whole thing on Maeva's hair and her pitiful frame, washing her the way you would wash a little girl. When she's put on clean jeans and a sweater and Rose has brushed her hair, Maeva looks almost pretty again.

Joey swings by the jail on the way to the bus station so Rose can tell Poe she will be gone for a while. She promises to be back before Christmas. Poe seems to be wasting away and Rose has the feeling that captivity is slowly killing him, despite the pies and cakes and pots of chili she carts to the jail.

By the time they climb on the bus, the drugs have worn off and the coffee has kicked in and Maeva is downright chatty. Rose is enjoying herself, feeling like the girl's mother, listening to her yack about what kind of lipstick she likes and how Alf always treated her bad but she's going to miss that pack of kids that come up every summer for the camp.

"I'd like to have a bunch of kids myself," Maeva says.

"So have them," Rose advises. "Find yourself a man that isn't Alf and have kids."

Maeva looks down, biting her lip. "Can't. Alf took care of that."

Rose doesn't pursue it. She remembers when Maeva was the prettiest girl in Belle Coeur County. Now she's past twenty-five and looking ten years older than she is. She's bird-boned and petite, with quick, shy gestures and a weary, wounded smile, but Rose is sure there's nothing wrong with the girl that a little tender care wouldn't fix. The first thing is to get her away from Alf for good, and the second is to get her off whatever drugs she's doing. One thing at a time.

Maeva dozes off with her head on Rose's shoulder. Rose cools her cheek against the window on the west side of the bus, watching the light drain out of the day, the dregs of the sunset spilling like molten lava down the dark hills.

It's dark when they reach the Port Authority Bus Station at Eighth Avenue and Forty-Second Street. They shoulder their bags, say goodbye to the driver and thank him for a pleasant trip, and Maeva leads the way on foot to the YMCA at Sixty-Third and Broadway. Rose can't stop gawking at the people, the traffic, the buildings that rise like steep cliffs on all sides. In every block, she stops three or four times to gaze up and up. Hurrying pedestrians bump into her, but Rose remains motionless until Maeva, who is shivering in the cold, yanks at her sleeve and says they have to be getting on. They take adjoining single rooms at the Y, both rooms smaller than most jail cells, and the only bathroom is down the hall. The rooms have been painted a shade of light purple, and Maeva says the color purple makes her sick. There's a tiny closet without a hanger rack, and the bed is on wheels, with a mattress about as thick as two of Rose's fingers held together, and every time she tries to turn over, it rolls away from the wall. The bed comes with a sheet, blanket, and one postage-stamp pillow, and the springs are so noisy and the walls so thin that when Maeva moves in the next room, she wakes Rose.

After one sleepless night, Maeva figures she can do better on a double room in a hotel. She locates a phone booth downstairs with the yellow pages intact, borrows a handful of change from Rose, and calls hotels until she finds them a room at the New World Hotel on the Bowery in Chinatown, a block from the Grand Street subway station and not far from an address they have for Skeeter in Alphabet City. The room is noisy and cramped and there is a pervasive smell of General Tao's chicken, but the beds are comfortable and they have their own bathroom. Rose sleeps like a baby. The police sirens, the car alarms, the maniacs screaming in the night don't bother her half as much as the birds back home.

Each time they registered at the camp, Skeeter and Moses gave a different address. Maeva also has various addresses for a dozen other boys from the area who were friendly with the pair and might know where to find them. They try all the addresses they have for Skeeter first, because they're in the neighborhood. It's frigid work. There's no snow on the ground and the temperature is ten degrees warmer than back home, but the wind whips through the canyons between the tall buildings and bites through their clothes. Rose doesn't complain, but Maeva has only a thin cloth coat and she shivers constantly. On the afternoon of the second day, they're trudging along Canal Street when Rose spots a pink parka and buys it for Maeva, along with a fleecy jacket and an oversized pair of mittens. Maeva puts it on and smiles gratefully at Rose.

The extra clothing fends off the cold, but Maeva is still frightened by the city. She carries a little spray can of Mace tucked in her hand most of the time, ready to zap anyone who looks at her the wrong way. Her eyes dart in every direction, watching for trouble, while Rose seems impervious to any threat. She strides through the crowds, saying hello to junkies, cops, wild-eyed streetwalkers, Wall Street brokers, subway token vendors, street magicians, cabbies, dog walkers, dope dealers, tourists from Indiana, and gangbangers with baseball caps turned sideways and pants riding around their knees. Even the gangbangers look her over and decide there's no point messing with a crazy white woman who is big as a house.

They have no luck finding Skeeter. The tenement address Maeva has for him in Alphabet City is gone, torn down to make room for a condo development. The elementary school that helped to place the boy with the Kids Kamp is still open, but it has been two years since Skeeter was registered there. Maeva and Rose give up on Skeeter and concentrate on locating Moses instead. That means taking the D train all the way to the Mott Haven neighborhood in the South Bronx. Neither woman has been on a subway before, but after taking the train the wrong direction all the way out to Coney Island, they figure it out. At the most recent address Maeva has for Moses, a sixth-floor apartment in a building that smells as though someone dumped a tub of boric acid down the stairwells, they pass a dead rat on the second-floor landing. Maeva wants to turn back, but Rose keeps trudging up the steps. They find a metal door with the number "609" spray-painted in fluorescent pink next to the doorknob. They can hear noises and a baby crying inside, but Rose has to pound on the door for five minutes before three or four locks snick open and a woman in her twenties peeks out between double chains.

"What you want?"

Maeva steps up to the crack so the woman can see her. "We're looking for Moses P. Washington."

The woman opens the door another crack. Braced on her hip, she holds a snot-nosed toddler with a smelly diaper. "What's he done this time? That boy ain't nothin but trouble."

"He hasn't done a thing. He might have seen a crime that was done last summer, that's all. He was at the summer camp I used to run with my husband. My name's Maeva."

The woman looks her up and down, like she's deciding whether to cooperate. "I heard of you, Maeva. Moe says you were good to him, but he ain't here anyhow."

"When do you think he might be back?"

"Moe? Might as well wait on the wind. He might be comin up them stairs right now, or we might not see him for a week.

You welcome to set out there and wait. You can't come in, on account of my baby-father is sleepin one off."

Across the street, there's a patch of what was meant to be green space, with a single park bench. The ground is littered with cigarette butts, used condoms, broken bottles, and syringes, but Rose and Maeva sit shivering in the cold, waiting to see if Moe is going to come home. They take turns warming up at a café up the street until early dark swallows the city. It's near eight o'clock in the evening when they give up and walk back to the 149th Street subway station. Maeva thinks they might as well take a bus back to Belle Coeur County, but Rose is determined to come back the next morning and to keep coming back every day until Moe turns up.

~

A crash like broken glass
They find Moe on the third day. He's coming back from the deli on the corner as they arrive in the morning, carrying a pack of cigarettes for his sister and milk for the baby. Maeva steps up to say hello.

"Hey, Moe. How are you?"

The boy eyes her warily, ready to run if that seems like the best option.

"You aren't in trouble if that's what you're thinking, Moe," she says. "It's me, Maeva. From the Kids Kamp?"

"Maeva! I didn't recognize you in all them clothes. Goodness, woman, what brings you all the way to New York City?"

"Looking for you and Skeeter. Do you have a few minutes to talk to us?"

He shrugs. "School's out for Christmas. I got nothin but minutes."

"Come over here and shake hands, then. This here is Rose, Poe's mama. Poe's a big fella who lives up on Manitou Mountain, you might have heard of him?"

Moe nods and says a polite hello to Rose. She shakes the boy's hand. "Nice to meet you, Moe. Listen, there's a café in the next block where we can get some breakfast. We'll buy you something to eat and we can talk where it's warm."

The boy lights up when she mentions food. "First off, I got to run this stuff upstairs. That baby is screamin its head off and my sister is about to have a nicotine fit. But I'll be right back down. Don't you leave without me."

Moses is gone so long that Maeva begins to think he's skipped out on them, but he comes whistling back out and leads the way to the restaurant, where they find a booth and Moe orders pancakes and bacon and a big glass of orange juice. Rose and Maeva settle for coffee and toast and when the coffee arrives, Maeva puts her hand on the boy's bony shoulder and looks him in the eye.

"Listen, Moses. This is real important. We thought you and Skeeter might've seen something that happened last summer, out by that old gravel pit. Poe is in a whole lot of trouble, and we hoped maybe you saw it and you might be able to help."

"Why would you think that?"

"I remember the way you boys looked when you came back that day. You came running into the yard like you were scared something awful. I thought it was only the lightning had you spooked, but you said you and Skeeter had been out by the gravel pit. When I heard they arrested Poe, I put two and two together."

"We like old Poe, me and Skeeter. For a while last summer we was tracking him most every day, only we didn't know it was him. At first we thought he was the Sasquatch or Bigfoot or one of them, cause we found these big tracks left by a beast that had six toes on each foot."

"So you were trailing him that day at the gravel pit?"

"We was, only we got there late. That was the day we figured out Poe and the Sasquatch was the same person. We followed his tracks out from town. Then we lost them for a while, maybe because he got a ride or somethin. We had to look around for two hours before we picked up the trail again. We followed them tracks along a road to the gravel pit, and we was still a couple of hundred feet away when we heard a lady screaming."

"Did you see what was going on?"

"Not really. We got up as close as we could, but we was hiding behind these big tall sunflowers because we was real scared. We heard this lady, sounded like somebody was killing her. We thought she was bein attacked by a Sasquatch. Then we heard a man talkin to her, kind of quiet, and she was tellin him to stop. Then you could hear he was hittin her. I knew for sure what it was because I heard that sound before, plenty. She was yellin for him to stop, only he wasn't goin to quit until he killed her was what it sounded like."

"Was it Poe who was talking to her?"

"I dunno what Poe sounds like. Well, we heard him sing a time or two, but we didn't never hear him talk."

"So what happened then?"

"After the lady was screaming?"

"Yes."

"The man yell."

"What did he yell?"

"I dunno. Somethin loud, like, *What?* Or maybe it was *Huh?* Then there was a big crash."

"What kind of crash?"

"Like a car wreck, maybe? Like broke glass, that kind of crash."

"Did you see a car there?"

"Nope. Like I said, we didn't see nothin. We was hidin behind the sunflowers."

"But you're sure it was a car? That sound you heard? Like a windshield breaking?"

"Coulda been. Or it coulda been a beer bottle. Or maybe neither one. Glass, anyhow. Some kinda glass. It sounded like a car window smashed, that's all I can say for sure."

"But you didn't see a car out there? Or a man who wasn't Poe?"

"Nope. We didn't see nothin. We only heard things, but I ain't exactly sure what we heard."

"What happened then?"

"Nothin."

"What do you mean, nothing? Something must have happened."

"Well, it was quiet awhile. Then we heard Poe runnin. Sounded like a freight train."

"How did you know it was him?"

"Ain't no normal man makes a noise like that. We tracked him back to the road and we got close enough once or twice to see he was carryin a woman. We wanted to get closer but we was afraid, and Poe was movin fast for a fella that big. We followed along until we seen him get to the highway, and that cop puttin the handcuffs on him, and the ambulance come and the paddy wagon. They put the girl in the ambulance and Poe in the wagon."

"And you didn't see anyone else out there? You didn't see a

man other than Poe?"

"Yeah. We seen the cop."

"That was the sheriff. I mean did you see anyone else, other than Poe and the sheriff?"

"No, ma'am. Just Poe and the girl and the cop and then the other cops and the ambulance people. Then we took off out of there because nobody wants to be around where there's cops and trouble. We wasn't gone far when that little fella picked us up on his motorcycle and gave us a lift the rest of the way. Never had a ride like that. We was home almost before we started."

"That was Airmail. He's a courier," Maeva says. "Friend of ours, or he was. He kinda disappeared around that time. Look, somebody stole Alf's camera, too. He was ready to skin one of you kids alive. It was gone for a couple of days, and then it was back where he left it. Was that you took his camera?"

"Yep. We was only borrowing it to take pictures of the Sasquatch we could sell to the papers."

"And did you take any pictures?"

"A whole bunch. Maybe a dozen pictures. Somethin like that."

Rose leans forward. "So you have twelve photographs?"

"Not exactly."

"What do you mean, *not exactly*?"

"Well, the pictures didn't turn out. We was holdin the camera up above the sunflowers, see, so we didn't notice the lens cap was still on. We took the film to a drugstore when we got back to the city here, and the fella there told us we had a whole lotta nothin."

Rose sags back in her seat. She lets her coffee go cold while she stares out the window at the river of yellow cabs pouring along Morris Avenue. It seems to go on day and night without pause. It doesn't seem natural to live in the middle of this, but she supposes that you get used to anything with time. Anything but Poe behind bars.

Moe tucks into his breakfast and finishes off every last bite. When he's done, he wipes his mouth on a napkin. "Look, I'd be happy to come up and tell a judge I seen somebody else beatin on that poor girl. Would that help?"

"We can't let you do that, Moe," Rose says. "If you did, you'd be tellin a lie, and then you'd be in trouble and it would go even worse for Poe. One last question: is there any chance Skeeter saw anything you didn't see?"

"No, ma'am. We talked about it. We always wondered what happened up there. Only other thing I can tell you is something strange happened a while before. We was trackin Poe one day, and a man in a big black car, maybe a Cadillac, was followin us. Fella pulled up right beside us on the county road, man in a funny hat. Looked at us real hard like we was dinner on a plate, but then he took off. Stranger for sure, outta state plates. I didn't get what state, though."

Rose looks at Maeva and shakes her head. "Poe says there was a big black car out there, but I don't guess it means much unless you saw it the same time you heard the girl getting beat on."

"I'm sorry, ma'am. I'd like to help old Poe, I really would. I hope we get to see him when we come up next summer."

"The Kids Kamp has closed," Rose says. "But if you want to come up next summer, you can stay with me. Help out with the goats."

"I'd like that. I'm gonna miss the camp, if it ain't there no more. Most fun I ever had."

Rose takes a napkin and prints her name, address, and phone number in careful block letters, then tucks the napkin in the pocket of Moe's hoodie. "You write to me and we'll figure out a way to get you a bus ticket to come up and see us next summer. Skeeter, too, if you know how to find him."

Rose calls the waiter over and orders a bunch of sandwiches off the menu for Moe, then asks the waiter if he can throw in a couple of quarts of milk from the refrigerator for the baby. She pays the check and they leave the restaurant and walk Moe to the door of his apartment building. He gives Maeva and Rose little hugs and takes the milk and sandwiches and heads on up the stairs. Rose turns and walks right out into the traffic, forcing the cabs to dodge her, and crosses the street to the park bench, where she sits down heavily. A weary sigh escapes her, like steam from a grate. Maeva waits until the light at the corner changes and darts across. She sits next to Rose and takes her hand. Rose says nothing, but she lets Maeva hold her hand. The wind picks up and Maeva feels it biting even through the pink parka. Finally, Rose struggles to her feet and heads toward the 149th Street subway station, with Maeva trailing behind.

Back at the hotel, they pack their bags and get ready to head home. Maeva asks if there is any point telling Lambert Cain or the sheriff about whatever it was that Moses heard or didn't hear, especially that last part about the black car.

Rose shakes her head. "I don't think so. Seems to me it would just confuse things. Put a twelve-year-old kid on the stand and you don't know what's going to come out. It's a damned shame they didn't stand up just the one time to peek over them sunflowers."

~ VI ~
The Trial

Erased by the hand of God

Poe's trial begins on the fourth day of January, with curiosity seekers packing the Belle Coeur County Courthouse, anticipating an irresistible concoction: beauty and the grotesque, sex and violence, a villain who will be satisfyingly pilloried at the end.

The first row behind the tables for the attorneys is reserved for families of the victim and accused, and the row behind that is for reporters. There are the local types who have known Poe all their lives, a couple of breathless TV reporters, even a distinguished writer for a national magazine who is thinking of writing a book on the trial, although he's rarely sober enough to attend. Behind the reporters, another hundred spectators are wedged into the benches of the lower gallery, with fifty more squeezed into an upper gallery behind a curved wooden railing, the first time it has been pressed into service since a murder trial in 1955.

Rose arrives early, but a plump reporter in a flowered dress has already claimed the seat directly behind her. She seems to have drenched herself in a cheap cologne so cloying that Rose has to fight down the urge to retch. The woman is there every day of the trial wearing the same stink like a second skin, so that whenever Rose thinks of the trial afterward, the stench of that cologne is the smell of Poe on trial.

The fluorescent ceiling lights give everyone present the pallor of late-night patrons in a fast-food joint. Rose sits behind the defense table, with Joey Ballew on one side and Maeva Miller on the other. Maeva holds her hand and gives her a little squeeze now and then. Rose wears a new blue dress she has sewn for herself, because the nice dresses they carry at the J.C. Penney don't fit a big-boned gal. She washes the dress by hand every night and hangs it by the fire to dry for the next morning. No one is going to look at Poe's mother like she's poor white trash and doesn't know how to dress proper.

The bailiff mutters something and the spectators rise. Rose hauls herself to her feet as the judge strides in. He looks like a buzzard, with a prominent beak and great black eye-brows that sweep back like a buzzard's wings. Lambert Cain has told Rose the judge's name, but it goes in one ear and out the other, so she thinks of the man as Judge Buzzard for the duration of the trial.

Poe is brought in by a paunchy bailiff. There are gasps in the gallery from those who have never seen Poe before and are overwhelmed by the sheer size of the man. "My God, he really is a giant," someone says, and Judge Buzzard raps his gavel. Poe is handcuffed and dressed in a freshly laundered orange prison suit. Rose blows him a kiss before he is seated in a special over-sized chair in the prisoner's dock. The thin-lipped state's attorney, whom Rose knows only as Savich or Savage, calls Sheriff Jim Dunn as his first witness. There is a scuffling and scraping as everyone leans forward to hear the questioning.

"Sheriff, you have been an officer of the law in this state for many years, is that correct?"

"Twenty years with the state police, the last seventeen as an investigator with Major Crimes before I retired. Then I got elected as sheriff here in Belle Coeur County."

"So you would characterize yourself as a very experienced criminal investigator?"

"You could say that, yes."

"And you have at one time or another investigated almost every sort of crime an officer of the law might encounter, is that correct?"

"I suppose there are a few situations I haven't come across, but if that's the case, I'd just as soon avoid them."

Rose misses the next exchange. Something about how often the sheriff had encountered perpetrators in the act during his career. Then Savich or Savage asks what the sheriff was doing on the day in question.

"I was patrolling that stretch of old Highway 116 out near the gravel pit. Not much traffic out there since the four-lane went through, but I'd been out to check the bridges after the storm. It was getting late in the afternoon, about a quarter past five, and I was heading back into town. Luckily, I was driving pretty slow, or I might have missed him altogether."

"Missed who, Sheriff?"

"The defendant, Poe. An individual known to me since we were both seven or eight years old. He was walking out of the woods with a half-naked girl over his shoulder, and she was in rough shape. I braked hard and jumped out of the car. Poe had blood all over his coveralls, and he was so exhausted he could barely walk."

"What did you do then?"

"I put in a quick call to dispatch to tell them I was going to need an ambulance and possibly backup if there was anyone available, in case I had trouble subduing the suspect."

"And did you have trouble with him?"

"No, I did not. I asked that he put the girl down gently, and he did as he was asked. She was unconscious, she had suffered bruises over much of her body, and she was bleeding pretty badly from the nose and mouth. I made sure that her airway was open and that her pulse and breathing were steady. I made her as comfortable as I could while I waited for the ambulance to arrive."

"Was the defendant saying anything to you at the time?"

"He kept repeating the same thing, over and over. 'Get help. Get help. Get help.'"

"Can you tell the court what happened next, Sheriff Dunn?"

"I did what I could in the way of first aid for the girl, then I put the handcuffs on Poe and read him his rights. I could see it was going to be a pretty serious situation because the girl had been badly beaten."

"You subsequently identified the victim?"

"I did. She was a young woman known to the defendant and to myself. As you know, the law says she can't be identified."

"Having taken the accused into custody, did you subsequently attempt to interrogate him?"

"I did, sir. Matters were delayed somewhat by the storm that broke as we were driving the suspect back to town. Because of his condition and because he did not have an attorney present, we delayed the first interview until the following day, the Monday, in the presence of his mother and his attorney, Mr. Lambert Cain."

"Can you tell us the result of that interrogation?"

"He kept repeating the same phrase, 'Get help, get help, get help.' He did claim that there was another individual who had attacked her and that he had grabbed this man and thrown him into a car window before carrying the girl to the highway."

"You made subsequent attempts to interrogate the defendant?"

"I did, always in the presence of his attorney, Mr. Lambert Cain. Altogether, we had six conversations with the defendant."

"And were the results any different?"

"Somewhat. He was calmer. The claim was made again that there was another man present and that it was this individual who attacked the victim, although the defendant claims not to have seen the man's face. He said only that he threw the man off the victim and subsequently carried her to safety."

"Did you attempt to verify this claim by examining the crime scene?"

"Yes, I did. Unfortunately, the crime scene had vanished by the time I got there."

"Can you explain that for the court, Sheriff Dunn?"

"The storm kept us away for a time because we were overburdened with public safety work in the county. When I got back out to the gravel pit, I saw that there had been a huge cave-in. The lake is a lot bigger than it used to be and I almost drove right into it. Everything out there was gone, including the tower for the old gravel chute. There was nothing left of the scene. It's all gone, like it was erased by the hand of God."

"Thank you, Sheriff. Now I'd like to show you State's Exhibit Number Thirteen. Have you seen this item before?"

"Yes. That's the white summer dress the victim was wearing when I encountered her. It was found to be stained with blood and semen and sent to the state lab. They were able to confirm that the blood was the victim's and the semen belonged to the defendant. The victim was partially clothed in this dress when I found her."

Poe gazes up into the fluorescent lights overhead. The lights make him feel sleepy. He wonders if they make everybody sleepy the same way. Some of the people have gone away, and those who are still in the courtroom look very tired. He tries to listen to the voices, the lawyer fellow talking to the sheriff, but he can't keep his mind on what they're saying. The lights make a humming noise and that noise makes him sleepy, too, so he tries to concentrate on the dress Miranda wore that day. It was a pretty white dress. Such a pretty dress, with so many buttons. Poe remembers seeing it once before that day at the gravel pit. Miranda was wearing it when she left the house late one afternoon right after she came back from Cane Bridge, and she waved at him before she drove away. The next time he saw the dress, she was wearing it at the gravel pit. She was wearing it, and she was lying down reading, and he could look up her legs at the seeing-through panties.

The lawyer fellow is done talking to the sheriff. The judge says it's time for lunch. Lunch is a good time, but after lunch Poe is even sleepier and it's hard to stay awake in the big wide chair.

~

Rose senses a tremor in the courtroom when Lambert Cain in his blue suit stands to begin his cross-examination of the sheriff. A straightening, as though people are sitting up, slouching less, minding their manners. Lambert has that kind of effect on people without trying. Something about the way he carries himself, tall and lean and graceful and dignified and always proper, but not snooty about it the way some people are. If Poe has a chance, it depends on Lambert Cain. The country doesn't seem to make men like Lambert anymore, but maybe it's just that you have to be a little older to have that air he has, like he's easy with himself and knows what he's about and how to do the right thing in any situation. She listens intently as Lambert begins.

"Sheriff, I hate to impose any more upon your time than we already have, but I do have a few questions, if I may."

"Go right ahead, Mr. Cain."

"Thank you. Now, Sheriff, I'd like to take you back to that first moment, when you were out on patrol on Highway 116. You came around a bend, if I understand correctly, at a fairly low speed?"

"That's right. I've never seen the point of patrolling at high speed. You don't see a thing."

"Makes sense. Now that was when you saw the defendant coming out of the woods, carrying the victim?"

"Yes, it is."

"And you hadn't been called to the scene? There was no reason to suspect that anything was amiss?"

"Correct."

"You've testified already, but I'll ask you to repeat it because I think it's an important point: you had no difficulty getting

Poe to give up the girl or in arresting him, is that right?"

"Yes, that's right. No difficulty at all."

"You didn't have the sense that he might not want to release the victim or that he would resist arrest?"

"Not in the least. He had run a long way with the victim and he was exhausted. All he wanted was for us to get help."

"Did you draw your firearm, may I ask?"

"No, I did not. I thought it far better to keep things nice and calm."

"I see. Of course, you read him his rights at the scene?"

"Yes, I did. Slowly and carefully because Poe can have a little trouble grasping things. He seemed to understand. I emphasized that he had the right to remain silent, repeated it a couple of times for his benefit."

"And did he? Remain silent, that is?"

"No, he did not. He kept repeating the same thing, telling me to get help."

"Is it fair to say that he was concerned about the welfare of the victim?"

"Yes, it is. Very concerned."

"Now, I'm going to ask you to draw on your experience, your thirty years as an officer of the law. Is it common for the perpetrator of a crime to show such concern for the victim?"

"Maybe not, but I've seen it before. A man gets angry with his wife, for instance, and knocks her around, and then afterward he's very contrite and anxious to see that she gets proper medical care. An individual's attitude toward the victim is not an indication of his guilt or innocence, one way or the other."

"Alright, Sheriff. I'd like to move on to the unusual situation we have here, in which a crime was committed but the crime scene has vanished. To what degree would you say the collapse out at the gravel pit that wiped away most of the physical evidence has compromised your investigation?"

"Well, it doesn't help. The crime scene itself is normally a key component of any investigation, and we've had to operate without it. That means I was unable to check the defendant's story about the black car that might have a shattered wind-shield. I could have looked for broken glass or tire tracks. He mentioned a wine bottle and the victim lying on a blanket having a picnic. I couldn't locate any objects to confirm that story. It also means that we could not find footprints that might have told us who the attacker was."

"And as you have already said, there was a considerable delay in getting out to the crime scene caused by the storm. What does that mean, in practice?"

"Well, under normal circumstances, we would have been out there that evening, using whatever light remained to examine the crime scene, probably working under the lights for a while."

"But at the gravel pit, there was no scene tape put down, no attempt to secure the area, nothing of that sort?"

"Nothing. As you say, we were dealing with unusual circumstances."

"So there were no tire tracks, no cigarette butts, no empty bottles, no blood or semen traces, no ejected cartridges, no hunting knife, nothing whatsoever that might be of use in an ordinary criminal investigation. No crime scene. The crime scene itself had effectively been completely erased, never to be found again?"

"Exactly. As though by the hand of God, I believe is how I put it before."

"The hand of God. It would seem, Sheriff, that the hand

of God — or chance, as an unbeliever might have it — has played a rather prominent role in this case?"

"I suppose that's true. God or chance, it hasn't worked in favor of a thorough criminal investigation."

"And in more human terms, we are also lacking any real testimony from the victim because she is suffering short-term memory loss?"

"That's about the size of it. Just about everywhere we turn with this case, something we'd like to have is missing."

"I must say, Sheriff Dunn, we are dealing with a unique set of circumstances here. I've been practicing law in this county for more than four decades, and you've been a law officer in this area for twenty-five years, and I think it's safe to say that between us, we have never seen a situation quite like this. Is that right?"

"Absolutely. I've never encountered anything like it."

"So we have no crime scene, we have no witnesses, we have a victim with no memory — and yet we have a defendant charged with aggravated assault and aggravated sexual assault, two very grave crimes that, taken together, might mean that he spends the rest of his life behind bars. Is that right?"

"I think that sums it up pretty well, except it's not quite true that there are no witnesses: I am a witness."

"Yes. And you are both the arresting officer in this case and the star witness for the prosecution, true?"

"I suppose that's true."

"Please understand, Sheriff. I'm not in any way impugning your integrity. What I am trying to get at here is the fact that in this particular case, you are missing so many of the tools you would normally have used to investigate a crime."

"I understand that."

"Thank you, Sheriff. That's all I have for now."

~

The Year of the Flood

When Poe sees Elmer Hepp called to the witness stand, he waves and calls out to him. "Hi, Mister Hepp. How are them Percherons doin?"

The judge bangs his gavel and warns Poe that he can be removed from the courtroom. There are titters in the gallery: Hepp is wearing an ancient brown suit that is three sizes too large, a white shirt with a filthy collar and a string tie, and he still has the gunnysacks tied with twine around his battered boots. He glares around the courtroom with one fierce eye, the patch on the other eye askew, as though daring someone to challenge his version of events. When he's sworn in, Hepp disdains the courtroom Bible, takes his own Bible from an inside pocket, and waves it around as though brandishing a sword.

The state's attorney approaches him cautiously. "Mr. Hepp, in order to establish a time line of the events on the day the victim in this case was attacked, we're going to ask you to take us through this. Is it true that on the day in question, you were driving your team out along Highway 116 when you encountered the defendant?"

"Yessir, it is."

"And you offered him a lift in your wagon, is that right?"

"That's absolutely right. I gave 'em both a ride."

"Excuse me? Did you say *both*?"

"Are ye deaf, sir? I said both."

"So you're saying there was more than one person on the road?"

"Sure there was."

"So you gave a lift to the defendant and to someone else?"

"I thought lawyers was smart. I believe that's what I said. Both."

Brendan Savage takes a cautious step back. "And can you tell us who the other person was, please? You picked up the defendant and someone else?"

"I most certainly did. I don't know the Jezebel's name, but I drove this Poe fella and that young harlot out to the gravel pit, where he did unspeakable things to her."

A wild buzz ripples through the crowd and the judge bangs his gavel. In the midst of the confusion, Poe protests: "Nossir! Nossir! Nossir! That ain't true at all. It was only me that took a ride in Elmer's wagon! There wasn't nobody with me!"

The judge hammers his gavel again and the gallery subsides into whispers and falls silent. Poe is warned again. Brendan Savage flips through his legal pad, buying time, trying to decide what to make of this new twist. He ventures another question: "You're quite sure, then? Two people, not one. The defendant and a young woman, is that correct?"

"How many times do I have to say it? Are ye as thick as that fella Poe yonder? There was two of 'em, the giant and the Jezebel. I said it already."

"And both of them got off at the same place, the turnoff to the gravel pit?"

"That's right. They was goin fishing, they said. But I knew damned well they had somethin else in mind. *And he shall lay his hand upon the head of his offering, and kill it before the tabernacle of the congregation: and Aaron's sons shall sprinkle the blood thereof round about upon the altar . . .*"

The judge bangs his gavel again. "Mr. Hepp, I am going

to have to ask you not to recite the scripture in my courtroom. Please answer the questions and leave it at that."

Elmer Hepp rounds on the judge. "Are ye telling me the word of the Lord is not accepted in your courtroom, sir?"

"That is not what I am saying. I am telling you simply that quotations from the scripture are not relevant to this case, so please confine yourself to answering the questions or I will have to hold you in contempt."

Savage steps forward gingerly. "Can you tell us why you didn't mention the young woman when the sheriff asked you about this the first time, Mr. Hepp?"

"Because he never asked me! That ought to be plain as the nose on your face. He asked me, did Poe ride in my wagon, and I said he did. That was an end to it!"

Savage, flustered, retreats to his seat, mumbling that he has no more questions. He doesn't dare mention that Elmer Hepp had told the sheriff in no uncertain terms that he had given a lift to Poe and Poe alone.

Lambert Cain approaches Hepp slowly. He can see that it will take very little to provoke an outburst from the old man, but it's hard to say whether that might benefit the defense.

"Mr. Hepp, I have one further question. I wonder if you can recall what the young woman, the victim in this case, was wearing when you picked her up in your wagon?"

Hepp doesn't hesitate. "She was wearing pants! I don't approve of a woman in trousers, and I told her so at the time. Only a harlot would dress in such a fashion. I tried to warn her that the giant Poe might be dangerous, if she sought to preserve her virtue. I spoke to her of the Year of the Flood, and I told her that the end time is upon us, but her ears were as closed as her mind and she would not listen."

"I see. Do you remember exactly what kind of trousers she was wearing?"

"They was blue jeans. So tight it was like she was poured into 'em. Blue jeans and a red T-shirt. Not what any proper young lady should have on her person, especially not on the Sabbath."

"Alright, Mr. Hepp. Now, I have one last question. How wide is the seat on your wagon?"

"Exactly thirty-six inches. Three feet. Built that wagon with my own hands, wheels included. Don't believe there's many here as could do that."

"You're correct in that, sir. It's a lost skill, the wheelwright's trade. Now, the wagon seat is three feet wide, and you all sat on it — yourself, the defendant, and the young woman, is that right?"

"Where else would we sit? I wouldn't ask a female to ride in the wagon box. Wouldn't be proper."

"Now you're a reasonably slender fellow, Mr. Hepp, but Poe — well, let's just say he's wide in the beam. But there was room for the three of you on the seat?"

"Are you calling me a liar? I just said there was!"

Lambert Cain lifts a hand. "Thank you kindly, sir. That will be all from the defense."

The judge nods to Elmer Hepp. "You may go, sir. We thank you kindly for your time."

Hepp rises, holds his Bible aloft, and begins to address the gallery as though he's delivering a sermon: *"And for his sister a virgin, that is nigh unto him, which hath had no husband; for her may he be defiled . . . And the daughter of any priest, if she profane herself by playing the whore, she profaneth her father: she shall be burnt with fire . . ."*

It takes three bailiffs to get Hepp out of the courtroom. He is still bellowing scripture as he is led away. The judge declares an hour-long break in the proceedings, and Lambert Cain confers with Rose in the corridor.

"I was a bit alarmed at first, but that may have been good for us," Cain tells her. "I could try to get that stricken from the record because we hadn't been told in advance that he would say he picked up both Poe and the girl. But there were so many holes in his testimony, it made our friend Mr. Savage look a bit ridiculous."

Rose bites her lip. "I surely hope so. I know it ain't the truth. I watched Poe leave, all by his lonesome. I'm sure he didn't go fishing with that girl."

"I believe you, Rose. I think we can simply leave that where it is. The dress speaks for itself. He had that all wrong."

~

Friday the 13th
"Good morning, Poe."

"Good morning, Mister Cain."

"How are you feeling today, Poe? Did you sleep well last night?"

"Yessir. I always sleeps well, especially since they brought in the long bed so's I got room for my legs and I don't hang over the end, like."

"Good. Then we'll get on with it. The first thing is that we need to be sure you understand why you're here. Do you understand that clearly, Poe? And do you understand that we can't say the name of the person who got hurt?"

"Yessir. I understand. I'm here 'cause she got hurt. And 'cause I went fishin that day."

"But you understand you're not charged for fishing, right?"

"Yessir, only if I hadn't have gone fishin, none of this woulda happened to me."

"Let's begin with that, Poe. How did you happen to go fishing?"

"I pretty much always goes to fish on a Sunday afternoon, only most times I goes to the river or one of the creeks. But they was all riled up on account of the flood, so I went back to my old fishin hole at the gravel pit."

"It's a spot you know well because you used to work there, I believe?"

"Yessir. I had a regular job, dumpin gravel in them trucks, till they closed down the pit."

"How did you get out there on this particular day, Poe? It's a long walk."

"Yessir, it is. But I had a ride partway from Elmer Hepp. He takes them Percherons out for a drive on Sunday afternoons, and he picked me up. Quoted a whole mess of scripture at me, then he let me off."

"He picked you up and you alone, is that right? Because Mr. Hepp has testified that you were with a young woman at the time."

"Yessir, I heard what he said and that's a lie. I wasn't with nobody. Well, except Elmer, after I got in the wagon. It's been ten years since I went fishin with anybody but myself."

"And did you have a good day fishing, Poe?"

"Sure did. Caught me a good mess of fish. Then I went up in the tower to play with the handles where I used to load them gravel trucks. That used to be my job when I worked at the gravel pit, see, to pull the handle and load the trucks."

"Is there another reason you climbed the old tower?"

"Yessir. Them old comic books that I used to look at was still there."

"What kind of comic books are these, Poe?"

"The dirty kind. The kind that shows stuff."

"Did you look at them this time?"

"Yep. I always do. I looked at them a bit, and I stroked myself some, and then I was done."

"You mean that you were masturbating, Poe, is that what you're saying?"

"I think that's the word, yep."

"And — I'm sorry to be so specific here, but it's important — when you ejaculated, did some of it fall on your coveralls?"

"You mean did I shoot it on myself? I sure did. Was quite a lot, too. I expect that's how it got on her dress, later, rubbin against her when I was carryin her."

Cain raises a hand. "Alright, Poe, I think you've said enough. We don't want to speculate as to how things got on her dress at this point. Now, can you tell us what happened next?"

"I went right to sleep. I ain't supposed to, on account of Mama says, 'Get them fish home before they stink.' But I was right tired."

"And when you woke up, what did you see?"

"I seen the girl. I know who she is. We been friends a long time, only I ain't supposed to say her name, on account of the law says I can't. She was just layin there on a blanket, up on that little rise that looks down over the river. It was like magic. She was not there and then she was there."

"And to repeat, she had not traveled out to the gravel pit with you, is that correct?"

"Nossir. She was there when I woke up. I don't know how

she come to be there."

"What was she doing when you first saw her?"

"Layin on that blanket and readin a book. She had a bottle of something, I think it was wine, and she was drinkin from a glass. Like she would have a little drink of the wine, and then she would start readin that book again. She was holdin the book up over her face, like to shade her eyes from the sun. And she was wearin a real pretty white dress."

"Can you tell us what happened next?"

"I heard her talkin to somebody. First I thought she was talkin to me, but somebody answered back."

"Somebody? A man or a woman."

"A man, for sure."

"Did you recognize the voice?"

"Nope. But he wasn't talkin loud."

"What were they saying to each other?"

"I couldn't make it out. But then he came around from the other side of the tower. He must've been watchin her, too, same as I was."

"Did you recognize him then, Poe? Do you know who he is?"

"Nope. I was mostly lookin at her, and I could only see him from the back."

"Could you tell if he was young or old?"

"Nossir."

"Tall? Short? Fat? Thin?"

"I couldn't say exactly. Kinda medium, I guess. More tall than short. A kinda big fella, only not big like me."

"What about his clothing, Poe? Did you notice anything about what he was wearing?"

"Yessir. He was wearing a hat."

"Can you describe the hat?"

"Like a big old round hat somebody wears if they don't want to get no sun on their neck or their eyes. I think it was brown."

"And what did he do, the man in the brown hat? Did he lie down on the blanket?"

"Yeah. Well, first he pours wine in her glass and he does somethin over it with his hand. Then he hands it to her and he waits, and I can see his shadow over her while she drinks. Then he moves real quick and he lays on top of her and starts grabbin her all over. And then he's hittin her in the face. Boom! Boom! Boom! And I was tryin to get down off the tower, only it was hard to squeeze through that little hole there, and I was caught in the hole and I couldn't get through. I could hear him hittin her, but I couldn't get there quick enough. I could hear her, sayin, 'No, no, no, you gotta stop,' only he wasn't stoppin."

"Can you tell us what happened next?"

"Well, then she went all quiet and I couldn't hear nothin at all. And I knew she was in real trouble then, somethin bad gonna happen, but I still couldn't get loose."

"How long did this go on, Poe? With you trapped and the victim not making a sound?"

"I dunno. I ain't real good with time. It seemed like a whole day. Then I put my arms up and I squeezed through, but some of the steps on the ladder busted and I fell real hard and it knocked the wind out of me. But I got up and I run at the sonofabitch fellow, hard. I run at him and I was hollerin. Then I grabbed holt of him and I throwed him."

"You threw him?"

"Yessir. I throwed him. I throwed him away."

"You hauled him off her and you threw him to the side?"

"Kinda. Only I throwed him more like up in the air, see. I didn't see exactly where he went, but I heard him holler and then *crash!* like he hit somethin. I think he hit the windshield on his car."

"So his car was nearby?"

"Yessir. Close to the blanket. Maybe about as far as I am tall. I hear *crash* when he hits somethin like maybe it could be the windshield, then I don't hear no more, but I doesn't look at him, 'cause I'm scared about her."

"Can you describe the car, Poe? What do you remember about the car?"

"Only thing I know is it's big and black. I ain't real good with cars."

"At this point, you decided to carry her to the road, is that right?"

"Yessir. First I checked she was breathing. Soon as I saw she was, I picked her up in my arms, like, and I started out tryin to run. I made it about as far as a football field is long, but I couldn't go no more like that. So I put her down and catched my breath some, and then I took her up in what you call the fireman's carry, like I learned in the army. Over the shoulders, kinda. It was pretty easy that way."

"You carried her all the way from the gravel pit to Highway 116, isn't that right? About a mile and a half."

"I don't have no idea how far it is, but it's a long ways. I carried her, yessir."

"And you didn't see the man again? He didn't come after you, nothing like that?"

"I expect not. I doesn't think about him no more, nor see him. All I was thinkin was to get help."

Lambert Cain lets that sink in with the jury for a moment, then starts on a tack that seems strange at first. "I'd like to ask you about that orange suit you're wearing, Poe. How do you find it? Is it comfortable?"

"Yeah. It's okay."

"When you put it on, say after a shower, does anyone help you?"

"Nossir, I doesn't need no help."

"And you have no difficulty with that big wide zipper, am I right?"

"Nossir."

"And what about at home, Poe? What do you wear at home?"

"I wears overalls. OshKosh B'gosh overalls, what you call bib overalls. And a work shirt."

"And you get dressed by yourself?"

"I does, yeah."

"What about the work shirt, Poe? You button that yourself?"

"Oh, no. Mama does that for me. I does everything else, but I can't do them buttons."

Lambert Cain turns away to ask the judge about Exhibit Number Thirteen. Rose hears the judge say, "Remind me again, which exhibit is that?" Lambert says it's the dress the victim was wearing when she was attacked. The judge asks what the purpose is, but Rose can't hear Lambert's answer.

"I'll allow it," the judge says, "but no cheap stunts. I'll ask the officer of the court to please remove state's Exhibit Number Thirteen from its wrapping and to hand it to the attorney for the defense."

Rose wonders what Lambert could possibly have in mind. Maybe he's trying to shock Poe into remembering something he's forgotten. She watches as Lambert stands over Poe, holding the dress for him to see.

"Alright, Poe. Now I'm going to ask you to look at this dress. Do you recognize this item?"

"Sure, I do. That's the dress she had on when that fella beat her."

"And what do you notice about it, Poe?"

"Well, it's real pretty, but it has blood on it."

"Yes. Anything else?"

"It sure has got a lot of them little buttons."

"Yes, it has. I've taken the liberty to count them. In all, there are twenty-six buttons from the neck to the hem. Even if a few at the top and bottom might have been undone on a hot day, that still leaves quite a number of buttons. At present, they are all buttoned up. Now, I have a little task for you, Poe. I'd like you to undo these buttons for me, please."

"Huh?"

"I'd like you to undo these buttons. Unbutton them. Do you understand?"

"All of 'em?"

"Yes, please. All of them."

"Well, I can't promise nothin, but I'll sure try. I expect it will take a while."

The lawyer hands the dress to Poe. Poe bends over it, his tongue thrust out to the side. He begins to work on the top button. A minute passes, and another, and he's still on the same button. Beads of sweat stand out on his forehead. He keeps trying, but his fingers, each as thick as a child's wrist, can't be brought to bear on the tiny buttons, which look like pearl-colored teardrops. The usual buzz and rustle in the courtroom hushes as the spectators, journalists, members of the jury, the judge, and even the court reporter and the bailiffs lean forward to watch Poe's struggle. Five minutes go by and he still hasn't managed to undo a single button. Lambert Cain has seen enough.

"That will do, Poe," he says. "In an emergency, can you think of any way you could get those buttons undone, if you absolutely had to do so?"

"I expect I'd have to tear up that dress, Mister Cain. Don't see no other way. And that would be a darned shame, it bein a real pretty dress and all."

"Thank you, Poe, that's all I have for you now."

Rose looks to the jury to try to gauge their reaction, searching for clues to Poe's fate, reflected in a dozen faces. A few she knows slightly. Steve Lynch, who runs a french-fry stand with a carnival and travels all summer. Bernie Michaels, who works the night shift at the 7/11. Candace Flynn, a teacher at the Henry Wadsworth Longfellow grade school. Try as she might, Rose can't read their faces. The one who worries her most is Grace Nagel, a thickset woman who is head cashier at the Grand Union. Grace is a hard woman to get along with. If Rose wants to use coupons when she buys groceries, Grace acts like Rose is trying to pay with cow patties. She always seems to have it in for Poe, and now she's the boss woman of the jury with power over Poe's life.

As she's leaving the courthouse, Rose sees a big shambling man in an expensive camel-hair coat walking ahead of her. It occurs to her that he had been there most days during the trial, but she has been so focused on Poe that she barely noticed. There's something familiar about him, but it's not until he opens the door of his car and turns briefly to face her that she realizes who it is: Rafe Skilling. Dr. Rafe Skilling now. His hair is mostly gray, but he's still a big strong handsome man. He smiles and Rose smiles back, but she makes no attempt to talk to him, because she understands. It wouldn't do.

~

Imaginary friend

Poe stares at the mouth of the state's attorney as the man questions him. He's never seen a fellow with lips like that before. It's almost like he has no lips, only gums and teeth. He gets to looking at that mouth and he misses the question, and the prosecutor has to ask it again, and Poe can see that makes him mad.

"Poe, you understand what it means when you put your hand on the Bible and swear to tell the whole truth, don't you?"

"Yessir. It means I got to tell the truth."

"You have to tell the truth or what, Poe? What are the consequences if you don't tell the truth?"

"You mean what's gonna happen?"

"Yes, Poe. What do you understand the oath to mean, in terms of what is going to happen if you swear on the Bible but you don't tell the truth?"

"Um, I don't understand what you're sayin."

"If you swear on the Bible and you tell a lie, what will happen?"

"Oh, that. Well, Mama says I'll go straight to Hell do not pass Go."

"And you believe it?"

"I got to. She said it was gonna rain cats and dogs the night before we got them floods, and sure enough they came and like to washed the whole county away."

"Alright. I'm going to ask you some questions, and we'll trust you to tell the truth, alright?"

"Yessir."

"I want to go back to what happened when you were in the tower. You said you had fallen asleep, yes?"

"Yessir. And when I woke up, them fish was stinkin to high heaven."

"When you were sleeping, did you have a dream?"

"What do you mean?"

"You know what a dream is? Like when you sleep at night, and you think something is happening, but it isn't real?"

"Uh-huh. I dreams that I can fly like a great big eagle. But then somethin happens, and I falls on my butt."

"That's a common dream. So when you fell asleep in the tower, did you have a dream?"

"I dunno. I don't remember nothin about no dream. All I remember is that I wakes up and them fish is stinkin, and I thinks how Mama is goin to be plenty mad."

"So you don't think it's possible this man you're talking about was actually in your dream? The man you say was attacking the young woman?"

"I don't know about no dream like that."

"Are you sure, Poe? Because this man seems to be someone you'd encounter in a dream — he has no face, no identity. Is it possible he didn't exist?"

Lambert Cain rises then. "I'm going to have to object, Your Honor. Poe has already stated quite clearly that he didn't have a dream when he slept in the tower."

"Yes, counselor. Let's move this forward."

The state's attorney gathers himself. "Now, I'd like to move on to another issue," he says. "You are unable to read, is that right, Poe?"

"No, sir. I can't read no words."

"And you can't add or subtract numbers? You can't do basic math?"

"Nope. I ain't got no editions nor suttractions."

"And yet you have an extraordinary memory for colors and events?"

"I don't know that word, extra-something."

"Unusual, special. You have a very good memory for things that happened, and you can remember the date by recalling something else that happened, like the day of a thunderstorm or the day a pickup truck was stuck in the mud, is that right?"

"Yeah. I does that real good."

"And your memory functions particularly well when it comes to the victim, whom you've known for many years, is that right also?"

"Uh-huh."

"You even remember the color of her toenails?"

"Oh, yessir. Unless she's got on regular shoes, I mean. Then I doesn't see her toes."

"Can you tell us what you remember about her toenails?"

"Well, sometimes they was red, and sometimes green, and sometimes she didn't have no paint on them at all."

"Can you give us specific examples?"

"Like on the day we had the big thunderstorm, her toenails was red. She has two pair flip-flops, one green, one blue. The thunderstorm day, it was green flip-flops and red toenails. She brought me a piece of cake on account it was her birthday, and that day they was blue flip-flops and she didn't have no paint on her toenails. Then the day Wild Bill's pickup truck got stuck in a mudhole, she had the green flip-flops and her toenails was green. We was both gonna push the truck while she drove, but I hoisted it outa there myself."

"Can you recall anything else about her dress on those occasions?"

"She wasn't wearin no dress."

"I'm sorry, can you tell us how she was dressed? What was she wearing?"

"The day of the big thunderstorm, I remember that, 'cause there was a mess of ravens flyin over. She was wearin them jeans that is cut off like shorts and a white T-shirt that said somethin on it in red letters, but I don't know what it said. The day it was her birthday, she had on long pants the color of skin and a black shirt with long sleeves and the two buttons at the top wasn't buttoned."

"That's an awful lot to remember about a woman and her clothes, Poe. A lot of men can't even tell you what their wives were wearing when they left for work."

"Well, I aint got no wife."

"We understand that, Poe. Now you can do that for the whole summer, remember everything she wore?"

"Yessir. Pretty much, I can. Maybe I forgets one or two. I don't think so."

"That's still remarkable. Poe, do you know what the word 'obsession' means?"

"No, sir. I doesn't."

"Well, obsession is when we think about something really a lot. Usually it's a person we think about, though it could be something else. We think about it all the time, until we almost don't think about anything else. Is this how you would describe yourself with her? Do you think about her all the time, and you think about almost nothing else?"

"I wouldn't say that. I thinks about lots a things. Not only her. But say at night before bed, yeah, I thinks about her. I goes through everything she wore all summer and I thinks about it. How she looks. How she looks when she bends over."

"And you want to do things to her?"

"Sure, I does. Who don't?"

"When you think about her at night, the things she wore, you want to have sex with her?"

"Does that mean screwin her?"

"Yes."

"Damned right. Real bad. It's worse now I'm in jail, 'cause I got nothin else to think about."

"And yet you want us to believe that when you had the opportunity, you did *not* attack this young woman on the afternoon of Sunday, August twentieth, is that correct?"

"That's right. I doesn't attack nobody. Well, except for the sonofabitch fellow, when I throws him."

"You did not hurt her? You didn't attempt to rape her?"

"Nossir. No way."

"Then how did she get these terrible injuries? Injuries that almost threatened her life?"

"The guy done it."

"The guy. Here we are, back with this mystery man, Poe. Can you describe him for us again, please?"

"Well, he was wearin a hat."

"A hat. You told us that."

"Yep."

"And that's as far as we can get. With your remarkable memory, which we have already established, you can tell us what color the girl's toenails were on a day when there was a thunderstorm last June, but you can't tell us anything about the man who was supposedly attacking her in August, except that he was wearing a hat. You can tell us about the hat and nothing else."

"No, sir. I'm sorry."

"And we're supposed to believe that? That a man with your uncanny memory can't even recall whether the man was young or old?"

"I'm right sorry. I wasn't paying no attention to him, that's all. I was scared about the girl."

"I find this hard to believe, Poe. I think this mystery man is like an imaginary friend. Do you know what an imaginary friend is, Poe?"

"Uh-huh. It's like make-believe. I know 'cause Mama says she had one of them when she was little."

"A make-believe imaginary friend. Exactly. So are we playing make-believe, Poe? Is this a make-believe man? An imaginary friend, so you can blame him for what happened?"

"Nope. That was a real fellow out at the pit. Sonofabitch fellow. I throwed him away."

"I don't believe you."

"That's okay you don't believe me; I know lots of folks don't. Mama says it's on account of I'm so big and kinda scary lookin. But I didn't hurt nobody. Was the sonofabitch fella done that."

~

"Is Mr. Didelot guilty?"
There's a hard wind blowing outside when the state's attorney stands to deliver his closing statement to the jury. Gusts hurl sleet against the courthouse windows, a sound like sand hitting glass. Poe hears something about serious crimes, before the lawyer says: "Your concern is to determine the simple

matter of guilt or innocence. Is Mr. Didelot guilty, or is he not guilty?"

"I ain't guilty," Poe says. The jurors grin. The judge threatens again to have Poe escorted from the courtroom. The attorney glares at Poe and turns back to face the jury, rocking back and forth on his toes as he speaks. After that, all Poe can make out is a lot of stuff he doesn't understand. His mind drifts. He watches Rose, who watches him. The lawyer keeps talking, striding back and forth. He brings up Elmer Hepp and a crime that was seen and a big black car, but mostly he sticks to somebody beating Miranda almost to death. The lawyer says the jurors have to find Poe guilty, and he pronounces the words with such drama that Poe feels like he ought to clap at the end, but he can't manage it with the handcuffs. Then it's Lambert's turn.

By the time Lambert Cain begins to speak, the noise of the sleet rattling on the courthouse windows is so loud that if not for his strong baritone voice, he wouldn't be heard at all. As it is, he has to pause to let the wind die down now and then before he resumes his oration. After one especially ferocious gust, he grins and shakes his head.

"I think that wind is going to huff and puff and blow this old courthouse down before I'm through. Maybe that's God's way of telling me to hurry this along so you can get on with your lives." A few of the jurors smile. Jurors have always liked Lambert Cain, because he never gets too big for his britches.

"Let us begin by stating the obvious," he says. "The defendant in this criminal case, Poe Revere Didelot, is not at all like you or me. He's more than a foot taller than I am, and I'm considered a tall man. He weighs more than the two lawyers arguing this case put together. He has a port-wine stain on his face and neck and a hump on his back. His eyes are two different colors. He has six fingers on each hand, and six toes on each foot. He is strong in a way that most of us cannot even comprehend. He can lift the back end of a pickup and heave it out of the mud, or he can heft a two-hundred-pound stone without assistance and place it exactly where he wants it on a stone wall. I confess that Poe has even given me a fright a time or two, when he appeared unexpectedly on a darkened street.

"Poe is different. He's unusual, in every sense of the word. His intellectual abilities are different from ours. He speaks in a different way. He has an extraordinary memory, but he can't read or write or do the simplest math. But under the laws of this state, Poe can't be found guilty simply because he is different. He's not guilty because he's over seven feet tall, or because he weighs more than four hundred pounds, or because he is remarkably strong, or because he has a rather prominent birthmark. I know that it bothers some of you that he occasionally drools, but that also is not a factor that can be taken into consideration in weighing his guilt or innocence of the heinous crime with which he is charged before this court.

"Essentially, there are only two pillars to the prosecution's case. One is that our county sheriff, James Dunn, saw him emerge from the woods near the old gravel pit carrying the victim. She had been badly beaten, sexually assaulted, and she was mostly nude. But the words Poe kept repeating over and over during his encounter with the sheriff tell you all you need to know: *'Get help. Get help. Get help.'* Poe was trying to rescue this girl, not to attack her. He had carried her a distance of a mile and a half from the point where she was assaulted to the highway, an act that should be seen as heroic, not dastardly. If you doubt me, you may want to try lifting an adult human being and carrying that person even a hundred yards.

"We have heard also from one Elmer Hepp, who insists that he found *both* Poe and the victim walking along the highway and gave them a ride on his wagon. This is contrary to testimony we have heard from both the defendant and his mother, who testified that Poe went fishing alone, and also from what we know the victim was wearing when she was attacked: a white dress, not blue jeans and a red T-shirt. Nor is it possible that Elmer Hepp, the victim, *and* a man as massive as Poe Didelot could *all* have squeezed onto that narrow wagon seat, so it should be pretty clear that Mr. Hepp has remembered something that did not happen — that is, the young woman was not with Poe when he accepted that wagon ride. We don't know how she got there, but she did not arrive at the gravel pit with Poe.

"There remains another pillar of the prosecution's case, the semen found on the victim's dress and on Poe's coveralls. We accept that the semen is Poe's. He has said as much himself, and he has explained how it came to be there. He had masturbated while looking at one of these obscene old comic books, and the ejaculate was left on his coveralls. While he was running with the victim in his arms, his coveralls rubbed against her dress. That explains why semen was found on the *back* of her dress, not the front. I should remind the jury that while you might find this act repugnant, he is charged with sexual assault, not public masturbation. When he realized what was going on, that the victim was being assaulted, he quickly descended from the tower, hurled the attacker out of the way with such force that the man's head or shoulders may have shattered the windshield of an automobile, and carried the victim to the highway, where he was fortunate to encounter the sheriff. Over the first hundred paces or so of that desperate run that saved her life, Poe was carrying her in his arms, in a position where the back of her dress rubbed against his coveralls and the fresh semen he had ejaculated there.

"Now, I know this sounds like a rather contorted explanation, but in my long experience of the law, the truth is rarely clear-cut, and often the truest version of events is the one that seems to depart most from our tidy sense of things as they ought to be. It's the clever liar who presents a neatly packaged narrative for our consumption, not the maladroit honest man who is incapable of concocting a meticulous lie. We all have a great respect for science, but science can tell us only so much: it can tell us that Poe's semen was found on the victim's dress, but not how it got there. And what, really, is the alternative explanation? That Poe deliberately ejaculated on the back of her dress, when she was partially nude in front? There are ways he might have ejaculated on the dress rather than her bare skin, but they are at least as contorted as the explanation Poe has offered, which has the advantage, I submit, of being the truth.

"You all watched as Poe tried and failed to open a single button on the dress the victim was wearing the day she was attacked. Yet, when Sheriff Jim Dunn found Poe carrying her out of the woods, *all* the buttons on the dress had been undone and it was completely open. Poe could easily have torn the dress open if he chose. In fact, had he attacked her, that would have been the obvious method. So why was the dress not torn? There are only two possible explanations. Either this young woman voluntarily undid the buttons for her attacker or there was a third party at the scene, the so-called mystery man who was responsible for undoing the dress. He was able to undo the dress one button at a time, the way a man with fingers more agile than Poe's would proceed, especially if his victim was drunk or semiconscious and he was attacking her at his leisure.

"I will leave it to you to draw your own conclusions, but in my view there's only one rational explanation for the fact that her dress was open: someone else undid those buttons, someone who was neither the victim nor the man who sits in the prisoner's dock today.

"I would ask you to consider also that there would be two consequences of a guilty verdict in this case. First, you would be sending an innocent man to prison, most probably for the rest of his life. But that's not all: you would also make it possible for a guilty man to remain free. Because someone *did* attack this young woman. Someone *did* almost beat her to death. And that someone is out there today, walking the streets a free man, laughing at us as we try Poe for a crime he did not commit.

"This is not an easy verdict. It's a complex case, with some elements I have never encountered before. The crime scene disappeared in the flood. The victim's short-term memory vanished and has not returned. It's complex, but it's simple at the heart of it — which is the very nature of Poe himself. Poe is many things, but he is not two people. What you see is what you get: the gentle giant, the man who wouldn't hurt a fly, or a young woman he adores. Given the facts of this case, you have only one real choice once you have weighed the evidence: that is to acquit Poe of the crimes of which he is charged, and to let him go free."

~

Judgment day

The jurors file out to begin their deliberations. Wild Bill and Matt Harrow head home to wait. Dan Gillespie goes back to the pub. Joey, Maeva, and Rose take a seat on a bench in the corridor and settle in, with Joey heading out for smoke breaks every half hour.

The day dims. Headlights pop on outside. It's rush hour in Belle Coeur, which means as many as four or five cars at a time idling at a stoplight. Rose finds it the worst hour of a winter day, when it's not quite dark, the time before the lights come on and you can smell good things baking in the oven. On these winter afternoons, she finds herself thinking of the time she will be buried someplace where the wind howls and the snow drifts high over her grave. Rose fervently believes that her soul will be in heaven singing the old gospel tunes, but there's no getting around the solemn truth that her body will be in the cold, cold ground, no matter what her soul gets up to.

Poe passes the time in his cell talking to Willie, a spider that has been in the same corner since the fall. *Willie, Mister Cain says I'm leavin' soon. Goin to the big jail or goin home. Either way, I can't be lookin' after you no more. I'd like to take you home, put you in the goat shed. You'd do real good there. Plenty flies. Or maybe the outhouse. You'd get fat in the outhouse. I know you don't say much, Willie, but you been a real good friend to me. I'll be sorry to go, but maybe they'll let me come by to say hello now and then.*

Poe doesn't mind the wait. He has always been good at waiting. He empties himself and floats with the current, so that he can't say whether he's waited five minutes, five hours, or five days. His sense of time is fluid and without fixed points, apart from the time he can distinguish on his fob watch. In here, he can't see the sun rise or set or the slow wheel of the stars at night. Time passes. Water drips. He hears the muffled sounds of traffic from outside. The song on the radio in the deputies' room changes from Hank Williams to George Jones. Willie the spider walks across the ceiling.

Poe hears a buzzer and his cell door slides open. Deputy Proulx is standing there. "Let's go, Poe. The jury is back. It's time."

Rose has dozed off on a bench in the corridor, with her chin down on her chest. She doesn't hear the bailiff when he pokes his head out the door to say the jury has reached a decision, but the flurry of activity wakes her. Joey takes her arm and leads her back into the courtroom. Her legs are stiff and her knees are weak. She can feel the thud of her pulse in her throat, and for a moment, she thinks she might faint dead away before they announce the verdict, but then Lambert Cain comes striding in, elegant as always in his dark blue suit, and she takes heart from his presence. He pauses at her side for a moment, rests his hand on her shoulder, and looks her in the eye without saying a word before taking his seat at the defense table.

Rose stands as the judge takes his seat. The jurors come trooping in, looking weary. She still can't read their expressions. She has to pee, but there isn't time. Her whole life comes down to this, to what a dozen people decide to do with her son.

Judge Buzzard asks the jurors if they have reached a verdict. They answer "yes," in unison. He asks for the verdict to be passed to him and scans it carefully before he speaks. "Alright, ladies and gentlemen. Do all of you agree with this verdict?"

Some of the jurors merely nod. Most mumble "yes." Only one or two speak up so they can be heard across the courtroom.

The judge leans forward. "Alright, jurors, now I am going to ask you to confirm your decision. Will the presiding juror please step forward?"

Rose watches as Grace Nagel stands. Grace, of all people. Rose experiences an awful moment of dizziness and takes Maeva's hand to keep from pitching forward out of her seat. The judge addresses Grace in a firm voice: "Madame, on the charge that Mr. Poe Revere Didelot committed aggravated assault on the person of the victim, how do you find?"

"Not guilty, Your Honor."

"And on the charge that Mr. Poe Revere Didelot did commit aggravated sexual assault on the person of the victim, how do you find?"

"Also not guilty, Your Honor."

"Mr. Didelot, you have been found not guilty on both charges and you are free to go. Bailiffs, please release the defendant."

Grace Nagel usually squawks like a parrot. On this occasion, she pronounces the verdicts so softly that Rose hears only the word "guilty," and it's not until the judge turns to Poe and tells him that he is free to go that she understands what has happened. Through all the months of waiting, she has envisioned herself leaping up with joy if Poe is freed, but now she sits motionless, staring straight ahead, unable to speak, struggling to breathe.

Lambert Cain bends over her, his hand on her elbow. He's saying something, but Rose can't make out what it is. Behind her is an odd buzzing sound, like a nest of angry hornets. The upper and lower galleries have mysteriously filled with people still in their parkas, their cheeks inflamed from the cold wind outdoors, huddling in little knots of anger, venting their displeasure with the verdict. When Rose glances back at them, they glare at her with such pure hatred that it shakes her to the core. How can people hate so? A jury has found Poe innocent. How could that be wrong?

Lambert and Maeva help Rose to her feet and lead her to Poe, who is rubbing his wrists, free of the handcuffs. He seems more baffled than she is. His eyes seek her out. "Is that all, Mama? Can I go home now?"

"Yes. We're going home."

Poe envelops Rose in his powerful arms and lifts her off the floor, swinging her back and forth until one of her shoes falls off. As he puts her down, Jim Dunn appears at his side.

"Poe, we've got to walk you back to the jail to get your effects and get you changed out of that jumpsuit. I'm going to send a couple of deputies to give you and your mother an escort home. There are some folks here in a very nasty mood. They'll calm down, but we'd best keep an eye until they do."

Rose waits in the corridor outside the jail until Poe emerges wearing his OshKosh B'gosh coveralls and the work shirt, which she has to button. She has with her an oversized shopping bag with his parka and mittens and a Russian hat she bought at a thrift shop in Bunker's Corner against the day when he would be released.

Joey drives, the three of them crammed into the cab of the pickup, Rose in the middle, a drift of snowflakes floating across the road in the mismatched beams from the headlights of the old truck. A deputy sheriff's cruiser leads the way, his lights flashing, and another follows along behind. They don't say much on the way. At the house, the deputies linger on the side of the road, the lights still flashing, casting a blue-and-red glow over the snowbanks. Matt Harrow, Maeva Miller, Dan Gillespie, and Wild Bill De Graaff all crowd into the kitchen and living room of the little yellow house. More friends and supporters keep arriving, until there are more than a dozen altogether. Rose has a beef stew she left to simmer just in case. She dishes up bowls of stew and slices of homemade bread with fresh-churned butter and hunks of her own cheese. Wine bottles are opened, caps popped off bottles of ice-cold beer, cups found. Matt breaks out his mandolin, Joey tunes his guitar, Dan gives them a riff on his harmonica, and Joey launches into "I'm Sittin' on Top of the World." Poe sits in their midst, feeling dazed and a little feverish, beaming at one and all.

It's past eight o'clock when Rose remembers the goats. Matt is trying to sing "Miss the Mississippi and You" and making a bad job of it, and Rose has to speak into Poe's ear to make him understand above the racket. "It's a cold night, Poe, but somebody has to milk the goats. Do you want to do it, or shall I ask Joey?"

Poe grins, the grin stretches into a smile, and he gets to his feet, keeping his head clear of the light fixture to avoid shattering the lightbulbs. "I'll do it, Ma. It's my job. Happy to do it."

Poe dons his parka and boots and mittens, and Rose wraps a thick woolen scarf around his neck. He grabs the empty buckets off the back porch and heads out to the winter goat-shed near the house, along the path that Joey and Rose have kept shoveled. He's halfway there when he hears the goats, bleating their urgent need to be fed and milked. He opens the door to the shed, closes it behind him, hauling it shut against the wind, and fumbles for the light switch. Their stalls are bathed in warm yellow light. The nannies are all around him, butting each other out of the way, butting him, licking at his hands. He inhales the warm fragrance of goat shit and hay and oats and goat milk. Two cats wind themselves around his ankles as he shakes out buckets of oats into the trough and grabs his stool to begin the milking. He calls them by name, Jenny-Girl and Ostrich, the twins Bertha and Pearl, Roxie, Little Dipper, Maude, Lula May, Olive, Susie Q, Thelma Pearl, Aunt Nell, and Princess Sally. As always, he begins with Little Dipper and finishes with Princess Sally. He milks them with his cheek nestled against their warm, fragrant hides. When he's done, he heads across to the cheese shed, carrying two full buckets in each of his six-fingered hands. Back in the house, he plunks himself down on the davenport in the center of the living room, the guest of honor in his own house, and watches the folks sing and dance when they aren't thumping him on the back and saying, *I knew it, Poe. I knew all along you wasn't guilty and they would figure it out sooner or later.*

It's past midnight when the last of them head home, including Joey. He offers to stay, but Rose wants to be alone with her boy. Joey thinks of opening the door to the shed to let the geese out to keep watch, but it's at least twenty below, cold even for a goose.

Rose and Poe sit in front of the little black-and-white TV, watching a blond woman laugh with a talk-show host. Rose doesn't know who they are because she's never up this late at night. They watch until one o'clock in the morning without saying much, then Rose switches off the television. "I expect we'd best get to bed," she says. "Places to go and things to do in the morning."

~ VII ~
Visions of the Apocalypse

Milk spilled across the sky

Deputy Travis Proulx leans his face against the icy window of the cruiser so he can watch the slow wheel of stars in the winter sky. The night is moonless. Out here, far from the big city, the stars are like milk spilled across the sky. That's what his mother told him years ago when he asked why it was called the Milky Way. She said it was spilled milk way up there, and Travis is embarrassed to think how old he was when he realized it wasn't true.

It's deathly quiet and Travis is cold. He watches the people who were celebrating the verdict at Rose's place leave the yellow house in twos and threes until the last rusty pickup has turned onto the highway and drifted away. Another hour goes by. He sees an owl fly past on hushed wings. He checks the clock on the dash. It's twelve minutes past one. If anyone is going to make trouble, surely it would have happened by now. He's under orders not to leave his post, but it won't hurt to dash into the twenty-four-hour donut shop in Belle Coeur for a coffee and donuts. He has a little thing going with Bridget, who works the night shift. He figures he can run into town, see Bridget, get his coffee, and be back at his post in twenty minutes.

Travis slips the cruiser into gear and drives toward town. He's making the turn onto Main Street when he passes a parade of vehicles headed in the opposite direction, most of them oversized pickup trucks with teenagers riding in the back despite the cold. He shrugs, figuring they're headed for a party somewhere. Same thing he'd be doing if he wasn't on duty.

Travis parks the cruiser and steps into the fragrant warmth of the donut shop. There are a couple of insomniac codgers seated at the counter, so there will be no slipping into the toilet for a knee-trembler with Bridget. She bags his favorite donuts, pours his coffee, whispers that she'll make it up to him when their shifts end in the morning. Travis lingers and Bridget obligingly undoes the top button of her uniform and bends over to give him an eyeful. They're still whispering to each other when one of the codgers clears his throat to get the deputy's attention. "You see all them pickup trucks heading out of town, Travis?"

"Yep. Figure there must be a party somewhere."

"There's already been a party, deputy. Expect you ought to know that much. They were down at the Bald Eagle the last six or seven hours, drinking hard. Albert Fall says they were bragging about how they'd go out to Rose's place and mess up old Poe, maybe drag him down to the gallows the Carney boys built. I expect it was all talk, but you still got another deputy out there just in case, isn't that right?"

Travis shakes his head. "Nah, not exactly. I'm pretty much it tonight."

He's trying to ignore the man, but the old coot won't let it drop. "Hell, I ain't one to tell a man how to do his job, Travis, but maybe you ought to get back out there and make sure everything is alright. Them folks was liquored up bad. They weren't lookin to get into a snowball fight."

"They were drunk, you're saying?"

"You gotta take the badge out of your ears, deputy. That's what I said before. They are drunk and hostile, and there's a big bunch. I don't think they'd be fool enough to try some-thing, but you never know. Thing with a mob, they get to egging each other on, you don't know what they might do."

Travis mulls it over. Chances are there's nothing going on. Among the bunch who drink at the Bald Eagle are some youngsters who don't mean much harm, but there are a few genuine hard cases in the mix, like the Carney brothers. He grabs his hat and treats himself to one last peek at Bridget's bosom. "I suppose I'd better get back out there, doll. I'll see you in the morning."

In the cruiser, he curses the old men. Busybody old bas-tards. They're on his case because they're jealous that he has Bridget and they don't, but they're just the type to call Jim Dunn and say his deputy was lollygagging at the donut shop when he should have been keeping watch. Four more hours and the long winter night will be over, he'll be off his shift, and he'll have Bridget to keep him warm.

~

A ring of stones

They come on snowmobiles and in muscle cars and on giant pickup trucks with oversized tires. They have been drinking for hours, working themselves to a frenzy. They park in a semicircle facing the yellow house. They're a wild crowd, always have been, but the worst they have done before this night is get drunk and spray-paint the high school or break the windows on a row of trucks parked outside the cement factory. They're still drinking hard, the drivers as drunk as their passengers. They have cases of beer in the beds of the pickups and bottles of rum and vodka and wine are making the rounds. The biggest of the trucks is blaring Black Sabbath at ground-shaking volume. The only ones missing are the Carney brothers, who egged the mob on and then said they were going to head home to oil up the trap door in the gallows and get it ready for Poe.

No decision is made. They're looking for trouble, but they don't know what sort of trouble. Some think they should haul Poe back to the gallows at the Carney place and hang him because a good, solid gallows like that shouldn't go to waste. Others just want to knock Poe around a little to scare him. More than anything, they are filled with an aimless, unfocused *hate* that has settled on Poe as its unsuspecting target. There is evil afoot in the land and someone must pay, and for reasons none of them could articulate, that someone must be Poe. Not one soul in the mob speaks up to say that given the verdict of the jury, Poe might actually be innocent. He's different, he's strange. They've been hearing all their lives that the man is a mutant, and for a mutant to do what he did to a beautiful human girl, well, it just won't do. They secretly thrill at the thought of the giant taking his enormous pecker out of those

OshKosh B'gosh overalls he wears and impaling the helpless girl with it, but he must pay nonetheless.

What happens next occurs as though preordained by some unholy stroke of fate. Someone produces a gallon jug that has been emptied of wine. Somebody else siphons gasoline from one of the pickup trucks to fill the jug. One of the girls reaches up under her dress to slip off her panties, laughing and holding them up for everyone to see before she soaks them in gasoline and stuffs them in the neck of the bottle.

"That's how you make a Malakhov cocktail, see?"

"Molotov."

"Huh?"

"Molotov. It's a Molotov cocktail."

"Well, Stevie, ain't you the little know-it-all teacher's pet? Maybe we ought to light your snotty little ass on fire. What's it matter what it's called? It lights things on fire, that's all I got to know."

A kid who has his father's Zippo from the Korean War offers to light the torch right there, and would have, except someone yells that they have to get closer to the house or it will blow up in their faces before they have time to throw it. The kid with the Zippo follows a tall blond youth carrying the bottle. The tall kid is so drunk he can't judge distance. He crouches in the snow thirty feet from the house, and the Zippo kid tugs at his jacket, hollering that they aren't close enough.

. They are too drunk to be quiet, but there's no sign of life from the house. The tall kid runs to a snow-covered bush a dozen feet from the front door and waits for the one with the Zippo to light the torch. He has to flick the old lighter four or five times before it catches. It's turned all the way up and the flame shoots six inches in the air. The gasoline-soaked panties in the neck of the bottle catch fire, and the boy holding the jug stares at the flame, mesmerized and immobile, with people yelling at him to throw it before it blows up in his hands. He panics and pitches it like a baseball, and the big window on the south side of the house shatters. They hear the crash of the flaming cocktail exploding inside. The blond boy and the kid with the Zippo run back to the trucks and stand with the rest of them to watch. A big football player who can barely walk stumbles over a pile of rocks hidden under the snow, stones Poe had collected for the wall. He digs out a rock and slings it at the house because he's mad that he fell. The cry goes up. "Rocks, rocks, we got plenty of rocks over here if you want to throw 'em." They dive into the pile and grab stones by the handful and start chucking them at the house in a gleeful, destructive frenzy.

Rose is a light sleeper, but on this night she's exhausted, in the deepest sleep she's had since Poe was jailed. She hears the crash of the exploding window as though in a dream, but doesn't wake. It's the smell of gasoline that finally rouses her, gasoline and the crackling of flames. From the shed out back, she hears the frantic honking of the geese. She sits up and pokes her feet into her slippers. She has just stepped through the door into the sitting room when the curtains burst into flames with a *whoosh!* and a wall of heat drives her back. She struggles into her robe and shakes Poe hard. He's easy to rouse when it's time to get up, but if you try to wake him in the middle of the night it's like waking a corpse. She bounces him up and down on the bed and shouts into his ear. "Poe! Poe! The house is afire! You got to get up, Poe!"

Poe rolls over onto his back, but he's still snoring. Rose tugs at his arm, trying to drag him out of bed, but she can't budge him. The room has started to fill with smoke and she can feel the heat from the fire. She tries to reach the kitchen to get a basin of water to throw in Poe's face, but the fire has spread and there is no way through. She smashes the bedroom window with her elbow, but the opening is far too small for either of them to squeeze through, and the oxygen simply feeds the fire. Frantically, she slaps his face, screaming, "Poe! Poe! You gotta wake up, honey! We're gonna die in here!"

Something, perhaps part of the ceiling, collapses in the living room and a shower of sparks shoots underneath the bedroom door. She slaps Poe again, putting all her strength into it. He lifts his head, still groggy, thinking he's back in jail, trying to understand why his mother is hitting him in the middle of the night.

Heavy black smoke pours into the room along with the stench of burning linoleum from the kitchen. Rose, gagging and coughing and overcome with smoke, topples to her knees, then falls onto her side, unconscious. Poe tries to open the door, but the doorknob is so hot he burns his fingers and jumps back, shaking his hand. He tries to get Rose to stand up, but her body is limp. He bends his knees, hefts his mother over his shoulders, and lifts her in the fireman's carry, the same way he had borne Miranda, only Rose is much heavier. He staggers under her weight, takes a deep breath, charges at the bedroom door, and bursts into the maelstrom of flames that is the living room. Poe stumbles back, but there is no other way out. He lowers his head and, with a roar like a wounded bear, barrels through the living room to the front door, shatters it with a heave from one shoulder, and bursts into the clear cold night. There he stands, teetering and barefoot in the snow with Rose over his shoulders, surveying the pickups and snowmobiles parked in a ring, the people screaming at him, their faces flushed from the fire and contorted with rage, the scene lit by the burning house and the halogen lamps atop the pickups.

The sight of him rouses the mob. *There he is! That's Poe! That's the goddamn rapist mutant who done that girl! Get him! Take the freak down!*

Poe feels a surge of heat down his back. Rose is on fire, her nightgown blazing. He lies her down and tries to douse the flames by packing her in big handfuls of snow, but the first stone catches him in the jaw and spins him around, and another thuds into his rib cage. He roars in pain and turns to face his tormentors. Most of them are at it now, even the girls, chucking rocks as hard as they can throw them. They're staggering drunk and their aim is terrible, but there are so many rocks coming that Poe can't dodge them all. He charges at the biggest of them, lifts the boy over his head, and throws him into the bodies of two others. The three of them go down in a heap, but scramble to their feet and back away, still hurling rocks at him as they retreat. A jagged hunk of granite opens a gash high on Poe's forehead. He backhands a boy who gets too close and sends him flying, but another catches Poe in the knee with a three-pound stone. The leg collapses and Poe falls.

"What'd I do?" he roars as he goes down. "What'd I do? I didn't do nothin. What'd I do?"

They laugh and point, chanting "Freak! Freak! Freak! Freak! Mutant! Kill him! Kill him! Kill the freak!" Some of the girls are laughing, too, although one girl is crying and begging them, "Please stop please stop please stop, you're going to kill him."

The bloodthirst is on them and they pay her no attention. A rock catches Poe behind the ear and dazes him. Blood from the wound on his forehead is pouring into his eyes, leaving him half blind. He is howling from the pain in his leg, and he feels lightheaded and weak. Behind him, Rose has stopped moaning. Poe thinks she must be dead, and he is collapsing under a hail of stones. A boy lifts a pitchfork like a javelin, preparing to hurl it at Poe to finish him off, while others cavort like devils, dancing in the wild yellow light from the burning house. With one hand, Poe reaches back for Rose, seeking her hand, finding it, pulling it to him as his world goes black.

In his cabin up the hill, Wild Bill De Graaff hears the commotion down at Rose's place and climbs out of bed, cursing. He looks out the window and sees the big gathering of pickup trucks and guesses the rest. He steps into his boots and pulls on a coat and gloves and is just heading out the door when he sees the little yellow house go up in flames. He jogs to the pickup as fast as his old legs will carry him, starts the engine, reaches back to make sure the shotgun is in its rack, and goes careening down the hill, leaning on his horn all the way.

To get to Rose's place, he has to go all the way down to the highway and double back along the path that leads to her house. As his old truck slips and slides along the icy track and he fights to keep it out of the ditch, he sees Poe surrounded like a bear fighting a pack of wild dogs, sees him catch a rock flush in the mouth and go down on his knees, trapped by an angry mob flinging stones at him from five or six feet away, closing in for the kill. Bill hauls the shotgun out of its rack and holds it out the window as he drives straight into the pack, feeling the solid impact as the truck sends two boys flying.

The pickup spins its wheels in the snow and stalls. Bill jumps out, desperation rendering him spry for his age, the shotgun at his hip. It's a pump-action twelve-gauge, and at close range it will wreak havoc. The first blast catches the hip of the tall blond boy who had thrown the Molotov cocktail into the house. The boy is fifty feet away, but it's still enough to spin him around. The buckshot at that distance has scattered too much to do real damage, but the kid yelps and limps off into the darkness, screaming at Bill. "Are you crazy, you old fart? You're trying to kill me!" Bill pumps another round into the chamber and fires straight over his head.

The mob scatters, the worst of the troublemakers running for their vehicles in the face of an assault from one crazy old man. A muscle car spins its wheels into a snowbank and stalls. A snowmobile takes off, runs twenty feet, and upends on a snowbank. Two or three pickup trucks get away, but there are still half a dozen boys chucking rocks at Poe from a safe distance. Bill turns to point the shotgun at them, but another snowmobile bears down on him. He has just enough time to raise the shotgun to his shoulder before the snowmobile catches him in the legs and sends him somersaulting into the snow. He knows before he lands that both his legs are broken, but he still manages to fire one last shell into the shins of a muscular kid who is still chucking rocks before he blacks out.

One of the boys is reaching down to grab the shotgun when they hear the siren. The remaining youngsters scatter. Snowmobiles speed off. The pickup trucks with their over-sized tires cut across the snow. Travis Proulx tries to block one with his cruiser, but the truck rams him out of the way. The cruiser spins and stalls and he sits with the engine steaming, surveying the scene. The house is almost gone and the sheds where the goats and geese are kept are blazing, showers of sparks erupting into the night sky, lighting the scene so that he can see the wounded where they have fallen. A blackened goat with half its face missing staggers toward the car on shaky legs and walks right up to him before it falls over, stone dead.

Travis is on the radio, talking to the dispatcher, unable to remember the police codes, if there was ever a code for any of this other than mayhem and catastrophe. "You got to get everybody out to Rose's place! Everybody. All hell has broke loose! Get the sheriff, get every deputy, get the state police, get the fire department. And ambulances, we're gonna need a shitload of ambulances. We got multiple individuals down, we got wounded, we got some that might be dead, we got buildings burning. It's like the freaking apocalypse out here."

~

Return of the messenger
Prosper Thorne is having one of his lucid nights, lying awake pondering the wreckage of his life: the broken alliance with the usurper Anthony Coyle that sent him into exile, the remnants of what had been a brilliant legal mind now like the shards of glass left at an intersection after a three-car accident, his beautiful daughter, Miranda, apparently healthy but still missing three weeks of her young life and part of her soul. She has not returned to Cambridge and now it seems that she never will. She makes up various excuses, but he knows that the real reason she isn't going back is because she has to care for him. He is old and helpless, and the very last thing he wanted for her has come to pass: she is tethered to him by the frailty of his mind. Only his death will set her free.

It sometimes seems to Thorne that old age is one long

aria of regret. All the mistakes a man makes in a lifetime wait until he has nothing left but to contemplate himself and the wrong turns he has made, and then they haunt him through every waking hour and filter into his dreams. He is still wallowing in that sea of regret when he hears the Kawasaki Ninja screaming up the county road, then Airmail pounding at the door as though he has come to announce that Judgment Day has arrived at last. So, the messenger has returned. Thorne sighs wearily, steps into his slippers, pulls on a dressing gown, and pads downstairs, cursing with every step.

When he opens the door, Airmail bursts through, bringing a blast of icy air with him. Thorne slams the door shut and turns to confront him. "What in God's name do you think you're doing pounding on my door at this hour?"

Airmail performs a little bow. "So sorry, boss. I come bearing sad news, but I have a terrible thirst. I'll just help myself to a beer from your fridge, good man."

"The sun isn't even up."

"Then it's still night and drinking time, is it not?"

Airmail pops open a Rolling Rock, pours half of it down his throat, wipes his mouth with the back of his hand, then shakes his head sadly. "I bring terrible news. The hounds of hell were turned loose in the night. They set fire to Rose's house, burned it to the ground, then they went after Rose and Poe. Seeking vengeance for the crime committed on the person of your daughter."

Thorne sits heavily, his face white. "That's impossible. Miranda said Poe was acquitted."

"He was found by a jury not to be guilty of the aforesaid crimes. As you say. But it appears there are some who didn't approve of the verdict. Teenagers, mostly. They got all liquored up down at the Bald Eagle and got to talking about how it was a travesty and such, and they firebombed the house. They say Poe carried Rose out of the burning house, but then the mob stumbled on a pile of rocks and stoned them both, and they were seen going down under a hail of stones."

Thorne's hands flap helplessly at his sides. "I made this happen," he says. "I created this."

"Made what, boss?"

"I'm not your damned boss, Airmail! I am an old man who has failed those he loves most. Listen to me, man. I created this. I don't know precisely how, but I know it has something to do with that walking stick yonder, the staff I carved with my own hands, my *fabula animi*. There is wizardry in that wood, Airmail, a frightening sorcery. I was fast asleep when it unleashed the tempest that turned our county into an island, yet my subconscious mind controlled the staff and caused it to happen. The storm, all of it. I used that magical staff in the most terrible way, because I was angry and jealous. It's all coming back to me. I remember now. You came here, didn't you? In August? Something you said drove me half mad with rage. Do you remember? What was it?"

"I most certainly did come here, boss. I came to inform you that I had seen a certain party visiting, and that his name was linked with that of your daughter, Miranda."

"It was more than that, Airmail. There was something more . . ."

"The name of the young man in question was Sebastian Coyle. Son of your nemesis, Anthony Coyle."

Thorne whacks the oak kitchen table with the palm of his hand. "That's it! Coyle! Of course! Coyle and Miranda. I believe . . . I believe I may have seen them myself, at a distance.

So far away that I couldn't quite place him. Then I forgot about it. All of it. What you told me, seeing them together. It all vanished, but the wrath inside me remained. I was consumed with a terrible rage, though I could not remember why. Then I had a terrible dream of a flood descending on the land, but it didn't merely descend, I summoned it! I summoned it, Airmail, d'you hear me? I made this happen. I brought on the tempest, the attack on Miranda, Poe in jail, all of it. I phoned the state's attorney — what's his name? Savage? I phoned Savage a dozen times, insisting that Poe be prosecuted to the full extent of the law. I brought these curses down upon us because I wanted revenge on Sebastian for interfering with my daughter. I wanted vengeance on all the Coyles. Oh, I have sinned, Airmail. I have sinned grievously."

Airmail places a tiny hand on Thorne's forehead to soothe him. "No, no. Not you. It is your fancy playing tricks on you. You give yourself too much credit. Surely you cannot summon storms and bloody mob attacks while not once leaving your mountaintop? You're not a sorcerer, boss. Your mind is not what it was. You imagine these things, I tell you. I am as acquainted as any with all the black arts, with necromancy, witchcraft, Santeria, voodoo. It is not in you to practice such sorcery. Where the heart is good, such wizardry will not follow."

Thorne will not be consoled. "Rose and Poe. I can't bear to think of them harmed. I would watch Poe from my window as I worked, a man who seemed born of the earth itself, the same earth where I have sown nothing but abomination and loathing."

Great sobs shake Thorne. He bows before them, as a man before a great wind. Tears course down his cheeks into his white beard. Airmail tries to comfort him, but Thorne remains inconsolable. At last, the old man lifts his head. "What about this Sebastian, then?" he asks. "Is he the culprit? Is it possible that he attacked my Miranda?"

Airmail shrugs. "I think not. I have seen him. He is a soft one. A pampered child of wealth. Miranda is a young athlete, sire. It would take a great deal to overcome her."

Thorne nods, puzzling on it. There is something vague in his blue eyes, and Airmail understands that the old man may be slipping away, beyond the reach of rational discourse. "Sire," he whispers, "Miranda will want to know what has befallen Poe. Perhaps you ought to rouse her?"

Thorne nods and trudges obediently up the stairs to wake Miranda. He returns with his sleepy daughter trailing him, fastening her robe and rubbing her eyes, her hair wilder than ever.

"Airmail! What are you doing here?"

"I bring terrible news. Rose and Poe have been attacked by a mob. House burned down, goat shed, geese burning, everything."

"Oh, God — what have those fools done? The jury found him innocent, what more do they want?"

"They wanted blood. They felt like they were cheated because Poe didn't hang."

"Are they alright?"

"This I can't tell you. I know they were taken away by ambulance. They're at the hospital or the morgue, one or t'other."

"God, no! I have to go!"

Thorne puts his hand on her arm. "There's something else Airmail needs to tell you. He told me last summer, but it slipped my mind immediately."

Miranda looks from her father to Airmail and back again. "What? What is it? Tell me quickly!"

"It's about Sebastian. Sebastian Coyle."

"What about him? Tell me!"

"I saw him last summer, lurking along the path where you hike."

"That's impossible. He wasn't here last summer. When was this?"

"Right before the storm. The first storm. Before you were attacked."

"Are you sure? I don't recall him being here at all."

"That's because your mind is temporarily out of order. Sebastian was here, alright. Knowing a little of the circumstances of your father's exile, I checked the register at the Manitou Mountain Motel, where he was staying. Sebastian Coyle, written plain as day. I was going to keep an eye on him, but when the first storm rolled in, I decided to sample other climes, and I climbed on the Ninja and rode south all the way to the sea."

Miranda glances at her father. Thorne is wild-eyed, on the verge of another explosion. "It's true then, isn't it? You betrayed me. You betrayed your own father with him."

"It wasn't a betrayal. Not at all. I ran into him at school. I thought he and I could bring our families back together, like we used to be."

"Our family and the *Coyles*? Are you mad? I would slit my own throat before I would have anything to do with Anthony Coyle."

"I know that now, Daddy. It was a pipe dream. I was foolish. I am so sorry."

Something in her father's eyes tells Miranda that he is thinking unbearable thoughts, but for the moment, she can't help him. "I have to go to the hospital now, Daddy. I have to see what's happened to Rose and Poe."

Airmail hops off the counter. "I can whisk you there in two shakes on the back of the Ninja," he says.

"Thanks, but in this weather I think I'll pass. I'll take my VW."

Miranda dashes upstairs to get dressed. Airmail helps himself to another Rolling Rock. Thorne takes up his walking stick from its place by the door and sits heavily, studying his handiwork, running his fingertips over the Alpha and Omega, the intertwined strands of DNA, the Buddha and Muhammad and Christ, wondering if the staff has turned him into a sorcerer. He feels as though he ought to toss the thing into the fire before it does more harm, but he can't bring himself to part with such a beautiful object.

~

With the angels

Poe knows that light. It's bus-station light. Flat light without shadows, light that takes the hollows out of things. He knows it from the army winter, when he and Rose took the bus across America. Rose always ordered the same thing in the bus-station diners, three grilled cheese sandwiches and an extra-large Cherry Coke hold-the-ice for Poe, a tuna-fish sandwich and a glass of milk for herself. The sandwiches in every bus station came with the same long thin slice of dill pickle and a heap of potato chips, just like you'd get at the Woolworth's counter in Bunker's Corner. People always stared, pretending not to stare but staring all the same, and the whispers started up until they attracted a gallery of watchers. *I swear as I live and breathe there's a man the size of King Kong sitting right there on two stools at the counter gobbling up grilled cheese sandwiches like they was going to outlaw them tomorrow, did you see him? Gawd how could a fella that size fit on a bus? I hope he ain't goin far.*

In the bus stations there were always lone soldiers in uniform headed in all directions and whole families who dozed piled against one another, shoulder to hip, head to knee, grandmas and grandkids and teenagers and pregnant mothers and worried fathers pulling out their billfolds to have another peek and count the singles one more time, wondering if there was any chance at all this money would hold out for the bunch of them until they got to Abilene or Valdosta or Tuscarora, waiting on the hard shiny pews where slender slack-limbed Indians slept with an elbow for a pillow, noses twitching at the ammonia stink of a mop bucket wielded by a stooped brown woman with gray hair who spoke no English and worked without pause, mopping around the sleepers and the lovers, the bankrupt and the desperate and the mind-gone crazies babbling at the moon.

No matter what he was doing, Poe always paused to listen enthralled to the voice of God booming from the loudspeakers above at regular intervals, intoning the names of places he'd never been: *Bus to Renton, Kent, Tacoma, Lakewood, South Hills, Centralia, Longview, St. Helen's, Portland, Beaverton, Salem, Albany, Corvallis, Eugene, Roseburg, Medford, Ashland, Redding, Red Bluff, Chico, Yuba City, Roseville, and Sacramento, leaving in five minutes from Gate 17.*

Poe hears footsteps and smells the perfume of angels. His head throbs. It feels like his arms are tied down and he can't move.

He can hear beeping sounds and he can see the bus-station light, and he thinks maybe he's dead and this is heaven, and he listens to the sweet-smelling angels talking.

"Can you believe it? A bunch of them rotten good-for-nothings that hang out at the Bald Eagle tried to kill this poor man and his mama. Burned their house down and then tried to *stone* them to death, like this is one of those godawful countries where they stone people. They would have killed them, too, except that young deputy came to the rescue. Travis Proulx."

"He's cute."

"Poe?"

"Travis, silly!"

"Oh, Travis! Yeah, but he's no brighter than he has to be."

"I don't care if he's bright. Long as, you know. He has those dimples and that cleft in his chin and the blue eyes."

"God, don't you ever think of nothing else?"

"Not if I can help it! My friend Annie says nurses are just plain hornier than other people. You think that's true?"

"Maybe. So much death. Makes you want to grab on to life while you've got it. That's my theory, anyhow, and I'm sticking to it."

They're quiet for a bit, working, then Poe hears them talking about him.

"So this is Poe. First time I've seen him up close. My God, he's even bigger than they say. He really is a giant. There's about two feet of him hanging off this bed."

"That's why they brought the other bed in. We had to put two beds together."

"He's the guy who attacked that girl, isn't he? The one we had in here last summer? Miranda Thorne? The one whose father was always after us for not doing our jobs right?"

"Yeah, her. Anyhow, they turned him loose."

"Who? The dad? They turned the dad loose?"

"No. This guy. The one with the bandage on his head. Poe what's-his-name. They had a jury trial and they turned him loose yesterday afternoon. I imagine somebody didn't like it, so those demented devils tried to kill him. Where have you been? On Mars?"

"No. I've been with Jimmy again. I haven't seen the news, read the paper, nothing. A month now it's been like this. I think it's true love. He never seems to get tired."

"Sounds more like true lust to me. That's what happens when you have a young boyfriend. Cradle robber."

"He's twenty. That's only three years younger than me."

"I'm jealous. That's what I need for these long winter nights, a guy like your Jimmy. All I have is Steve, and he's snoring before I can get Arianna down, same thing every night. Geez, did you see this IV? Marlene must've had trouble finding a vein in that big old arm when they brought him in. He looks like a pincushion. Poor man."

"So what are we dealing with?"

"Concussion. Lost a lot of blood. Head wound, other gashes all over him from the rocks. The head wound bled like a stuck pig. He got two units before he stabilized. Dr. Jennings said he put a hundred and eighty stitches in the man. He took a rock in the mouth and lost four teeth, too. Some ribs are broken and his legs are black and blue, up and down. He got hit all over the place. Worst of it is they shattered his kneecap. He'll need an operation to put that back together, if they can do it at all on a man his size. Some burns, too, but the burns were first and second degree, could have been worse.

Oh, and frostbite. He was barefoot out there and it's freezing. He has six toes, did you notice? Six fingers, too. I heard they might have to amputate one toe on each foot, make him like everybody else."

"There isn't *anything* they could do that would make this man like everybody else. What about his mother?"

"Second-degree burns on her back and arm and smoke inhalation. She's bruised pretty bad. I heard they were throwing rocks at her when she was out cold. Imagine stoning an unconscious woman? Who does a thing like that? She's in the burn unit, but they say she'll survive. Could have been a whole lot worse. They say the big fella carried her out of that fire, saved her life. We got a bunch more came in, too. One old man, a friend of theirs, Bill something-or-other, he has two broken legs. A kid ran him down with a snowmobile. One of those boys got an ass full of buckshot, serves him right. A few of the others are banged up pretty bad, but they'll all live. Kind of a miracle that everybody got out of this alive, I guess."

Poe tries to speak to the angels, but his jaw won't move. He hurts all over, but the bus-station lights are making him very tired, and he falls asleep.

~

Aftermath

Belle Coeur hunkers down after the blaze, sullen and contrite under the winter sun, licking its wounds. The temperature drops and drops again. At thirty below zero, everything in the county grinds to a halt. The few cars that will start without jumper cables groan in protest, and the drivers shiver as they head out to run the errands that have to be run.

Fourteen men and two young women from the county face charges ranging from arson to public drunkenness to attempted manslaughter in connection with the attack on Rose and Poe. The father of the blond youth whose buttocks caught thirty-seven pellets from Bill De Graaff's shotgun attempts to sue Wild Bill, but he's laughed out of court by a judge who points out that Bill's intervention might have saved the boy from a murder rap. Four of the accused are descendants of Lambert Cain's clients. When the parents and grandparents come calling, expecting the youngsters to get off with a slap on the wrist and a warning, Cain refuses to represent them. He'll lose a few clients, maybe, but the money doesn't matter. After what they've done, these young people deserve to take their chances with Gerald B. Nye, the public defender. Having won the most important case of his life, Lambert has decided that it's time to take down his shingle. The wealthy folk of Belle Coeur County will grumble, perhaps, but they will survive without him, because people do.

At the end of what seems like an eon of winter, the ice on the Belle Coeur River cracks with a noise like cannon fire. A few bedraggled tulips stagger out of the ground, peek at the sun, are buried by fresh spring snow, and pop out again, stronger and brighter. The denizens of Belle Coeur County surface from their homes, blink at one another, and begin convincing themselves they had nothing whatsoever to do with the stoning of Rose Didelot and her son, the giant Poe.

Jim Dunn is having none of it. He has seen the worst of what his fellow citizens are capable, and it's more than enough. The verities of his youth — scout's honor and never tell a lie and respect your elders — have long vanished, replaced by a viciousness in public discourse that sickens him. For most of his career as a lawman, he has loved his job, but the events out at Rose's place, the things people already call "the Happenings" as though what occurred was a divine accident, have left him wondering if the people of Belle Coeur County deserve his protection. Teenagers did the burning and hurled the stones, but they were egged on at home by their parents, taught a malignant brand of hatred that has poisoned the water and fouled the air. Dunn wants nothing more to do with it. His retirement is approaching and he's ready to make that blue highways tour around the continent he's been promising himself for twenty years, but there is one item of business that must be taken care of before he can leave. He has an unsolved sexual assault on the books, and he wants that case closed. For Poe's sake, for Miranda, for himself as an officer of the law. Once it's solved, he can ride away with a clear conscience.

Miranda has supplied one missing bit of evidence. She has informed him that her ex-boyfriend, Sebastian Coyle, had indeed been in Belle Coeur County shortly before the attack. She doesn't recall seeing him, but the courier Airmail, a friend of her father's, had seen the young man and found his name on the register at the Manitou Mountain Motel.

When the sheriff attempts to interview the young man, he is informed that Sebastian Coyle is traveling somewhere in Southeast Asia and cannot be reached. It could be a coincidence, or it could be that Coyle is hiding out on the other side of the world until things cool down. The fact he was in the area when Miranda was attacked is enough to make him a suspect, but not enough to bring charges.

In Coyle's absence, the only tangible thread that might lead to something is the windshield on the black car, possibly a Cadillac, which Poe says was parked at the scene. Poe says the man he pulled off Miranda hit that windshield with enough force to shatter it. If Dunn can find the shop that repaired the windshield and track down the car, it might be enough to file charges. He's already checked the hospitals and private clinics to see if any of them treated a man with head wounds that might have been caused by a car windshield and come up empty. Now he's down to the windshield itself. If it was shattered, then someone had to repair it.

The deputies are far too busy, so the investigation is Jim Dunn's and his alone. He does most of the work on Saturdays, and he has to do it in person. Phone calls don't work. It's too easy for a harried garage owner to claim he hadn't repaired any such vehicle in August and hang up. A man with a badge at the door is another matter. Long experience has taught him that few small garages are entirely above the law. Some are out-and-out chop shops for stolen cars, more operate on a cash basis for at least half their jobs. No bills, no credit cards, no taxes. The only thing they want when a lawman shows up is to make him go away.

The big chain outfits are easy to cross off the list. They're no less crooked than the little guys, but they stick to ripping off the customers and they keep good records: a quick check and he can move on. In Belle Coeur County, he turns up repairs on the windshields of two black cars in late August: one belongs to a female schoolteacher whose windshield had been cracked by a rock thrown up by a passing truck. The other is owned by a car salesman named Vince Wright, who has three domestic violence raps on his sheet. Wright looks like a possible suspect, but he was in Florida at the time of the attack. His windshield, it turns out, was damaged when a tree branch fell on the car during the first big storm.

Dunn works in a widening circle from Belle Coeur to the east, west, and south, under the assumption that a guy with a shattered windshield would not have driven the vehicle into Canada. He's surprised how many small, out-of-the-way garages operate on back roads in the country and in back alleys in small towns. A guy with some tools starts fixing cars for his family and buddies, then rents a cinder-block building some-where, goes into hock for a hoist, and he's in business. They aren't in the yellow pages, they aren't on any list of garages, but they're out there. Any garage in a fifty-mile radius might be the one that repaired the windshield of a black automobile in August.

On a Saturday in late April, Jim Dunn drives his daughter to the mountains for a final bout of spring skiing. He watches her make a few runs for the sheer joy of seeing the fearless way she flies down a ski hill. She's spending the day skiing with friends and plans to ride home with them, so he leaves the slopes in mid-morning. On the way home, he runs into heavy traffic on the highway and detours south onto a two-lane blacktop road he's never taken. Ten miles along, he sees a hand-lettered sign off to the side advertising a place called Dean's Auto that offers bodywork and windshield repairs. Dunn pulls off the highway, parks the Jeep, and follows the sound of hammering to a concrete-block building out behind a tiny white house. When the mechanic glances up from his hammering, he flashes his badge.

"Belle Coeur County Sheriff," he says. "Jim Dunn's the name. Are you Dean?"

"That's me. What can I do you for?"

Dunn extends a hand. "Good to meet you, Dean. I wonder if you can help me a bit. I'm sorry to trouble you. I'm looking for a shop that might have repaired the windshield on a big black car, maybe a Caddy."

The mechanic squints at him through the grime that has worked its way into the creases around his eyes. "That doesn't narrow it down much."

"This would have been around the twenty-first of August. Right in the middle of that second flood we had, unless the fellow hunkered down someplace. The driver might have been cut up some himself."

The mechanic thinks it over. "That might fit," he says. "I can check my receipts, if you can wait a minute."

"I'm in no rush. I can wait till you've got time to look."

Dean shakes his head. "Don't matter at all to me. This is my mother-in-law's transmission I'm working on. I don't give a damn if she ever gets her car back."

The mechanic has a thick wad of receipts impaled on a spindle. He lifts them off the spindle, licks a greasy forefinger, and pages through them, frowning intently. Finally, he holds up a receipt that seems to be even greasier than the rest.

"This is it. Monday, August twenty-first. Fella in a new-model black Cadillac came in while it was raining cats and dogs, wanted it fixed pronto. I couldn't believe he'd driven it any distance at all, the shape that windshield was in. Claimed he hit a deer, but it's usually way worse with a deer. There was a fair bit of blood on the windshield and he was cut up some, nothing too serious. He had to wait around while I drove over to the dealership in Preston to get a new windshield, then it took me two hours to change the windshield. He paid cash and I sent him on his way."

"What did he do while you were working?"

"Set around. Nothing else he could do. Didn't say much. I

could tell he didn't want to get grease on his pants, that type."

"You have any kind of description?"

Dean scratches his balding head. "Thirty, or a bit less. Blond. Trying to grow some kind of mustache, wasn't working out too well. A little under six feet, a bit overweight. Not fat but soft, know what I mean? Like a man who never did a day's work in his life. All decked out in this outfit, like he was an African explorer or something, all brand new. Like the car. And a hat. Bush hat, I think you call it. Kept it pulled down over his eyes."

"Did you get a name, a license number, anything like that?"

"He paid cash, like I said, so I didn't take nothing down."

"You happen to notice what state was on the plates?"

"Massachusetts. Now you mention it, I remember the plate. One of them vanity plates. ANTHONY1, like that, the name Anthony and the number one."

Dunn takes out his notebook and jots it down in case his memory fails him. "So I'm guessing the fellow's name is Anthony. Would you recognize him if you saw him again? If you had to point him out in a lineup, for instance?"

"Hell, yeah. I guess he's in some big trouble, is that it?"

"He might have attacked a young woman over in Belle Coeur County. That's what we're looking into."

"I got no use for a man that hits a woman. My wife was married to a fella like that, knocked her around. After she told me, I went over and beat him almost to death. Guess I shouldn't tell you that, but I just couldn't hold back."

"Not my worry. I'm the sheriff in Belle Coeur County, not over here, and I've got even less use for men who beat women than you have. I've had to clean up the messes they leave behind. You've been a big help, Dean. If we find this guy, we'll let you know."

"You happen to know what happened to the windshield, Sheriff?"

"A man saw him attacking this girl, picked him up, and threw him off her."

"*Threw* him! That must be one strong sonofabitch. Fella who was in here with that Caddy had to weigh two hundred pounds."

"You don't know the half of it."

Dunn jots the mechanic's phone number in his notebook. He's almost back to the Jeep when he thinks of one more question and heads back into the garage. "I don't suppose you would have kept that windshield by any chance?"

"Didn't throw it out, if that's what you mean. It's somewhere out back, but it isn't going to be easy to find."

They spend more than an hour digging through the leaning tower of junk that has accumulated out back of the shop. Rusted radiators, old bumpers, split rubber hoses, gas tanks with bullet holes through them, carburetors, axles, worn shock absorbers, broken fan belts, a chassis or two with all the windows smashed out. Dean finally locates the windshield atop an old radiator. To the sheriff's eye, it looks as though the windshield was shattered in the shape of a man's head and shoulders. Maybe a deer did that damage, but it sure doesn't look like it. Dean locates a big plastic bag used to wrap tires, slips the windshield inside it, and Dunn carries it to his Jeep.

Three days later, the Massachusetts DMV confirms that there is indeed a black Cadillac with a vanity plate reading "ANTHONY1" registered to one Anthony Coyle of Boston. The woman from the DMV provides some additional unsolicited information: Anthony Coyle is sixty-two years old, and he's the senior partner at the biggest criminal law firm in Boston.

~

Fragments shored against our ruin

Miranda loves the old stone of New England. What began with the search for the stones to build Poe's wall has become her passion. As she ranges farther and farther afield, she learns to identify more and more specimens and, when they aren't too large to carry, she adds them to her personal collection: chlorite schist, white marble, Monkton Quartzite, Lake Champlain limestone, greenstone, magnetite schist, dolomite, Cheshire quartzite, serpentinite, micaceous marble. She is especially fond of the granite in all its varieties. Poe's wall is built, for the most part, with granite and gneiss, the gneiss striated in undulating patterns, the granite like a pointillist painting, all tiny flecks of crystal that catch the light in a thousand ways.

The university has given her a year to recover from her injuries, but she has already decided that she will not return. Studying law at Harvard, she understands now, was always her father's ambition, not hers. Instead, she has already applied to study geology at the University of Vermont, where she can be close to home, close to her father, and immersed in her passion at the same time.

As she recovers and the weather improves, Miranda spends more and more time hiking — searching for new varieties of stone, searching for herself. On the first really fine day of spring, she leaves the house shortly after daybreak, carrying a backpack with a large bottle of water, an apple, and a tuna sandwich. Somehow, it is only while she is hiking that she finds it possible to recover bits and pieces of the things that happened to her in August. Fragments of memory come to her like strobe lights in the darkness: a quick flash and then it's gone, but the fragments accumulate. She recalls a detail or a scene and then pieces it together with something else. She's begun writing down what she remembers so that it can't be lost again. It's hard to be patient when it's so important for her to understand what happened, but she can't force it. When she tries to pin down the fragments that have come to her, they vanish, only to return when she's thinking of something else. Somewhere, she's convinced, her memory of that time remains intact, just beneath the surface.

She hikes on, enjoying the day without paying attention to where she is, until she reaches a rocky outcrop next to the trail. When she pauses to rest, she sees an empty bottle someone has cast aside. She picks it up in disgust. That's exactly the kind of thing Sebastian would do, she thinks. He's so careless about the world we live in, as though it's his to spoil.

She has to brace herself against the rock to keep from falling. *It's exactly the kind of thing Sebastian would do, because Sebastian was here.* Precisely here. He *was* here, waiting for her, watching her through his binoculars. She was furious with him. They quarreled. She had looked up and seen her father watching them. She pretended she hadn't seen him and turned and hiked away in the opposite direction, walking quickly so that her father couldn't catch them, forcing Sebastian to jog to keep up. That was exactly how it had happened.

The rest of it comes back to her in waves. Her mind is racing, putting it all together. How she had called Sebastian's cell to break it off with him and found that he was still staying at the motel. How he wanted to meet at a breakfast spot, but she suggested the old gravel pit because she didn't want to be seen with him. It hadn't occurred to her that she would be in danger if she met him in a place where there were no witnesses. He stalked off and left her sitting alone. When he returned, he attacked her.

Miranda falls to her knees and vomits until her body shakes. She sees the gravel pit as though it's right in front of her. She's lying on a blanket, sipping a glass of wine. Then she feels very dizzy, and Sebastian is on top of her. She can't push him away. Why not? She's stronger than he is, why can't she fight him off? Her arms and legs feel like water, as though she can't control them.

She remembers how odd her voice sounded when she tried to speak. Her tongue was thick, she was slurring her words. Now she understands: she was drugged. Of course. Sebastian had slipped something into her wine. She had no control over her limbs. He bore her down and she couldn't fight him off. When she did try to fight, he punched her. He held her down and unbuttoned her dress, and when she managed to knee him in the groin, he punched her harder. Once, twice, more. She remembers trying to twist away from the punches, his knee forcing her legs open, the moment when she knew it was going to happen because she didn't have the strength to fight him off — then everything goes black.

What else? She tries to remember, but it's as though someone has pulled a string and yanked the scene offstage. She can recall nothing else. But Poe was telling the truth. He *had* thrown Sebastian off her. Everything happened exactly as Poe had said, but almost no one believed him. He had saved her.

Miranda digs the water bottle out of her pack, washes her

face and hands, rinses out her mouth, then drinks deeply. She's still shaking, but she can walk. She has to tell Sheriff Dunn. She has wondered for months why Sebastian had disappeared after the attack. It wasn't like him. Even after she told him it was over, he would have kept pestering her. She hikes quickly back to the house, repeating over and over to herself, *Sebastian, you bastard. You absolute bastard. You're going to pay.*

When she strides into Jim Dunn's office half an hour later, he smiles. "I was just about to call you," he says. "I located the mechanic who repaired the windshield on a black Cadillac the day after you were attacked. I have a description of the guy who I think attacked you, and the plate number on the vehicle. It's registered to an Anthony Coyle, of Boston."

~

The suspect

On his return from Asia two months later, Sebastian Coyle is arrested at Logan Airport and held until Sheriff Jim Dunn arrives to question him. After two hours in an interrogation room with the younger Coyle and two of his lawyers, Dunn decides that it's just as well he's about to retire, because after three decades and a spotless record, he's as close to striking a suspect as he has ever been.

Coyle has longish dirty-blond hair and a wisp of mustache that doesn't suit him. The only surprise is that Coyle doesn't deny having sex with Miranda. Instead, he brags about it. Apparently, this is going to be his defense. Miranda *loves* sex, he claims, and she loves it rough. She likes to be slapped and spanked. What happened, in Coyle's version, is simple.

"Miranda and I were about to have sex. I had unbuttoned her dress, I remember that. Poe must have been watching us from up in that tower and he got jealous. I knew that she was friendly with that big freak, and I had warned her about him, that he could be dangerous. I saw him through my binoculars while he was working on the wall, but I had no idea how big he is. All of a sudden, I heard this terrible roar, and here was this big freaking ape, coming after me. I tried to fight him off, but he picked me up and just threw me. I landed hard on the hood of my car. My head slammed into the windshield. I must have been knocked out because when I came to, there was no one around. Miranda was gone, the big freak was gone. He must have taken advantage of her while I was out."

"So what did you do when you came to?"

"There was a terrible storm coming. I picked up the blanket and the picnic stuff and I got in the car. I could see enough to drive because my head hit the passenger side of the windshield. I was bleeding some, but I thought I was okay. I got to the highway just in time to see the sheriff's cruisers and the ambulance heading the other way."

"If Poe had attacked you, why didn't you follow us into town so you could tell me what happened? Why try driving your car with a smashed windshield when the closest mechanic was in Belle Coeur?"

"I figured Miranda would tell you what happened. I just wanted to get out of there before the storm hit, and I wanted to get away from that monster. My head hurt like hell. I probably had a mild concussion, and I was feeling confused. I went the other way, and in the first town of any size I came to, I found a twenty-four-hour clinic where I got stitched up. I checked into a motel until the storm was over, got the windshield fixed the next day, and went on my way."

"So a man injured you seriously enough that you needed

stitches, and he damaged your car, but you didn't want to see him arrested?"

"Sure I did. But Miranda had seen what happened. I figured she would tell you all about it. You didn't need me."

"And what about her injuries? She was so badly beaten that she was unconscious for a week. How did that happen?"

"Well, Poe did it, obviously. I didn't hurt her. He must have done it while I was unconscious. I didn't even know she was injured."

Dunn leans back and studies this child of wealth and privilege. If this is how they turned out, he is pleased that he never had the money to spoil his offspring in this way. He leans forward.

"Your story doesn't make a damned bit of sense. If Poe attacked you for no reason at all, you would have wanted us to charge him with assault. If you weren't guilty as hell, you would have had your car window repaired right here in Belle Coeur. There are a dozen holes in your story that I can think of right off the top of my head, and that yarn about how she liked rough sex isn't going to fly: she was examined at the hospital after the attack. Miranda is a virgin, so you can drop that one now. Her memory is crystal clear. You attacked her, most probably after drugging her. We didn't test for date-rape drugs, because it's a new thing and we haven't made it standard procedure in the county yet, but we will. It doesn't matter, because we have Miranda's testimony. And we have Poe's testimony, an eyewitness who saw you assault her. Now, you talk it over with your lawyers, son, but if you want to take a piece of advice from an old country sheriff, you'll plead guilty and save all of us a whole lot of trouble. If you make that young woman face a courtroom and tell the world what you did to her, I'll make it my personal business to see that you don't walk out of that prison until you're old and stooped and gray. I should think that a young man of your attractions wouldn't suffer unduly from loneliness in jail, but I wouldn't know. That decision is up to you."

Sebastian Thorne confers with his lawyers for more than an hour before Dunn is called back in. The decision is made: he will accept a plea bargain.

Miranda is sitting in the courtroom, flanked by Rose and Poe, the day Sebastian is sentenced to five years for aggravated sexual assault and five years for aggravated assault, the sentences to be served consecutively. She watches his sallow face as the judge pronounces the sentence. He's going to prison, and it's going to go hard for him there.

Rose holds her hand. Miranda rummages through her emotions, looking for something, anything. She doesn't feel a thing except a pervasive numbness. Joy, anger, elation, sadness, a sense of revenge, nothing. She thinks that she ought to feel pity for Sebastian, but that tank is empty.

That night, she tries to explain it all to her father, how Sebastian Coyle is going to jail. Thorne stares at her, his watery blue eyes a complete blank. "Sebastian?" he asks. "Coyle? Do I know him?"

~

Atonement

Once Sebastian Coyle has been sentenced for the crime they had blamed on Poe, the remorseful citizens of Belle Coeur County begin to take stock. There are conversations in hushed tones. Some are truly penitent. Others feel the whole thing is a black mark against the county and that something ought to be done to erase it.

When they learn that Rose had no insurance on her home, Dan Gillespie and Lambert Cain take on the task of raising money for her to rebuild. Shame is a useful tool in soliciting contributions. Money is still tight, but tradesmen and skilled craftsmen volunteer time and materials. The site of the original house is cleared with a bulldozer, the burned wreckage hauled away. Excavation is done quickly and the concrete poured free of charge. The frame for a four-bedroom home with a finished basement goes up almost overnight on the site of the old yellow house. Toilets, pipes, sinks, and insulation are donated, and granite tabletops installed. For the first time since she was a child, Rose will have an indoor toilet. A local alarm company provides an alarm and security cameras to help Rose and her son sleep better at night. An electronics store in search of good publicity donates a TV. Solid outbuildings go up to house the goats, geese, and the cheese business.

Rose insists on only one thing: her bedroom has to be large enough for Poe to sleep beside her, as he always has. Maeva leaves her home at the old Kids Kamp and moves into one of the spare bedrooms. It takes some effort, but she's able to convince Rose that with the brand-new refrigerator and freezer, she can get along without her root cellar.

Rose recovers from her burns with only a few scars, but it takes Poe much longer. He walks with a bad limp from the fractured kneecap, he has trouble seeing out of his right eye. He trembles at the sound of snowmobiles throbbing in the night. He's terrified of fire. He flinches at any loud noise. He mourns his lost goats, and he can never milk the survivors or the new goats provided by their friends and neighbors without remembering those that are missing, especially Susie Q, Little Dipper, and Princess Sally. He trusts only a handful of people: Rose and Maeva, Joey Ballew and Dan Gillespie, Wild Bill, Matt Harrow, Jim Dunn, Lambert Cain, Miranda. When strangers come to buy cheese, he hides until they're gone.

But he's a free man, and each morning for the six months of the year when the goats are up at their summer pasture, he rises before dawn and scrambles up the mountain with the aid of a beautiful walking stick carved for him by Prosper Thorne himself — six-fingered and six-toed and still barefoot, singing his wild song. He nestles his cheek in the warm flanks of the nanny goats, he squirts milk into the mouths of feral kittens, he watches the red sun burst over the horizon, listens to the church bells ring, and checks the time on his fob watch, the big hand between the "1" and the "2," the little hand on the number that looks like a bucket with a curved handle.

Miranda spends the last week of her father's life at the hospital. He takes her hand and calls her "Elena." She weeps, as much for her lost childhood as for him. Rose sings "Amazing Grace" and "Farther Along" at his funeral, and a week after, Miranda hikes down to Rose's place and finds Poe outdoors, trimming the cedars.

"I want you to go back to work on the wall, Poe," she says. "I want you to finish it for me. I'll pay you well, better than you were paid before. You can repair it where it's damaged and when you finish that, you can begin again with the stones we have, or we can look for new ones."

"Okay, Miranda. New stones."

"It will be a beautiful wall when we're done, Poe. The most beautiful wall in all of New England."

"We'll make it pretty."

"Yes, Poe. We'll make a pretty wall. Rose will be proud of you, and so will I."

"You doesn't need to pay me, Miranda."

"Oh, yes, I do. I need to find some way to repay you, to make it all up to you."

"I don't understand."

"It's alright. You don't need to understand. All you need to do is help me finish the wall."

Poe goes to work on the wall the next day. He and Miranda work together. She is studying geology now, but they still have the summer to work. Miranda also hires a big strapping neighbor boy to help, and Poe teaches him how to place the stones. Young and strong as the boy is, he still can't begin to lift some of the stones that Poe hefts onto the wall by himself. They work through May, June, July, August, and September. The work goes much faster with Miranda and the boy to help and they place the last stone in the middle of October. Miranda walks the length of it and pronounces it straight and true, a beautiful wall, the best stone wall in all of New England. She takes photographs and has the neighbor boy take a picture of her and Poe standing side by side, with Poe towering over her and the length of the wall curving into the distance behind them, and she has a shop in town frame a large blow-up of the photo and gives it to Poe to hang above the fireplace in the new house.

~

The quality of mercy

Rose forgives them all, without exception. She forgives the teenagers who burned down her house and nearly stoned Poe to death. She forgives Melody Crowder, who spat on her in church. She forgives the Reverend Hank Tattersall, the new minister at the Lamb of Jesus Gospel Church, for telling her it might be better if she didn't attend service until things blew over. She forgives the anonymous vandals who spray-painted "Rapest!" on the side of the yellow house. She forgives the prosecutor, Savage or Savich, who did his best to put Poe behind bars, because that's his job.

Her customers come back, and her new notoriety brings in dozens more. The cheese business thrives. Maeva is now her partner. It turns out that she's a born saleswoman and that to shift from selling dope to cheese is the most natural thing in the world. Alf Miller is doing fifteen to twenty years for dealing drugs, so he's out of the way, and Maeva can get on with her life. She makes deals with cheese shops in tourist towns, and soon Rose has to start depositing some of her money in a bank, the first time in her life she's kept it anywhere other than in the little strongbox in her cellar. The first time she needs to make a withdrawal and the bank teller hands it over without complaint, it seems like a small miracle.

Summers, Maeva and Rose run a little camp on the side for a few of the boys from the original Kids Kamp, beginning with Skeeter and Moe. They teach the boys how to milk the goats and how to make cheese, and Maeva's cousin Donnie, a real outdoorsman, takes them deep-woods camping. After the first summer, Skeeter and Moe stay on year-round, moving into the extra room at Rose's place and enrolling in the high school. Skeeter becomes the quarterback on the high school football team and the point guard on the basketball team, while Moe turns out to have a gift for mathematics. When they have little else to do, they tag around after Poe. When they call him Sasquank, he rubs their heads with his six-fingered hands and laughs.

The prostate cancer finally gets Matt Harrow. Matt is the first of Rose's close friends to go, and it gets her to thinking. After considering it from all angles, she draws up a will. The house, the land, the cheese business, and the goats she leaves to Maeva, on condition that she look after Poe once Rose is gone. It has been a constant source of anxiety to Rose these past few years, what will happen to Poe if she goes before he does, which is almost certain. Knowing that Maeva will care for him is an enormous relief. Maeva is fiercely loyal to Rose and fond of Poe. She's a good cook and she likes watching the big fellow eat. Once the will is drawn up and signed, Rose feels free to go when her time comes. She's in no hurry, but neither is she reluctant. The Good Lord will call her when it suits His bidding, and she will cross to the other shore knowing that her boy is in good hands.

Two years after the will is done, Rose is loading a heavy crate of cheese for shipment to Maine when she sighs, brushes the hair from her eyes, mumbles something about the goats to Maeva, collapses facedown and lies motionless, unable to hear Maeva's scream. The doctor says later that the heart attack Rose suffered was so massive, she was dead before she hit the ground.

So many people want to attend Rose's funeral that the pastors of the First Gospel Church of the Pentecost and the Lamb of Jesus Gospel Church across the street agree to hold a joint service outdoors, where the whole county will be welcome. At least a thousand people turn out. Poe stands nearest the casket, towering over everyone, great tears streaming down his cheeks. Lambert Cain delivers the eulogy, and everyone agrees he has never been more eloquent. Maeva Miller, watching from the shade of an oak tree apart from the rest, curses the mourners under her breath, all but the handful who had stuck with Rose through thick and thin. The preachers hadn't wanted Rose in church while Poe was on trial, and many of those who are weeping now had also helped fan the fear and hatred that almost got both Rose and Poe killed. Rose might have forgiven them, but Maeva never will.

For months after, Poe cannot be consoled. He wanders the hills alone. He claws at the earth as if to dig down to a place grief can't reach. He sleeps in the woods or in the shed, surrounded by the warmth of the goats. His keening lament echoes over Mount Manitou through the cold rain of late autumn and on the coldest days of winter.

Then one spring day, he eats a big breakfast for the first time in months. That night, he sleeps in the house. Maeva, lying awake listening to him snore, smiles to herself. Poe will go on.

~

The beast that lopes these dark hills
A fisherman from the city, lingering on a riverbank, hears a strange, wild song in the distance. He shivers, wondering what manner of beast lopes these dark hills. He reels in his bait, packs up his tackle, jogs the half mile to his pickup truck, and drives four miles downriver before he dares to cast his bait again. When he does so, it's with an eye over his shoulder for a creature not of this earth.

Poe scrambles downhill along the rocky path. He pauses for a moment atop a knoll to sniff the scent of loam and moss and new growth. From there he can see the new house, which is painted yellow like the old one, set in the grove of cedars far below, smoke curling from the stovepipe in the cheese shed, the geese pecking at bugs, the old rusty hay-rake that has been parked in the same spot in the weeds since before he was born, the creek that trickles down from just north of the goat pasture to a hundred yards beyond the house, where it veers sharply down and down again toward the river.

Maeva is waiting for him. She pours him a glass of milk in a big beer stein and he drinks it and she pours another. When he's finished, she wipes his lips with a napkin and pats his bald head.

"I have an errand for you, Poe. I have letters for you to mail at the post office and I need you to pick up a package for me. Can you do that?"

"Uh-huh. I likes goin to the post office."

"I know you do, Poe. That's why I saved this errand for you."

He whistles as he heads out, taking a different path from his usual route. On the outskirts of town he passes the French Mountain Cemetery where Rose is buried. It's the first time he's passed this way since the funeral. He doesn't understand why the place affects him so, why there is a slight tremor in his hands. He's munching an apple, so he pauses to finish the apple and fling the core away. Then he stops to pet a mewing black cat that is curling its way through and through the wrought-iron bars of the fence before he pushes the rusty gate open. Inside the cemetery, he searches up and down the rows of graves until he finds the slab of pinkish granite that bears his mother's name. He can't read what it says, but he remembers the color of the gravestone and the spot where he watched the men lower Rose's casket into the ground. An enormous old crabapple tree near the grave is in full bloom. The heavy boughs hang low, as though sheltering her from the elements.

Poe bends to trace his finger over the name, "Rose Didelot," and the years of her birth and death. Someone has left a bunch of daffodils on Rose's grave, so he picks some dandelions and heaps them next to the daffodils.

It still doesn't seem quite right. There's something else he is supposed to do. He circles the grave, making low keening noises in his throat. Something that goes with a visit to the cemetery, something a person is supposed to do for his kin. He rocks from one foot to the other. He looks around, but there isn't a soul to tell him what to do. He can't do the remembering.

Then it comes to him. A wide, beatific smile crosses his face. He unzips the fly on his OshKosh B'gosh overalls. It takes a while to get it going, but at last the urine begins to flow, and he pees on Rose's grave in a mighty yellow stream that arcs through the spring air and splashes the long mound of earth all the way up to the gravestone itself. He has to go badly after drinking the two big glasses of milk, and he soaks the earth until his bladder is empty. He thinks, too late, that maybe he should have saved some pee for Huguette's grave nearby, but that will have to wait for another time.

A great shaggy raven watches him from the highest branch of the crabapple tree. Poe waves and says hello. The raven hops to a lower branch for a closer look. Poe says hello again and the raven answers. Then the bird flies away, its wings black against a cobalt sky.

Poe zips up his coveralls and heads on into town, bare

six-toed feet scuffing in the dust along the shoulder of the road as he walks along, whistling Rose's favorite hymn: "*Oh, they tell me of an unclouded day . . .*"

Acknowledgments

I must thank my friend Bob Batos-Parac, Merchant Marine Chief Engineer, poet, and master carver, for the loan of his magical walking stick, the *fabula animi*, which I have attempted to reproduce faithfully.

I also wish to thank Catherine Wallace, Laurie Mitchell, Magnolia Kahrizi, Judy Riggs, Lina Basile, and John Cooper, Sally Harding for her faith in the giant Poe, Susan Renouf for seeing what it could be, Laura Pastore for her dedicated work on the manuscript, and Irene Marc for her sacrifices and understanding.

Finally, I am indebted to the Canada Council for a grant, without which *Rose & Poe* might never have been written.

Jack Todd was born and grew up in Nebraska. He came to Canada during the Vietnam War and eventually settled in Montreal, where he has been a columnist for the *Montreal Gazette* for nearly 30 years. He is the author of a memoir and three previous novels.

Published by ECW Press
665 Gerrard Street East
Toronto, ON M4M 1Y2
416-694-3348 / info@ecwpress.com

Library and Archives Canada Cataloguing in Publication

Todd, Jack, 1946–, author
Rose & Poe / Jack Todd.

Issued in print and electronic formats.
ISBN 978-1-77041-399-3 (softcover)
ISBN 978-1-77305-100-0 (PDF); ISBN 978-1-77305-101-7 (EPUB)

1. Shakespeare, William, 1564-1616. Tempest. I. Title. II. Title: Rose and Poe.

PS8589.O633R67 2017   C813'.6   C2017-902411-6
C2017-902990-8

Editor for the press: Susan Renouf
Cover design: Natalie Olsen | kisscut design

The publication of *Rose & Poe* has been generously supported by the Canada Council for the Arts which last year invested $153 million to bring the arts to Canadians throughout the country, and by the Government of Canada through the Canada Book Fund. *Nous remercions le Conseil des arts du Canada de son soutien. L'an dernier, le Conseil a investi 153 millions de dollars pour mettre de l'art dans la vie des Canadiennes et des Canadiens de tout le pays. Ce livre est financé en partie par le gouvernement du Canada.* We also acknowledge the Ontario Arts Council (OAC), an agency of the Government of Ontario, which last year funded 1,709 individual artists and 1,078 organizations in 204 communities across Ontario, for a total of $52.1 million, and the contribution of the Government of Ontario through the Ontario Book Publishing Tax Credit and the Ontario Media Development Corporation.

Printed and bound in Canada by Norecob
5 4 3 2 1